OBSESSED

OBSESSED

G. H. Ephron

St. Martin's Minotaur
New York

www.minotaurbooks.com

Library of Congress Cataloging-in-Publication Data

Ephron, G. H.
    Obsessed / G.H. Ephron. — 1st ed.
      p. cm.
    ISBN 0-312-30531-1
    1. Zak, Peter (Fictitious character) — Fiction.   2. Forensic psychiatrists — Fiction.   3. Stalking victims — Fiction.   4. Boston (Mass.) — Fiction. I. Title.
    PS3555.P49O23   2003
    813'.6 — dc21

                               2003046823

First Edition: December 2003

10 9 8 7 6 5 4 3 2 1

For Nora, Delia, and Amy
Nelson Butters and Ethan S. Rofman

Acknowledgments

With this book, we needed a lot of expert help to get the technical details right. We are grateful to Jonathan M. Levin, M.D., of the Brain Imaging Center at McLean Hospital; Francine M. Benes, M.D., Ph.D., and George Tejada, M.S., of the Harvard Brain Tissue Resource Center; Carolyn Kraut Roth, William Faulkner, Karen Rich, and Vera Miller, who generously shared their expertise in MRI safety; D. P. Lyle, M.D., author of *Murder and Mayhem: A Doctor Answers Medical and Forensic Questions for Mystery Writers*, and Joseph Kennedy, M.D. Any errors are solely our own.

Thanks also to Bruce Cohen, M.D., Sumi Verma, M.D., Cindy Lepore, Adriana Bobinchock, and McLean Hospital for their support. Also thanks to Steve Feldman, Gus Rancatore, and Kevin Brown. To fellow writers: Linda Barnes, Connie Biewald, Maggie Bucholt, Kate Flora, Carolyn Heller, Naomi Rand, Pat Rathbone, Sarah Smith, and Donna Tramontozzi. Special thanks to editor Jonathan Ostrowsky. To Michael Getz and the folks at Illumina Interactive for nurturing our Web site at www.peterzak.com.

To Louise Quayle for getting all of this started and to Gail Hochman for getting us to the finish line. And to our editor, Kelley Ragland, for her steady encouragement and support.

And special thanks to our spouses, Susan and Jerry, for their love and support, and for the time and space that writing takes.

OBSESSED

1

NAKED BULBS every twenty feet or so did a feeble job lighting the gloomy underground passageway that connects the two dozen buildings of the Pearce Psychiatric Institute. My footsteps echoed on the concrete floor. Even well into spring, the powdery cement walls held winter's cold in their bones, and icy water dripped from the ceiling.

I opened a door and emerged into deepening twilight. For once I wasn't taking work home. I was meeting Annie Squires at eight at the Casablanca in Harvard Square. Mediterranean spices beckoned, plus a beautiful companion whose day hadn't been spent dealing with hospital bureaucracy and five new admissions. It wasn't a record for the Neuropsychiatric Unit—we'd once had nine in a single memorable day, nearly a fifty percent turnover. But five was enough to frazzle Gloria Alspag, the nurse in charge, which meant the rest of us got thoroughly frazzled as well.

Dinner with Annie was just the antidote I needed. We'd share a good bottle of red wine, maybe a Ridge Zin. She'd tell me about her day—I knew she'd been planning to spend it tracking down and interviewing the associates of some millionaire businessman whom attorney Chip Ferguson was defending against charges of fraud. Maybe we'd split a bread pudding for dessert. Linger over some espresso. Come back to my house for a glass of port with its rich, almost chocolatey taste. Nice, but not nearly as nice as the taste of Annie. I felt the tingle of anticipation.

I walked along the side of Rose Hall. The decommissioned—our euphemism for "derelict"—building had a red-brick façade and a handsome white-columned portico. Even though most of the buildings that graced the Olmsted-designed grounds had been built at the same time, each was unique. Rose Hall was Greek Revival, the building that housed the neuropsych unit was Victorian gingerbread with a mansard roof, the administration building resembled an Italian villa. Perhaps the founders of the Institute craved architectural diversity—or maybe it had been a board that couldn't agree on anything. I'd been on more than a few of those myself.

Patients and staff had long since moved out of Rose Hall as clinical units closed while cinderblock-and-glass research facilities opened. Now the first-floor windows were boarded. One of the sheets of plywood was painted white with a big black X across it, marking it for demolition.

A side door was slightly ajar. When I got closer I could see a lock dangling from a hasp that had been pried loose. As a kid, I'd have found an open door to an abandoned building irresistible. I'd have rounded up Danny Ellentuck and we'd have set out to explore what we fervently hoped would turn out to be a haunted house.

I'm not a kid anymore. I pulled the door open and peered inside. I tried not to inhale the mildew and rot. There was a rustling inside, as if something were scuttling about. Probably rodents.

The door squealed as I pushed it shut, and I made a mental note to call Security and let them know the building needed to be secured. Again. Vandalism was a constant problem at the Pearce. For years we'd talked about setting up a checkpoint at the entrance gate, but that would have been like spitting in the ocean. Anyone could walk onto the grounds just about anywhere along the ten-plus-mile perimeter.

I started down steps that were nothing more than timbers set into the side of the hill. That morning, I'd snagged one of the last spots near the lower end of the two-tiered parking lot. Now more spots were empty than taken and the place felt like a deserted stage set. Shadows from the surrounding trees stretched across the asphalt.

I heard a high-pitched screech, *pee-yah*, and thought I saw something swoop across the parking lot. Now a breeze rattled the trees and undergrowth. The Pearce had a staff of twenty whose job it was to keep the encroaching woodland in its place. I put on my jacket and turned up the collar. Spring in New England didn't mean warmth.

I walked toward my car, a brand new silver Subaru WRX, which I was growing to hate. I passed Emily Ryan's Miata. Emily was a post-doc I was supervising. She'd been working part-time with us for the last few months on a fellowship. Neat car, I thought as I took a detour to admire it. The red looked nearly black in the twilight. Not as sexy as a Corvette, or as classy as my deceased '67 Beemer. I felt a pang just thinking about that car. No point in bellyaching. It had been totaled and no amount of sweat, wishing, or money was going to get it back.

Yes indeedy, that Miata was pretty cool. I wondered if it had the leg room I needed. What the hell was I doing with a Subaru anyway? Contrary to what the nobs at the car magazines were saying, the WRX was *not* the hottest ride of the new century. For my money, it felt like plastic and drove like a windup toy. Only consolation was that finding replacement parts was a cinch.

As I ran my hand over the Miata's sleek front fender, something felt odd. It wasn't smooth like I'd expected. I crouched to get a closer look. The entire length of the passenger side had been keyed. To some people, I suppose, a brand-new, shiny red car is as irresistible as an unbitten candy apple.

Uneasiness seeped into my chest. The damage was recent—little curls of paint still adhered to the groove.

I hung there, crouched. When it was your car, this was the kind of thing that made you sick to your stomach, then angry as hell. Then it frightened you as you wondered if it was random, the luck of the draw—or personal, and you were handpicked. I checked out the rest of the body, the headlights. One of the rear tires was nearly flat. Damn.

I started across the parking lot and back up the steps, already refiguring my timeframe. Emily was probably still in her office. I'd find her, we'd call AAA, then I'd wait until the tire got fixed and she got off safely. I should still make it to the Casablanca in time to meet Annie.

I hurried back through the tunnel and let myself into the building. I took the stairs two at a time up three flights and knocked on the door of the oversized closet where we parked post-docs. Office space was a scarce commodity. No answer.

"Emily," I called, knocking harder. I tried the knob. The door was locked.

Maybe she was on the main floor. I took the elevator down. Gloria looked up from the nurse's station—the broad counter surrounded by chart racks, file cabinets, and an assortment of mismatched chairs that serve as our hub and nerve center. Gloria's day should have ended at five, but being her superconscientious self, she was still there slogging through unfinished paperwork and orienting the night shift to our new patients.

"You seen Emily Ryan?" I asked.

"What's wrong?" Gloria stands small but mighty at about five-three, with close-cropped light brown hair and glasses. Very little gets past her.

"When I went out to get in my car I noticed she's got a flat tire."

"Her *new* car?"

Like I said, very little gets past Gloria.

"Yeah. And someone keyed it all along one side."

Gloria looked outraged. "That's awful. Security"—she said the word with a snort of contempt—"bet they were off somewhere busily handing out parking tickets." It was a sore spot with Gloria that five perfectly good parking spots alongside our building were marked NO PARKING. "Emily left about forty-five minutes ago. She was wearing her running clothes. Carrying her briefcase and her work clothes."

Forty-five minutes. She'd probably dropped her things in her car, stretched, and then gone for a run on one of the trails that snaked through the woods and across the lawns of the Pearce. She could be getting back to her car right now. She could easily miss the flat tire and start home, then end up broken down on the side of the road, might even ruin the wheel.

I thanked Gloria and raced downstairs and out through the tunnel. I'd just reached the top of the stairs when I heard what sounded like a single clap, then a woman's scream cut through the twilight, sending chills down my back.

"Goddamn you, you miserable sonofabitch," Emily screamed,

backing away from her car. She stumbled over her own feet.

The parking lot was now deep in shadow. I couldn't make out another figure. Who was she talking to?

"You bastard. Oh, God, get away from me."

"Emily!" I yelled, starting down the stairs.

"Stay away," she shrieked. She ran across the parking lot, heading for a stand of birch at the far end.

"Emily, it's me, Peter," I shouted, flapping my arms.

She froze for a moment. Then she ran straight at me and hurled herself into my arms, nearly knocking me over.

"Oh my God, he's out there," she said, sobbing and shaking. "Someone's—" She gave a startled leap. "There, did you hear that? Over there. In the bushes?"

She held on to me tighter. I smelled sweat, and something else, like the inside of a tin can—fear.

"Whoever you are," I thundered in that general direction, "the party's over. Go away. Stop bothering her."

Emily clung to me tenaciously. Tendrils of dark hair had come loose from her ponytail and were now stuck to the perspiration at the back of her neck. Though she was small and slight, Emily was anything but weak. She could move fast, and shoulder and back muscles rippled through her thin Lycra top as she pressed against me.

I managed to pull out my cell phone and called Security. They picked up on the second ring. I asked them to send someone over right away.

With my arm around her, I walked Emily back to her car. She put out a trembling hand and rested it on the open door on the passenger side. Her face had gone pale as chalk.

"The door was open when I came back," she said. She leaned

into the car and felt around on the floor, on the seat. "He took—oh, God, I don't even know what he took. Some underwear. And I thought I left an earring on the seat."

A helpless fury was building in my chest. The underbrush surrounding the parking lots was now in deep shadow. Was he waiting for her there? Lurking in Rose Hall? Or had he been there earlier, watching me, too?

"Oh no," Emily said groaning, touching the place where a key had been scraped along the car's body.

"Your right rear tire's flat, too," I said.

She moaned.

One of the white Pearce security vans pulled into the lot. An officer climbed out, keys jingling from a ring attached to his pants. He hooked his fingers over his belt and did a 360 after Emily told him what had happened. Then he got out a flashlight and walked the perimeter of the parking lot, shining the light into the trees and bushes.

"I think he was over there," I said, indicating where Emily said she'd heard a noise.

The officer waded into the underbrush. He crashed around, strafing the area with his flashlight beam. Anyone or anything hiding out there would have had plenty of warning and time to relocate by now.

When the guard reemerged, he took off his cap and scratched his head. "I don't see anyone now. We've had a couple of coyote sightings the last few weeks."

Sounded more like the Wild West than suburban Boston. "Coyotes don't key cars and let the air out of tires," I said. I told him he ought to check Rose Hall. The side door had been jimmied open.

He got out a notebook and wrote. Then he unhooked his walkie-talkie from his belt. "I think we'd better have the police check this out."

"Please don't," Emily said. She'd gone a shade paler as she touched her fingers to her throat.

The guard and I looked at her in disbelief.

"It's probably just kids," she said. "Really, I don't want to bother the police. They'll make such a to-do about it."

"But—" the guard started to protest.

She put her hand on his sleeve. "You do understand, don't you?"

He looked at her uncertainly.

"Emily, are you sure you know what you're doing?" I asked. Why was she suddenly minimizing her obvious terror?

"I'll be more careful," she assured us both. "Get an alarm installed. Change the locks."

The guard put his walkie-talkie back on his belt.

"You'll file a report internally at least?" I asked him.

He nodded. "As for you, little lady, I'd suggest you do your running when it's still light. And you might get yourself a whistle."

"Little lady?" Emily grumbled as we watched him drive off. "What a jerk." She pulled a zippered sweatshirt off the floor of her car and put it on. She overlapped the front and crossed her arms. "Why is this happening to me?"

I called AAA and asked them to send someone over to change the flat.

"Why didn't you want to call the police?" I asked while we waited.

"I just didn't want to make a fuss. Stir things up."

Stir what things up? I was about to ask when my cell phone beeped. I had a message waiting. Uh-oh, I thought with a jolt. I'd completely lost track of time. Annie had already been waiting for me at the restaurant for twenty minutes. I had no good explanation for why I hadn't remembered to call her. I hadn't been thinking.

I dialed voice mail. The message was from Annie all right—but not what I'd expected to hear.

"Peter, sorry I'm late. I got tied up and lost track of time," Annie said. "You should go ahead and eat. I'm not going to be able to make it. I'll call you later at home."

At first I was relieved. At least she hadn't been sitting in the restaurant wondering where the hell I was. Then I felt irritation—though I knew I had no right. When I got past that, worry set in. It wasn't like Annie to be late, never mind stand me up.

I called her back. I tried her at home, at the office, and on her cell phone. In three places I left the same message: "Don't worry about it. Call me."

"You want me to follow you home?" I asked Emily after the tire had been changed.

"No. Really, I'll be okay." She rose on tiptoe and gave me a light kiss on the cheek. "Thanks."

"Don't mention it," I said.

When I opened the driver-side door, I noticed an odd, almondy-sweet odor. A bottle of hand lotion was lying open next to the gas pedal and a puddle of white oozed onto the mat. I crouched and felt around for the top. I started to tell Emily what I'd found but the words died in my throat. Across the dash in white streaky letters someone had scrawled BITCH.

2

I GOT to work late the next morning. I still hadn't been able to reach Annie. I sprinted from my car, up the steps to the tunnel, barely registering the gorgeous spring day—air that smelled like cool, fresh water, trees just leafing out in that amazing lime-green color that lasts only until the first heat wave.

I hoped Emily had managed to get some sleep. I wondered if she'd be up to working with patients. Thinking someone is out to get you, true or not, can have insidious consequences. I knew that from firsthand experience.

A blast of warm, humid air greeted me when I unlocked the door to the unit. The pinkish basement walls seemed to shimmer like overheated flesh. It wasn't that the a/c was on the fritz. The heating system never knew when to quit. I took the stairs up to the first floor and let myself out onto the unit.

I ducked into the little room behind the nurses' station, poured myself a cup of coffee. The mail hadn't yet arrived. Gloria's philodendron plant, nearly hacked to death a few months ago, was now thriving. Affectionately known as Audrey, its vines snaked from the pot, up and over the window and around a mirror. Between the heart-shaped leaves, my own dark eyes looked worried as they stared back at me from beneath a tumult of black eyebrow hair flecked white. I straightened my tie and cleaned my glasses.

I walked down the corridor with its nine-foot-high ceilings, past the common room where sun streamed in through floor-to-ceiling windows behind the once-grand piano. It was a room that deserved a red velvet Victorian settee, gents' and ladies' chairs. Instead it had vinyl sofas and molded plastic chairs, a fiberboard bookcase, and a large-screen TV. There was mesh screening over the windows— today's psychiatric hospital's stand-in for bars.

"If it isn't the hero of the hour," my colleague and resident fashion consultant Dr. Kwan Liu announced when I arrived at the conference room. He was looking his usual spiffy self in a custom-made charcoal suit and red tie, his dark hair gleaming. "Heard you rescued a damsel in distress last night."

"Never mind him," said Gloria. "Security sent out a bulletin for everyone to be on the alert for an intruder. What happened?"

I told Kwan and Gloria how I'd found Emily in the parking lot. How her car had been vandalized and she'd been terrified, convinced that someone was taunting her from the shadows.

"A stalker." Gloria breathed out the word.

"You think so?" Kwan asked.

"It looks that way," I said. "Someone got into her car. Wrote 'bitch' on the dash and took some stuff—underwear and an earring."

"Creepy," Gloria said, fingering one of the tiny gold hoops in her own ears. Gloria rarely wore jewelry. She might even have been wearing a touch of lipstick. "Is she okay?"

"She's fine," came a voice from the doorway. It was Emily Ryan, leaning her head wearily on the doorjamb. She had on a navy blue suit, the jacket buttoned. The clothes were a somber contrast to the dark hair tied back in a ponytail. Between her Miata, the preppy outfits, and her all-American good looks, you'd have thought Emily came from somewhere like Connecticut and money. But she didn't. The scar on her cheek and more on her arms were the only visible traces of a hardscrabble childhood in central California. Her father, a trucker, had been mostly absent while her mother struggled to keep them all fed. Somehow Emily had managed to lift herself out and put herself through school.

She gave a half-smile, not wide enough to turn on the dimples at either side of her mouth. Her complexion seemed even more pale today, and she had smudges under her eyes. She walked over and settled into a spot at the table.

"You get any sleep?" I asked.

"Can I get you some coffee?" Kwan offered.

"You sure you're okay?" Gloria asked.

"Listen, you guys are great," Emily said, looking at each of us and turning up the smile, "and I appreciate your concern. But I can take care of myself."

"No one's saying you can't," Gloria said. "We're a team here. If one of us is hurting, we're all in trouble."

"You can't do this kind of work if you're afraid," Kwan added.

Emily's smile vanished. "I've been managing so far."

"This wasn't the first time?" Gloria asked.

Emily looked down at the table. She shook her head.

Gloria moved into the chair and put her arm around Emily. "How long?"

"A few weeks. Maybe a couple of months."

A couple of months? I wondered why she hadn't mentioned that to me or to the security guard last night.

"Phone calls late at night. I think someone's been following me to my car in the garage at the MRI lab. I've been asking one of the guys over there to walk me out."

That was disturbing. Emily had a half-time clinical fellowship with us and a half-time research fellowship at a magnetic resonance imaging lab near Central Square. Whoever the stalker was, he was following her there, too.

Emily got up, went to the window, and stared out. "It's so infuriating. I hate that it's made me change my life. I used to run at Fresh Pond, but halfway around it's pretty isolated. I realized if *he* was there, I'd be a goner. He'd drag me off and—" Emily shivered. "That's why I started running here at the Pearce. I figure there's more people, there's Security. Hell, they tow your car in about thirty seconds if you park where you're not supposed to." She bit her thumbnail. "I felt safe."

Emily didn't look as if she felt safe now. For the moment she looked small and vulnerable, a little girl in dress-up clothes.

Kwan was massaging his chin as he listened. Gloria reached out and squeezed Emily's hand.

"Any idea who it might be?" Gloria asked. "Your ex?"

"Kyle wouldn't, no way."

"Someone you broke up with?" I asked.

"A couple of months ago."

"Isn't that when you said this all started?" Gloria said.

"Yeah, but Kyle? I just don't think he's the type."

What type of person got his jollies from following a woman? Vandalizing her car? Taking her belongings? I knew what the literature said. Most often a stalker was an ex-partner who couldn't accept the end of a relationship. Or a suitor whose overtures had been spurned. Celebrities got stalked by adoring fans. And like the rest of us working in mental health, Emily's occupation put her at a higher-than-average risk of crossing paths with an individual capable of forming an obsessive attachment.

I'd never been stalked by a patient, but I had been stalked by a man I helped defend. Ralston Bridges had been on trial for murdering a woman he'd met in a bar. He'd blown up at me when I suggested an insanity plea, banged his fist on the table and bellowed, "I'm not insane. No one calls me that and gets away with it." Then he'd turned off the emotion like a faucet. And besides, he'd said with the supreme confidence of a man who'd gotten away with murder before and expected to do so again, he didn't need anyone to convince the jury that he was crazy.

He'd been right about that. After deliberating for six hours, a jury of his peers found Bridges not guilty. They bought his blue-eyed baby face and his lies. When he got out, he'd stalked my wife, Kate, and me, learned our routines so that he knew when she'd be home and I wouldn't. He broke into the house and took his revenge, killing Kate.

Now I could rattle off those details in a matter-of-fact way, hold them at a distance like a news story that had happened to someone else. But the feeling of devastation, of catastrophic loss could still ambush me when I least expected it.

I was glad I'd been there last night for Emily. I took any kind of stalking threat very seriously—who knew if her stalker would be satisfied with merely scaring her to death?

Our social worker and the music therapist arrived, followed shortly after by the physical therapist and the occupational therapist. Everyone took places at the table and I started morning rounds. The rhythm of this daily routine where we review the patients on the unit made last night's trauma seem distant.

After the meeting I caught up with Emily in the hall. She was standing close to Gloria, their arms linked.

"You're looking very chic today," Emily told her. "Nice outfit." In addition to the gold earrings, Gloria had on a white silk blouse instead of her usual crisp, button-down oxford shirt with a pair of dark belted trousers. "Got a date?" Emily asked, her voice teasing.

Gloria gave a self-conscious laugh and looked around, as if to see who was listening. "Just meeting Rachel for lunch," she said. Rachel was Gloria's life partner. "It's our fifth anniversary."

Good thing it wasn't a job interview. Gloria could pretty much have had her pick of jobs at the Pearce, or any psychiatric hospital, for that matter. So much of the order and sanity on the unit depended on her.

"No donut today?" Emily asked, reaching out and patting Kwan's stomach as he squeezed past. "You're looking very trim."

Kwan stopped, beaming. "Well, I'm glad someone around here notices," he said, eyeing me.

I had to admit, he was looking a bit less paunchy. It was only a month ago I'd been teasing him that he'd had to let his belt out a notch. And the vest that now buttoned comfortably—I remembered how it had strained across his middle.

"Of course we notice," I said. "We're just polite."

"I've lost twelve pounds," he said, glowing with pride.

"No wonder you've been in such a pleasant mood."

"I've been a prince," he said, and ambled off.

Now it was just me and Emily in the hall. She pulled a pack of gum from her pocket and offered me a piece.

"No thanks," I said. I hated Juicy Fruit.

"Helps me not smoke," she said. "And boy, would I love a cigarette right now." She slid the gum into her mouth.

"You okay working with your patients?" I asked.

"I think so. I've got Mr. Black later this morning. Otherwise, nothing I can't handle." Mr. Black was a clinic outpatient whom Emily had been treating since before she began her rotation with us.

I took out my datebook and checked my appointments.

"Maybe I can observe. I expect you're still feeling the aftereffects from last night. Wouldn't hurt to have a backup."

Emily realized that I wasn't asking permission. As her clinical supervisor, it was my job to be sure she had the oversight she needed.

"Actually, that would be great. Maybe you can tell me if he's getting anywhere or if we're both spinning our wheels."

• • •

I closed myself into the little room behind the nurse's station, poured myself another cup of coffee, and tried Annie at home. No answer. Then I tried her office number. "Ferguson and Associates. Squires Investigations," said the familiar recorded voice. I'd done many forensic evaluations for her business partner, attorney Chip Ferguson, assessing the psychiatric status of defendants. "If you know your party's extension . . ." I punched it in.

"Annie Squires." Annie's voice was clipped, as if she'd grabbed the phone on her way out the door.

"You're busy?"

"Actually I was just heading out. I'm really sorry about last night."

"At least you called. Don't worry about it. I never got to the restaurant myself." I told Annie what had happened.

"Did you see anyone?"

"No, but it was dark. I waited with her for Triple-A."

"Stalking isn't something to mess around with."

"That's what I told her. I didn't realize it had gotten so late until I saw your message."

"So that's a weird coincidence. Each of us standing the other one up."

"Where were you?" I asked.

"Family emergency. I'll tell you about it. Right now I've got to run."

"Sounds like you're pretty busy."

"Wouldn't you know. After all those months of struggling to make the rent, business is booming."

"And tonight?"

"Busy. How about tomorrow night? I'll be hungry by then."

"I'm hungry now and we don't even have to have dinner," I said.

"Hold that thought. How about dinner at my place? Eight o'clock?"

"You're going to cook?"

"Did I say that? I was thinking Chinese take-out. Or pizza."

I didn't care what we had to eat. "I'll bring the beer," I said. I'd been strictly a wine drinker before Annie educated me to the finer points of beer. I made a mental note to pick up some flowers, too.

I hung up. I'd never given Annie flowers. I smiled, remembering the daisies she brought me after I mangled my ankle tackling a man who turned out to be a murderer. It was much too long after the daisies that we finally made love. That had been months ago, but I could still feel my groin tightening and a grin tugging at the edges of my mouth at the memory.

After Kate was killed all my passions seemed to dry up. Food had no taste. I gave up Bordeaux for bourbon. I buried myself in work. It had taken nearly two years for me to start feeling again.

I was still getting used to what I was feeling now. Lust. I savored it.

WHEN I got up to my office, there was a piece of notepaper stuck to the door. "Appointment with Mr. B at 11," it said. It was signed "E." The note had printed at the top: FREUDIAN SLIPS. Cute.

A little past eleven, I entered the observation room and took a seat. Through one-way glass I could see a room the same size as the small one I was in. The room was anonymous but pleasant with its table lamps and eye candy impressionist landscape print. A vase of artificial irises and daffodils stood on the coffee table, and among the flowers was a microphone which connected to speakers on my side of the wall. We weren't trying to hide the microphone, just make it inconspicuous. Mr. Black had given his permission to be observed back when he'd started treatment.

I sat in the dark with the lights off and shades drawn. Emily was in the therapy room on the other side of the one-way glass. She sat in an armchair, legs crossed, light streaming in through the window behind her.

Facing her was Mr. Black. The middle-aged man with a receding hairline and a face and stomach that had gone to paunch was scribbling in a notebook he had balanced across his lap.

"You know, you won't be able to do that if you go ahead with the operation," she said.

He lifted the pen and looked at his arm. "I'll learn to write with the other hand."

"What are you writing?"

"Just a note to remind myself of a bunch of things I need to do—find my passport, get a Spanish phrase book." He closed the notebook. "I'm waiting to hear when they can take me. Sometimes they get a cancellation and you've got to get down there right away." I suspected they had quite a few last-minute cancellations—patients who fantasized about having a limb amputated and then, when the moment of truth came, backed out. "This is going to save my life."

"It's a very big step."

"Don't you think I know that? It's not like it's a sudden decision," he said, setting the notebook down alongside his chair. "It's like I said, this is about becoming whole, not becoming disabled." He looked at his arm as if it were a piece of meat past its expiration date. "I feel like I've got this . . . this alien object attached to me."

"And what if something happens and the operation falls through?"

He gave a sly smile. "Don't worry. I won't lie down on a railroad track."

It was a brutal thought, but I remembered reading about a man who'd been obsessed with amputating his legs. Unable to find a doctor to do the job, he'd lain on a railroad track and let the train do the job. Even survived to tell about it.

Though an obsession with limb amputation was rare, the syndrome had a name—apotemnophilia. The phrase had been coined by an expert in sexuality at Johns Hopkins. Apotemnophilia victims, he wrote, wanted to cut off their limbs so they could have better sex. The suffix *philia* grouped it with the psychosexual disorders that the average person thinks of as perversions. Emily and I had discussed whether this diagnosis fit Mr. Black. To both of us, the way he talked about his desire for amputation seemed more about being stuck in the wrong body—body dysmorphia—than about sexual desire.

"And how do you think things will be different after the operation?" Emily asked.

"Much better. Infinitely. With this"—he stretched out a perfectly normal-looking arm—"I know how odd I look." He crossed his other arm over the one he despised.

"So you think your arm makes you look deformed?"

"It doesn't belong there."

"Um-hmm."

"I don't feel right, and it's all I think about. It's cost me my marriage. My job."

"Your boss fired you because of your arm?"

"Yes."

"That's what he said?"

"No, of course not."

"What did he say?"

"Some mumbo-jumbo about inadequate job skills. I didn't swallow it for a minute."

"Did he offer you job training?"

He shrugged. "It wasn't about that. I could've learned the goddamned computer shit. It was about *this*, not that."

"But they'd promoted you before."

"Out of pity. That's all it was. They felt sorry for me so they gave me the promotion. But I know the truth. No one can stand to look at me. I've never had a healthy relationship with anyone. It's why my wife left me. How could she make love to someone as deformed as I am? Not when I've got this thing that doesn't belong to me. I get such an overwhelming sense of despair sometimes." He glanced quickly up at Emily, then back down. "I don't want to die, but there are times I don't want to keep living in a body that doesn't feel like my own."

"I'm sorry—" Emily started.

"I don't need your pity," he said, spitting out the words. "I just need to fix what's wrong with me. It's so simple. Why is it such a big deal?"

"Think about what it's going to mean," Emily said. "You cut off your arm, you won't be able to write, shake hands."

He blinked at her, as if unsure how to respond. Then he seemed to stare right at me with a look of loathing. I realized he was looking at himself in the one-way glass.

"If I had a great big nose, no one would think twice if I got a nose job. And what about all those Hollywood actors who get half their body fat suctioned away? My brother rubs Rogaine into his scalp every day and no one tells him he's nuts."

"Those are different, and I think you know that."

"My brother actually suggested maybe what I needed instead of an amputation was a new car. After his divorce he got himself a Hummer." Mr. Black rolled his head around so the bones in his neck cracked. "You drive a red Miata. Isn't that about the same thing?"

Emily opened her mouth. She seemed at a loss for words. *Course correction* . . . I tried to telegraph the thought. Therapy is about the patient, not the doctor. This was classic resistance. Mr. Black was using this remark to shift the focus onto the therapist. The next thought wouldn't have occurred to me if Emily hadn't been stalked: How the hell did Mr. Black know she drove a red Miata?

"Are you sure this is what you want? You won't be able to change your mind later."

"I know what I want. I've known it ever since I was seven. I still remember the first time I saw a man who had one arm. It was like a light went on in my head."

"You were seven years old."

"That's when I realized why everyone was staring at me. It was my arm. It didn't belong there, and they could all see it just as clearly as I could. Now I can't wait until it's fixed and I can get on with my life. Get *started* with my life."

"Did you tell your parents about this?" Emily asked. "Or a teacher?"

"Of course not. It would only make them stare more." There was a pause. "Like you're doing now."

Emily recrossed her legs. "I'm just trying to understand what makes you hate it so much."

Mr. Black leaned forward. Now he was staring at Emily's legs. "It's easy for you to say. You have a beautiful body."

She shifted her notebook so it covered some of the exposed knee.

Mr. Black sat back. "One thing that *has* changed. At least now I know I'm not alone."

He talked about the people he'd met on the Internet, men and women who wanted to have parts of themselves amputated. One man had already had a leg removed and claimed he felt reborn, at peace for the first time. A woman had had four fingers from one hand removed and was waiting for surgery on her other hand.

Mr. Black showed Emily where he wanted the surgeon to cut, precisely two inches above the elbow. Then everything would be better. He could begin looking for a new job in earnest. Reconnect with his estranged daughter. Go out in public without feeling like a leper.

The session ended and Mr. Black got up to leave. He collected his notebook. Emily shook his hand and then held on, her other hand on his forearm. She didn't seem to notice Mr. Black's shudder.

"I'll see you tomorrow evening at the lab?"

He nodded, his gaze riveted on the arm that Emily held. He cleared his throat.

"You gave me the address already."

"Right. Park in the building. If anyone asks, tell them you have an appointment with Dr. Shands."

When she let go, a look of relief washed over Mr. Black's face. He stumbled as he left the room.

• • •

After the session Emily and I went to my office to talk. She stood, surveying my walls. Her eyes flicked over my Wines of Provence poster. She pointed to the crayon drawing of the brain and gave me a questioning look.

"I did that when I was eight. My mother had it framed when I got my doctorate in neuropsychology."

Emily gave a wry smile and shook her head. "You're amazing. You knew from the get-go that this is what you wanted to do."

I laughed. "Who knows? She saved *all* my drawings. If I'd become an astronaut she'd have framed one of my moon rockets. A baseball pitcher? I drew a whole series of Yankee Stadium."

"You played baseball?"

"Stoop ball. We didn't have ballfields in Flatbush, we had front stoops. You throw a Spalding," I said, pronouncing it *Spaldeen*. "You know, a pink rubber ball."

"How fascinating. And?" Emily said, facing me now, her chin resting on her fist.

"You really want to hear this?" She nodded, her eyes wide. It had been ages since I'd thought about stoop ball, though I'd played it with Danny Ellentuck just about every day after school. "You throw it against the steps and the other guy tries to catch the ball on the rebound. After one bounce it's a single, two a double. Catch it on a fly and you're out. Three outs and you switch and the other person gets to throw the ball. The real object of the game is to hit the edge of the step on the stoop because then the ball goes flying and you get a home run."

Emily smiled appreciatively. "Where I grew up there were no front stoops, or ballfields either."

She picked up a matted photograph I had lying on my bookcase. It was a black-and-white picture of a woman in black with a mournful face and long flowing hair. She stood intertwined with the sinuous trunk and limbs of a tree. Undulating lines merged nature and woman into a single form.

"A patient gave that to me," I told her. "She knew I liked Annie Brigman's work."

"It's a pretty disturbing image."

"I guess that's why I haven't put it up. Not something I want patients to have to confront while they're in therapy." I paused. "That's the thing about therapy. It's why that therapy room is so neutral. The point is for the patient to deal with what *they* bring into the room, not what we put in there or what we bring of ourselves."

Emily sat down in a chair. She tilted her head to one side, alert to the nuance. "Are you saying that I'm bringing something into that room?"

I ducked under the ceiling overhang and sat at my desk, my

back to the dormer window. "I noticed you trying to keep a therapeutic distance. That's good. But shaking Mr. Black's hand, holding on to his arm the way you did—it made it uncomfortable for him."

"But I was just—" Emily started. She took a breath and started over. "Yalom says therapists should make a point to touch a patient during each session. Touch makes a patient feel valued."

"I know there are therapists who make a point of shaking hands when the patient comes and when they leave. That's not inappropriate. But perhaps touching a man with this particular disorder is pushing it. For him, it may be as intrusive as if your own therapist patted you on the behind."

She swallowed. "Do you think I upset him?"

"He definitely reacted. It's hard to gauge whether he took it as an aggressive intrusion, as a sexual overture, or just as a too-friendly gesture." I rested my elbows on the blotter and folded my hands. "You want to be a neutral presence and deal with his *mishigas*, not yours."

"Of course. You're absolutely right. I guess I'm a toucher. And it's not always the right thing to be doing." Emily wrote in her notebook. "I'm so glad you called me on it. It's something I need to watch."

It was gratifying to work with a bright post-doc who didn't go all defensive in the face of constructive feedback. Who actually wrote down suggestions. Who knew she hadn't arrived at this rotation knowing all the answers.

As she leaned toward me, her buttoned suit jacket gaped. I caught a glimpse of skin and a transparent, flesh-colored camisole that Emily wasn't wearing anything underneath.

"And, uh . . ." I tried to remember what I'd been saying. "Everything you do, what you wear . . ."

She tugged at the hem of her skirt.

I needed to say more. But how to do it without sounding like a lech or a prig? "You have to be careful about the signals you're sending," I said, raising my eyebrows and looking at her suit jacket as I touched my hand to my chest. "You might be encouraging the wrong kind of attention."

It worked. Emily glanced down and then shrank back. "I didn't realize—" she started.

"Any patient is going to notice. Someone like Mr. Black, with body dysmorphia, is going to be riveted. He's already made a remark about your body. It's like having a clanging bell in the room providing a constant source of interference."

"Of course, you're right." Emily looked up at me. "How inconsiderate of me. Do you think that's the reason I haven't been getting anywhere with him? I keep trying to get him to examine other aspects of his life, his personality, when this first arose—and he always comes back to 'I need to cut off my arm.'"

"That's classic resistance," I said. "You poke around where he's sensitive and he becomes intractable. He redirects the dialogue."

"Every time. *I need to cut off my arm.* It's like a mantra that he keeps chanting at me." Emily gave an anxious glance at her front. The suit jacket had stayed in place.

"I'm sure there's more to his resistance than what you're wearing," I said. What a therapist wore was easily fixed, once he or she was aware. "I had an obsessive patient who drove me nuts. He'd go on and on about how miserable his life was. Nothing I could do could make him shift perspective. With people who are obsessed like that, it takes on such intensity that no matter how logically you argue, you lose."

"That's Mr. Black all right," Emily said. "Remember, we talked about whether the roots of his obsession might be organic?"

It was an interesting idea which Emily had begun to investigate. At first I'd dismissed the notion that something in Mr. Black's brain was telling him that he shouldn't have an arm. Then I reconsidered. Why not? People with phantom limb syndrome continue to feel sensations in an arm or leg long after that limb has been amputated. We'd speculated about what a functional MRI might show. Maybe arm movement on one side elicited qualitatively different responses in the brain. One of the pleasures of working with a bright young psychologist, new to the field, was wrestling with fresh ideas.

"I was able to convince Dr. Shands to give me an hour on the new system."

"*New* system?" I asked. In recent years, magnetic resonance imaging technology had taken huge strides. Scanners had become smaller and less intimidating, and at the same time more powerful. And unlike PET and CT systems, huge magnets didn't give off radiation.

"It's a four-point-five tesla machine."

I whistled. That made it nine times as strong as the one we had at the Pearce. Must have cost a fortune. But then, the medical schools would be flocking to it with their research grants. It would pay for itself long before it became outdated. In the meantime Shands had his own his own high-tech playground—a researcher's dream.

"I've never seen a system that powerful. I'll be very interested to see what you find out."

"You want to observe? It's tomorrow night," Emily said, her color rising. "There's usually a no-observers policy, but I'm sure he'll make an exception for you. You can sit in the control room with me. You'll actually see the images as they come in. The computer synthesizes them to three-D. It's like watching a movie of the brain in action."

I glanced up at my crayon drawing of the brain, at the plastic model of the brain I kept on my shelf. I remembered the excitement I'd felt when I dissected my first brain. I couldn't turn down a ringside seat, watching a brain in operation.

Tomorrow night? Shit. That was when I had a date with Annie. I heard myself saying "What time?" Immediately I felt a rush of guilt. I'd just stood Annie up and now I was about to do it again.

"Eight." She turned to a new page in her notebook and wrote, tore off the sheet, and handed it to me. The note said "University Medical Imaging Center" with a Sidney Street address in Cambridge.

Surely the test wouldn't take more than an hour. I'd call Annie and see if we could get together after. As I tucked the paper into my pocket I wondered what the hell was wrong with me anyway. Most men had the problem of letting the little head control their actions. I seemed to be letting my big one run amok.

"Thanks for the feedback." Emily stood, reaching out to shake. I got up and grasped her hand. "I was also wondering what you thought about my questioning. Did I overstep?" she asked. Her hand was warm in mine. I felt a moment of discomfort as she held on, her eyes rapt.

"Not for the most part," I said, jerking my hand away and reaching to straighten my bow tie. Okay, she's pretty and you're flattered by the attention, I told myself. You're her supervisor. Where's your clinical distance? "The only place I thought you skated the line was when you reminded him that he wouldn't be able to change his mind. It wasn't so much *what* you said as *how* you said it. It felt somewhat confrontational." My voice sounded stiff and formal.

"I guess I don't want him to make a terrible mistake."

It was the kind of thing you typically heard from an inexperienced therapist. "Remember, you never know what's best for your patient." I opened the door for her.

"But what if he makes the wrong decision? I mean, amputation? It's barbaric."

"It's his decision to make. His life to live. You can't help him unless you truly believe that."

She was halfway out the door when she stopped and turned back. "How do you think he knows I drive a Miata?"

I'd wondered the same thing. "You think it could be him?"

"I wouldn't have thought so," she said.

I agreed — Mr. Black seemed far too self-absorbed to have formed an obsessive attachment to Emily. On the other hand, I'd evaluated enough murderers to know that villains took surprising shapes. Ralston Bridges had fooled a jury.

"I wouldn't rule anybody out unless you know for sure," I said. "Please be careful."

4

"I'M SURE you'll be dazzled by it," Annie said dryly after I told her I had an opportunity to see a functional MRI on this new machine, and could we postpone our date. "Actually, I was going to call you. Something has come up—"

"I could be there by nine-thirty. Ten, the latest," I tried.

"No, really, it's okay. I'm probably going to be tied up."

"Another family emergency?"

"Something like that."

"Is there anything I can do to help?"

"Maybe." I heard some papers rustle on her end. "I'll let you know."

I hoped "family emergency" wasn't just a convenient excuse. I was coming up with one bad scenario after another. I'd been crowding her and she needed some space. An old boyfriend was in town. She was doing round-the-clock surveillance on a particularly dangerous case and didn't want to worry me.

"You could try calling me when you're done," Annie said. "I may be finished."

"Sounds great. I can pick us up some takeout from Mary Chung's, maybe a pint of French vanilla from Toscanini's?" I get that from my mother, a belief in the power of good food.

"Mmm," she said, but it sounded as if her mind was already somewhere else.

Her good-bye was distinctly distant and our conversation felt unfinished. It was still gnawing at me the next evening when I drove to the imaging center. My stomach rumbled, reminding me that I hadn't eaten anything since a bowl of tepid minestrone soup and a packet of saltines at lunch. Some dun dun noodles from Mary Chung's sure would hit the spot. I hoped Annie would be home when I was done.

I turned down Sidney Street. This area had been transformed over the last five years. Once the home of the Simplex Wire and Cable Company, the area was now the poster child for urban renewal, Cambridge style—a mixture of residential buildings, office space targeting before-the-bust dot-coms and biotech startups, with a hotel and giant supermarket thrown in for good measure. A historic brick-and-beam factory building, where myth has it they baked the first Fig Newton, was now artist lofts.

I drove past the modern glass-and-granite office building. The entrance to the basement parking garage was around the corner. I had to go two levels down to find a spot. Then I rode the elevator up to the main floor.

The lobby had a high ceiling with an old-fashioned crystal chandelier that would have felt right at home at the Met. The interior, with its warm wood and brass fittings, was designed for tenants who could afford to pay plenty of overhead.

A uniformed security guard behind a circular mahogany counter asked me to sign in. He pointed me to the two-story archway that led to the University Medical Imaging Center. A pair of potted trees, taller than I, flanked the double glass doorway.

In the waiting area, the large window in the wall was slid open. A young woman at a desk on the other side had her jacket on and was shutting down her computer. She was tall and blond, like she was fresh off Malibu Beach. I told her who I was and why I was there. She disappeared into the back.

While I waited I looked around the empty carpeted waiting room. Rows of straight-backed chairs were punctuated by low tables loaded with magazines. The photos on the wall were blow-ups of historic Boston. I was admiring a picture of the Old Howard—a burlesque house in Scollay Square, that mythic part of Boston long ago torn down to make way for a soulless Government Center— when the door to the inner area flew open. A tall, handsome man with a chiseled profile and a mane of silver curls came toward me, his hand outstretched. He wore wire-rimmed glasses and his teeth glowed.

"Dr. Zak?" he said. "Dr. Ryan has told me all about you. I'm Jim Shands."

He had the firm handshake of a seasoned politician. He ushered me into an antiseptic-smelling area where harsh fluorescent lighting bounced off a white vinyl floor.

"Please, call me Peter. I've read your papers on Lewy body dementia. Very interesting."

"And I've read yours on memory," he said. "Impressive."

His gaze fell to a FedEx box on the floor. "What the . . . ?" he started. Labels on it read WET ICE and STORE AT 4° C. "How the hell long has this been here? They know I've been waiting for this." He looked around and, seeing no one, raised his voice. "Why in God's name didn't someone tell me this was here?"

He picked up the box like someone might pick up a newborn baby and cradled it in his arms. "Amanda," he barked. "Where is that girl?"

"I think she went home," I said.

"Incompetence." He muttered some more about how he'd told her a million times. Then to me, "Sorry. I need to take care of this. This won't take a minute."

He disappeared down the corridor. When he returned a short time later he seemed fully recovered.

"I appreciate your allowing me to observe," I said. "I don't know nearly as much as I'd like to about MRI technology."

"If you're going to see it, this is the place. We've got the strongest whole-body magnet used for clinical imaging in the country."

We started down the corridor.

"I understand you do some forensic work?" he said.

"I evaluate people who are accused of crimes." I didn't mention that I always work for the defense. I'd learned not to the hard way, having sat through more than my share of lectures that began with raised eyebrows and a knowing look, followed by *Oh, so you're one of those hired guns.*

"Have you read about the recent Johns Hopkins work, examining brain scans of convicted criminals?" Shands asked. "They found abnormalities in the prefrontal cortex."

I'd read the study. Their findings confirmed what had been hypothesized for years—that the prefrontal cortex plays a role in controlling emotions and behavior. It invited the question: Could we "fix" a criminal's frontal lobes so he'd stop committing crimes? This kind of speculation had encouraged a flurry of work exploring drug therapies and brain surgery. Cingulotomies—operations to excise a portion of the brain's limbic system—were in vogue. The operation seemed to help certain patients, especially extreme obsessives. Still, the thought of it made me shudder. I hoped we weren't headed back to the good old days of frontal lobotomies à la *One Flew Over the Cuckoo's Nest.*

We approached a pair of double doors. There was a sign on one of them, a bright yellow triangle with a picture of a horseshoe magnet on it with zaps of lightning coming from the ends. Below it were the words STRONG MAGNETIC FIELD, and below that NO METALLIC IMPLANTS.

Shands pointed to the sign and gave me a questioning look.

"No implants," I said. "At least none that I know of."

I'd heard that the magnetic pull of an MRI system could be powerful enough to stop pacemakers. The magnet could dislodge an aneurysm clip in the brain, tearing the artery it had been used to repair.

Shands pushed one door open; I pushed the other. On the other side was what felt like the hub of the lab. There was a large, semi-circular counter in the center with rolling desk chairs and low file cabinets arrayed around it. Everything was white except for dark red chair cushions. Corridors radiated off in three directions.

"The magnet is always on, even if the power to the unit is shut down," Shands said. "So even though the scan room is shielded, you have to be careful what you take any closer." He gave me a plastic container. "Something as innocuous as a paperclip has a terminal velocity of over a hundred miles an hour when pulled into the magnet. Not to mention the magnetic field erases all your credit cards."

Emily Ryan came in as I was taking off my watch and emptying my pockets, dropping my credit cards, spare change, cell phone, and car keys into the container. She had on a white lab coat over her dark suit, and her ponytail swung from side to side as she walked toward us.

"Dr. Zak," she said, her face lighting up. She hoisted herself up onto the countertop and swung her legs. She was obviously comfortable here. "I'm just about finished getting Mr. Black set up. Should be another ten, fifteen minutes."

"Why don't I take Peter back with me, then?" Shands said. "I can tell him about the work we've been doing."

• • •

Shands's office was spacious and bright with a view overlooking an atrium courtyard. Green and pink spotlights illuminated a jungle of tropical plants. A few tall trees reached up toward the light. Unlike the vegetation we had adorning the neuropsychiatric unit, I was willing to bet that not one of these was plastic.

"So Dr. Ryan is working for you, too?" He raised his eyebrows, as if "working for" were code for something else.

"She's doing a post-doc on the neuropsychiatric unit."

"She's very eager," he said. "A hard worker." I wondered if he always sounded so condescending talking about the people with whom he worked. "She tells me you rescued her the other night. Did you see anything?"

"What kind of anything?"

"Oh, like the person who she says is following her. It's got her so spooked she's afraid of her own shadow."

"I may have seen something," I said. It was a lie, but I didn't want to undercut Emily's credibility and make her look like a kook. Her terror had seemed so real.

"And?"

I shrugged. "I didn't get a good look at whoever it was."

"I'm glad you made sure she got home safely," he said, as some of the tension lines in his forehead erased themselves.

I felt a pang of guilt. I probably should have. "Actually, I offered to, but—" I adjusted my tie. Why was I doing this? I didn't owe him an explanation. "Nice office," I said, looking around.

There were the usual diplomas and awards hanging behind the massive mahogany desk. Less usual was a bank of light boxes. One had a film of a brain scan clipped to it. It was a slice looking from the top down with areas highlighted in color. In the neighboring light box was a transparency of what looked like a tissue sample. I leaned in to get a closer look at the red cells with white halos around them, floating on a mottled reddish background.

"That was our breakthrough," Shands said. "The first patient we diagnosed with Lewy body dementia from a functional MRI and later confirmed. Those are cortical Lewy bodies." Shands pointed to the deformed brain cells with their white borders. "They're actually cytoplasmic inclusions that seem to kill brain cells, resulting in Lewy body dementia and Parkinson's disease. What we've discovered is that by altering cell membrane permeability, we can stop the formation of Lewy bodies and prevent the death of brain cells."

Among the dementias, Lewy body was once thought to be extremely rare. We'd come to realize it was actually much more common. But it could only be diagnosed definitively by examining brain cells.

"Autopsy?" I asked.

He nodded.

That was the frustrating thing. You could look at behavior, test results, brain scans, blood work, and X rays until you were blue in the face. Still, a diagnosis on a living patient was usually at least part guesswork. Too bad patients had to die to satisfy scientific curiosity.

"Must have been very exciting," I said.

"Probably the most satisfying moment of my career." He pointed to an area of the MRI scan. "Here's the marker. We could actually see the change in the diffusion of water molecules. See here, and here. The cells are less permeable." He was pointing to the basal ganglia. I nodded, though I didn't know what I was supposed to be seeing.

"That would account for the movement disorders," I said.

"Of course, this was only the first case. We've had lots more since. We'll need hundreds to convince the medical community."

Hundreds of brain scans. Then hundreds of autopsies to confirm the diagnosis. At least patients with Lewy body dementia died fairly quickly—within a year or two. It would only take a few decades for Shands to make his case.

My mother had refused to authorize an autopsy after my father died. Didn't matter to her one way or another whether it was Alzheimer's or something else that had taken my father's soul long before his heart stopped beating. She wanted no more indignities inflicted on him. I'd been the one who wanted to know, but it was her decision to make.

"Now we can give a definitive diagnosis early," Shands continued. "Before there are even symptoms. We're looking at extremely early intervention. Medication that increases the permeability of brain cells. We're administering Cimvicor."

Cimvicor had been approved by the FDA for the treatment of high cholesterol. It had long been known that many drugs that reduced cholesterol also increased cell permeability.

Shands went on. "Within just a few weeks we're seeing changes in the brain in response to the drug. That's a whole lot faster than the months it takes for us to see definitive cognitive improvement."

"Does it delay the onset of the disease?" I asked.

"Delay? Prevent? That's what we're trying to find out." He gave a wry smile. "That's why the research is so important. If we can identify patients early, confirm the diagnosis with a functional MRI, treat it aggressively, we may even have what amounts to a cure. Hold out some hope to families suffering through the nightmare of this disease."

There was a light tap at the door. Emily stuck her head in. "Ready when you are."

Shands offered me his hand and we shook. "Nice meeting you." He held on and put his other hand on my forearm. "By the way, if you're interested in having your brain scanned, we're always looking to add normals to our library. The only way data makes sense is when we can do comparisons to an overall population."

I grinned. "Me? Get an MRI?" I couldn't help the enthusiasm. It sounded pretty neat. Wouldn't hurt to have the experience, I told myself—that way I'd be in a better position to advise my own patients about what it was like.

Shands knew just how to seal the deal.

"Sure," he said. "Why not? We'll even give you a souvenir image for your wall."

I wondered what my mother would think if I installed a light box in my living room and displayed a scan of my own brain. I'm sure she wouldn't find it nearly as charming as the crayon drawing of an eight-year-old.

"Talk to Dr. Ryan about it before you leave," Shands said. "She'll schedule you."

"ISN'T HE amazing? His work is completely original," Emily said as we headed back into the central area. I suspected Shands inspired this kind of hero worship in many of the young researchers who came to work in his shadow. "And he's so dedicated—beyond anything I've ever experienced."

I followed her into another hallway. We passed the open door to a small room filled with person-sized dewars marked LIQUID HELIUM. I assumed they used cryogenic gas to cool the coils through which electrical currents passed to create the magnetic field. There were also a few smaller tanks marked OXYGEN, one of them set on a narrow handcart with wheels. In the hall were a pair of yellow sawhorses and more warning signs: CAUTION and NO METALLIC OBJECTS BEYOND THIS POINT.

Sitting on one of the sawhorses was what looked like a flattened hockey puck. Emily picked it up. "You don't mind if I just check to be sure you haven't got anything on you that'll be attracted to the magnet?" When I looked puzzled, she added, "This is our test magnet. We use it to check anything metallic before it goes into the scan room—and we double-check people, too."

"Sure," I said, and held my arms out like I was at the airport about to get wanded.

As she ran the magnet up and down each side of my body, then front and back, she said, "I love working here. The excitement of being at the edge of what's possible. Imagine, the third most commonly diagnosed dementia, and we're going to cure it?" Emily's cheeks had turned pink. "The hard part is working with patients who are dying. Seems like you just get the chance to know them and they're gone."

That was one of the hallmarks of Lewy body dementia—death came more quickly than with Alzheimer's.

Emily put the magnet back on the sawhorse. Across the hall I noticed a door marked PRIVATE.

"What's in there?" I asked.

"That's Bluebeard's chamber," Emily said, giving me a wink. "Honestly, I don't know what's in there. It's the only lock with a different combination from the other ones in the lab." I noticed the keypad lock on the doorknob. "Only senior staff gets to go in there."

As she moved on I tried the door, like a little kid unable to resist. It wouldn't budge.

I followed Emily to a heavy metal door that was propped open. I assumed it was part of the shield Shands said protected the scan room. Beyond, in a large bright room, Mr. Black was lying on a narrow table attached to a massive white cube that was the MRI scanner.

"Just a few minutes more," Emily told Mr. Black.

Then she led me through a door connecting the scan room to another room. "This is our control room."

The overhead lights in this room were off. In the half-light, computer monitors and wall-mounted light boxes glowed. Through a wide window in the connecting wall to the scan room we could see Mr. Black on the table, and directly beyond him, into the horizontal tube that ran through the magnet from front to back. No wonder some patients freaked, unable to tolerate having to remain motionless in such tight quarters.

Emily sat me at a monitor by the window. "We'll be able to watch from here." To one side, there was a control panel with an array of buttons.

I heard someone cough and looked around. "That was Mr. Black," Emily explained, indicating a speaker mounted in the console. "We'll be able to hear everything that goes on in there."

A short, heavyset man in a white lab coat slunk into the room. He had thinning hair, glasses, and the pale, unhealthy look of someone who didn't see daylight often. A folded newspaper was tucked under his arm.

"Hey, Lenny," Emily said. "This is Dr. Leonard Philbrick, the real expert on this stuff. Lenny, this is Dr. Peter Zak. I work with him at the Pearce."

Philbrick gave me the once-over through thick lenses. "Shands say he was okay in here?" he asked, his voice high-pitched. Sweat stains were just visible under the arms of his lab coat.

"Uh-huh. I was just about to explain how all this works," Emily said. "But you're much more eloquent—"

Philbrick seemed to take the flattery as his due. "It's not complicated." He set down the newspaper and slid a well-chewed pencil into his pocket. "You know how a functional MRI works?"

"Sure," I said. "I get the general idea." I knew that in a regular MRI of the brain, the scanner took picture after picture, slice after slice. In a functional MRI the same thing happened, only much more quickly so you got a series of images of the brain. Somehow, with the help of a computer, the images got assembled to show changes in the brain over time.

Philbrick said, "Then you know that the data shows us where blood supply increases during mental activity. Our experiments generate huge amounts of information quickly. It used to take days to process the data into a high-rez three-D image."

He avoided eye contact, his gaze darting around the room as he talked.

"Our scanner is one of the most powerful in the country. We use helium to cool the superconducting magnet coils. The system holds almost a thousand liters of liquid helium." I wondered if that explained the thickness of the cube walls.

"Our scanner records data from the brain and transmits it via high-speed network to a Cray T3E in there"—he indicated a glass wall through which I could see a massive black multisection cabinet with a jaunty red racing stripe—"which converts the raw data into three-D images, compensates for head movement, and identifies the level of activity in different areas of the brain. From the T3E the data travels here where we can watch what areas of the brain light up. Functional imaging in real time," he said, his voice caressing the words.

Philbrick kneaded his hands together. "We've already got one of the largest libraries of brain scans in the country."

I could imagine him poring over the data bank, Midas counting his gold.

"It's the first comprehensive collection of MRIs of patients with Lewy body dementia," Emily added. "Plus lots of normals for comparison. Mine's in there. So's Lenny's. Lenny modified the controls so we can even do it ourselves. Just push a button and the program takes care of everything. Slides you in, administers the test, slides you out. It's pretty amazing to see your own brain working."

I could relate to the "amazing" part. But I wasn't too keen to slide myself into that narrow tube without knowing that someone could haul me out if something went wrong. "Dr. Shands said you could set me up for a scan."

"Sure. I'll do it before you leave."

"You staying late?" Philbrick asked Emily, squinting at his watch.

"Dr. Shands is letting me use the scanner for a research project." She blinked at him. "Oh, gosh, Lenny." She put her hand on his shoulder. "I'm sorry. I forgot we were going grab a bite later. You want to hang around? We can —"

Philbrick's mouth turned down, pinched at the edges as his eyes darted at me and away. "Not a problem," he said. "I can't make it tonight anyway."

"Lenny's worked for Dr. Shands for ages," Emily said brightly.

I couldn't read Philbrick's look. "Yes," he said. "I've collaborated with Dr. Shands for more than ten years." There was a big difference between "worked for" and "collaborated with."

"Of course, that's what I meant." Emily gave a nervous laugh.

"Though it's Dr. Ryan here who scored a credit on his latest paper. Quite a coup. Took me three years to do that." His words were addressed to the computer monitor.

"Thanks." Emily was glowing. "It just got accepted in the *Journal of Neuroimaging*. Real snappy title. 'Neurocognitive Correlates of Lewy Body Dementia.' I did the neuropsych testing and wrote up the methodology."

Philbrick hung his lab coat on a hook and grabbed a rumpled raincoat. "Make sure you get someone to walk you to your car later." He addressed the warning to his own shoulder.

"Don't forget this," I said, picking up the newspaper he'd left on the table. It had been folded over to the obituaries.

He grabbed it and left, leaving behind a slightly sour smell.

"Lenny was with Dr. Shands and Dr. Pullaski at Harvard," Emily said. "He helped set up this place. Got the designers to remove an entire floor so the magnets wouldn't affect the other building tenants. Lenny knows more than anyone about this technology but he stays behind the scenes pretty much. He's not so weird, once you get used to him."

"He walks you to your car?"

Emily smiled. "He's a sweetheart."

Emily picked up two fist-sized pink rubber balls from the table and unhooked a pair of high-tech goggles and a set of headphones from the wall. "The system makes quite a racket during a scan. These muffle the noise," she said indicating the headphones. "Plus I can communicate with him through them."

"You playing stoop ball in there?" I asked.

Emily laughed, looking down at the rubber balls. "No. I'm going to give them to Mr. Black. You'll see. He'll use them during the test."

• • •

"Mr. Black, can you hear me?" Emily said, addressing the question to the microphone in the control room.

From inside the scanner, Mr. Black answered that he could. Emily turned up the volume so we could hear him better.

"Get ready now. I'm going to start the scan. You'll hear noises. That's perfectly normal. I'd like you to just lie there. Relax." Emily put her hand over the microphone. "First we take a baseline."

Now the machine was making loud, rhythmic, buzzing sounds.

The window in a corner of the screen flickered and an image started to materialize. Instead of slice after slice of brain, an integrated, three-dimensional image of a brain hovered in front of me. It blurred and came back into focus. Mr. Black must have moved.

We sat there in silence for about a minute. Then Emily leaned into the microphone. "Mr. Black?"

Now the machine was making thumping sounds along with the buzzing. It was the kind of noise you'd expect in the bowels of a manufacturing plant. What we saw was amazing. There were pulses of yellow in the bluish green on either side near the temples, and immediately more pulses closer to the center as Mr. Black heard, then processed what he'd heard.

Emily began what seemed like a test routine. She asked Mr. Black to open and close his eyes, say his name, his mother's maiden name. She logged the time at which she made each request. I watched, fascinated, as different areas of the brain were activated, pulsing in a spectrum from green to yellow to orange. It was like watching a supersonic pinball game. I wanted to slow it down.

The door to the control room opened and a woman stepped in. She was an imposing presence with her stylishly cut short black hair streaked with gray and her dark eyes, eyebrows nearly meeting over her nose. She had on a lab coat, and an ID tag hung from her neck. "Dr. Ryan? I didn't realize you were using the scanner."

"Mr. Black, I'm going to pause the scan for just a moment," Emily said into the microphone. She pressed a button and the scanner fell silent. "Yes, I'm working with a patient," she said with her hand covering the microphone.

"I can see that. Who gave you permission?"

"Dr. Shands said it was okay."

"And we don't allow visitors." The woman's nostrils quivered as she eyed Emily, then me.

"Dr. Pullaski, this is Dr. Peter Zak. He runs the Neuropsychiatric Unit at the Pearce."

I could feel Dr. Pullaski lower her hackles. *The Pearce* bestowed an instant patina of legitimacy on anyone associated with it.

I stood and offered my hand, told her how I'd heard such wonderful things about University Medical Imaging and how I was grateful to have a chance to see their amazing system in action. She gave me a thin smile. This was not a woman to be patronized.

"And where is Dr. Shands?" she asked.

"He's around." Emily waved her hand distractedly. "Somewhere. I'm sorry. I thought you knew."

"I'm sure you did," Dr. Pullaski said. Then she wheeled around and left.

"That," Emily breathed the word, "was Dr. Estelle Pullaski, the executive director. She and Dr. Shands are like this." She held up two fingers. "She runs this place, right down to the last latex glove and hypodermic syringe. She's always got a bug up her ass about something. I mean, the system was going to be idle anyway."

Emily removed her hand from the microphone. "Mr. Black, we're going to start again." She pressed a button on a control panel and the system started up again. "Now I'm going to show you some pictures."

To me she explained, "Those goggles I gave him? We project images from here onto the insides of the lenses."

A window had opened up on the monitor screen showing a photograph of a bouquet of flowers. Emily noted the time. Then she pressed the button again. Now the picture changed to a person's arm. She went on, changing the images and marking the times on the test protocol. With each change in the image, there were subtle but perceptible changes in Mr. Black's brain. But it was all happening too fast to make any sense to me.

"That's very good. Now could you squeeze the ball in your left hand?"

I watched carefully, seeing the activity I expected in the right motor strip and the areas around it.

"Excellent," Emily said. "Now squeeze the ball in your right hand." This was the arm he wanted amputated.

We both watched intently. There was some activity in and around the left motor strip. Definitely not the zero response Emily must have hoped for. But was it what you'd expect in a "normal"? I had no idea.

Emily continued giving Mr. Black tasks to perform. Flex one foot, then the other. Hyperextend each knee. Shrug each shoulder.

By the end, Emily's breath had quickened and she could barely stay seated, she was so excited. "I'll have to analyze it, of course. But there's something here, I'm sure of it. I'll just save this — " She clicked a few times, typed something.

Quickly she showed me how to rerun it, how to control the speed of the replay. Then she went off to release Mr. Black.

It was just after nine-thirty. Plenty of time to pick up some food and get over to Annie's. I used the phone on the wall to call her house. There was no answer. I tried her cell phone next. No answer there either. She probably had it turned off. Damn. Still, it was early. Maybe by the time I left here, she'd be home.

I returned to the computer and stared into the screen. *She'll tell you what it's about when she's good and ready to,* I told myself.

I ran the animation again, fast-forwarding through the beginning, slowing down in the part where she'd asked him to squeeze the balls. The right squeeze had definitely elicited a different response on one side of the brain than a left squeeze had elicited on the other side. But was it a random difference or was it measurable and consistent? What about the legs — was there a generalized effect right to left? What if he'd been asked to create a mental image of his right arm and then of his left arm? What if he'd closed one eye and then the other? What if he'd been shown pictures of amputees? My mind was throwing off ideas like sparks from a grinding wheel.

I sat back, enjoying the rush of intellectual energy. None of this technology had existed when I'd been in grad school. If it had, I might easily have ended up a researcher instead of clinician.

I fingered a sheaf of stapled papers Emily had left on the desk. "Consent by Subject for Participation in Research Protocol." It looked as if she'd quickly revised the standard one Shands used for his research. Purpose of the study. Procedures. Risks and discomforts. She hadn't had to change much. The procedure, an MRI, was the same. Some paragraphs just above Mr. Black's signature had been deleted, the text marked over with thick-tipped black marker and initialed by Mr. Black. I wondered what Shands routinely had as part of his consent form that Emily found inappropriate for her research. I was about to turn the paper over and see if I could read it from the back when the door opened and Emily returned.

"He's on his way home," she told me. "No worse for wear."

She picked up the consent form and the test protocol and I followed her up the corridor, out into the central area. I'd pocketed my change, wallet, and credit cards and was about to use my cell phone to call Annie again when I heard raised voices. Emily had grown still.

"I don't understand why you're taking chances." It was a woman's voice. "We've been at this too long—"

A man's voice cut her off. I could only catch bits and pieces. ". . . overreacting . . . off your high horse . . . it's my business . . ."

"You're a fool, James—" Dr. Pullaski stormed out into the hall. Her words died when she saw us staring at her. "Next time," she said, directing her words like darts at Emily, "please get *my* permission before you commandeer the resources of the Center." She stalked off.

Shands came out, looking decidedly pissed. "Estelle!" he called after her. When he saw Emily, his look softened. "Emily, I'm sorry. I'll get this straightened out." He followed Dr. Pullaski down the hall.

Emily's hands were shaking as she tried to slide the sheaf of papers into her briefcase.

"I'll walk you to your car," I said, helping her off with her lab coat.

"You don't need to do that."

"Humor me."

We rode down in the elevator in silence. Emily's mouth was set, the clenching and unclenching of the muscles in her jaw the only indication she didn't have her emotions in check. She hesitated when the elevator doors opened. I looked out into the garage. There were plenty of shadowy corners between cars where someone might have been lurking. I found myself wanting to put my arm around Emily, to protect her from whatever bogeyman was about to jump out at her.

The Miata was parked across from the elevator. She opened her trunk and tossed in her briefcase. When I put my hand on her shoulder, Emily shuddered.

"Sure you're okay?" I asked.

"Sure I'm sure. I'm fine." Her voice was tense.

She got into her car. I stood aside as she started it up and pulled out. When she stopped at the top of the ramp, no taillights came on.

I didn't like it. If someone had tampered with her brake lights, there was no telling what else they'd messed with. And what was that gasoline smell? Maybe he'd punctured the tank. I didn't see any wet spots on the floor, but the smell seemed overpowering to me.

"Hey," I shouted, starting to run after her. But she'd already taken off.

I RAN to my car and jumped in. I pulled out and gunned it. By the time I got to the attendant's booth, the wooden barrier was coming down and Emily's Miata was gone. I threw a ten-dollar bill at the guy and bit my tongue while I waited for change.

I knew she lived in Brookline. Best guess, she was headed down toward the river. The tires screeched as I peeled out. With the three- or four-block head start she had and without any taillights visible, I'd have to go on instinct. I'd never be able to see her ahead of me in the maze of back streets. I thought I caught sight of a red sports car crossing the BU Bridge. I tried to zigzag around other drivers to close the gap between us.

On Comm. Ave. I got stuck at a light behind a bus. When the light turned green, I swerved around it, my tires scraping against the curb of the trolley platform that ran down the middle of the street.

I caught a glimpse of the car again as we crossed the border into

Brookline. After a few streets, she took a left. I'd almost caught up with her when she pulled into the well-lit parking lot of a multistory brick apartment building, one of those sturdy ones built in the forties. I slid to a stop under a tree. I was about to get out when I saw a shadowy figure, skirting the corner of the building under cover of trees.

Emily got out carrying a pile of clothing. She'd popped the trunk. She went around and pulled out her briefcase.

I flipped off the dome light, opened my car door, and slipped out. Now Emily was walking across the parking lot, her heels tapping on the concrete. She gave an anxious look over her shoulder.

There was definitely someone out there, pressed up against the side of the building, moving closer. Now Emily was almost under the ornate carved archway. I debated what to do. I could slam the car door and call out her name. That would scare him off. Or I could stalk him the way he was stalking Emily, catch him in the act. It was no contest. Unmasking him was far preferable to getting him spooked.

I moved closer. The figure moved closer, too. Emily was at the door. She was rummaging in her bag for her key. Using a row of parked cars for cover, I crouched and made my way to the building. I was almost clear of the last car when I heard the front door of the building close. I hovered, just able to see Emily inside, waiting at the elevator. She punched the button impatiently.

I scanned the parking lot. The base of the building. Whoever had been lurking there had vanished. I froze and listened. A car whooshed past. The trees rustled in a light breeze. Then I heard footsteps behind me and adrenaline shot through me. Before I could turn and rear back, something large hit me from behind and I was flat on the ground, gasping for breath. Someone was pushing my face down into the concrete.

"You got a problem, buddy?" the man growled at me. He ground his knee into my back. I couldn't move, never mind argue with him. It felt like I had a two-hundred-pound gorilla sitting on me.

He had me by the collar now and was lifting me up. "Get your fucking hands off me," I said, gasping as I scrambled to my feet. His fist connected with my face and I staggered back.

I was coming at him, ready to punch him out when Emily came running across the parking lot.

"Kyle!" she shouted. "Leave him alone!"

Kyle? I wondered if this guy, who looked like he could play fullback for the Pats, knew that Emily referred to him as her "ex"-boyfriend.

"I caught him in the act," Kyle said. "Lousy sonofabitch."

"You idiot," Emily said. She stood in front of Kyle, her hands on his chest. "Take it easy. Time out." She touched his face.

I'd never seen anyone hypnotize an alligator, but this must be what it was like. Kyle went from tense and raging to calm and docile in about ten seconds. The guy was handsome in a frat-boy kind of way, dark wavy hair that was beginning to recede, broad shoulders, and a strong chin and jaw that was starting to grow jowls.

"I know you think you're protecting me," she said, "but I don't want you hanging around anymore. This has to stop. I mean it."

"But he was . . ." Kyle gave me a hard look.

"Kyle Ronan, this is Dr. Peter Zak. He's my supervisor at the Pearce."

"At the Pearce? But I thought . . . aw, shit," he said. I wondered what he'd expected. "I'm sorry." Kyle started straightening my jacket. I pushed him away.

"You thought I was stalking Emily?"

"You followed her."

"Her taillights were out," I said. "And I smelled gas. I thought maybe someone punctured her gas tank, too."

"What?" Emily said, turning pale. She walked back to her car. "They're not broken."

"Open the trunk. Let's have a look," I said.

She opened the trunk. I felt around inside. There were loose wires.

"Wires have been yanked."

"Let me see that," Kyle said, pushing me aside.

"But it's a brand-new car," Emily said, her voice trembling.

Kyle was down on his hands and knees, looking under the car. "I don't smell any gas leak," he said. "Still, you should get the rest of the car checked out. You never know what else he might have screwed around with."

"Goddammit," Emily said. "This isn't going away."

"Now we know why I'm here," I told Kyle. "Why were *you* skulking around in the shadows?"

"Give me a break," he said, getting back to his feet. "I wanted to catch the bastard." Kyle gave Emily a sideways look, as if gauging her reaction. She looked exhausted as she tucked back a strand of hair. "Double-lock your door, babe. You know where to find me if you need—"

"I'm not going to need you," Emily said wearily. "Not now. Not ever." She turned on him, her eyes blazing. "And if you keep creeping around, I'm going to get a restraining order."

Kyle took a step back.

"I'm not kidding. Stay away."

Kyle's mouth turned down and his expression turned ugly. "Ungrateful bitch," he muttered, and slammed his fist into the side of the car. Then he turned on his heel and strode over to a black

Range Rover. He climbed in. The engine roared to life and he took off.

"You okay?" Emily asked.

"I'm fine," I said. I brushed the dirt off my pants and tucked in my shirt. Then I took off my tie and stuffed it into my pocket. I took a deep breath. It felt as if I'd been run over by a truck, but nothing seemed broken. "Promise me you'll get your car checked out before you drive it again."

Emily smiled. "Promise." She reached up and smoothed my collar. "And you'd better put something on that eye." Then she went into the building.

The flesh felt singed where her fingers had grazed my neck.

• • •

I got into my car and turned on the dome light. I examined my face in the mirror. My right eye was starting to swell shut. I was going to have a formidable shiner. A shower and an icepack, that's what I needed. I tried Annie one more time before heading home, but no luck.

On the way, I rolled into a Dunkin Donuts and got myself a coffee and a cup of crushed ice. I wrapped the ice in my hand-kerchief and drove one-handed, pressing the makeshift icepack to my eye.

When I got home I dumped the leftover ice in the driveway. My mother had left the porch light on. She'd lived in the other half of my side-by-side two-family ever since she and my father moved in five years ago at the start of his slide into Alzheimer's.

I mind my business, and my mother minds mine, too. If she heard me say that, she'd shoot back: "Just like your brother — always with the jokes." Truth is, we watch out for each other but pretty much stay out of each other's hair. Like that light that she'd left on for me. She didn't want me to call or knock when I got in. Just turn off the porch light, she'd tell me, "So I shouldn't worry."

She's never been happy that one of the things I do is evaluate accused criminals. Seeing my face turning various shades of purple wasn't going to allay her fears. I hurried up the walk. I didn't want to have to figure out an explanation.

I was just unlocking my door when my mother poked her head out. "It's about time," she said.

Time for what, I wondered. I looked at my watch. It was nearly ten.

I bent down to get a peck on the cheek. I knew she was preoccupied when she didn't notice my eye.

Annie was standing in the hall behind my mother. Her curly reddish hair was tied back and her gray eyes looked tense. She had on jeans and a Boston University sweatshirt that I knew she sometimes pulled on in the morning over nothing. This was her standard hanging-around-the-house outfit. There was some dirt streaked across her cheek, and her arms were folded tight across her front, as if she were cold, but I knew my mother's apartment was always toasty. What was she doing here? I knew something was wrong.

Annie noticed my eye right off.

"What happened to you?"

Now my mother noticed. "You evaluated another criminal?"

"I didn't. Actually it was a case of mistaken identity. This guy thought I was someone else."

"This guy?" my mother asked, her voice laced with skepticism.

I followed my mother and Annie through the living room, with its comfortable stuffed furniture and dark patterned carpeting, and into the kitchen. The countertops gleamed. My mother was taking an ice tray from the freezer.

"I tried calling you," I told Annie.

She reached into her pocket for her phone. "I'm sorry. I forgot I had it turned off."

Now my mother was at the sink, knocking ice cubes into a dishcloth.

"What's wrong?" I whispered to Annie, my stomach doing flip-flops. It was amazing how little it took to catapult me back to where I'd been after Kate was killed, sure that any moment another person I cared about would be tossed off the precipice.

"I needed to talk to you." She had her arms across her middle again, as if she were protecting something fragile. "I need your advice."

I realized this was the first time I'd ever heard Annie say she needed me.

My mother handed me the ice, now wrapped in a moist dishtowel. She pressed it into my hand while giving the rest of me the once-over.

"Your mom heard me knocking," Annie said. "I knew you were going over to watch that brain scan but I thought you said you'd be home by now."

"I didn't realize you were here. I'd have brought Chinese take-out."

Annie managed a smile. "And Toscanini's?"

"You haven't eaten?" My mother sucked in her breath. "Neither of you has eaten?" Her look dared either of us to deny it. "Sit."

As ordered, I sat on one of the vinyl-seated chairs with metal tube frames that had been in our kitchen in Brooklyn. My mother had already taken a pot roast out of the fridge and put it on the stove to warm. Now she was taking out a casserole of leftover noodle pudding and sliding it into the microwave. She started it up. We weren't going to starve.

"So?" I asked over the oven's hum.

Now my mother had a can of fruit cocktail wedged into the electric can opener. A minute later she'd plopped two bowls of the stuff on the table. I've never understood why my mother, a woman who waxes eloquent about healthy eating, doesn't understand that fruit cocktail is to fruit what Styrofoam is to bread.

My mother bustled about, putting out silverware, napkins, and water. She propelled Annie to the table and made her sit. My mother had her rules, and hearing bad news on an empty stomach was strictly *verboten*. I stifled myself and had a spoonful of fruit cocktail. The microwave dinged.

"What is it?" I tried once more.

"It's my Uncle Jack," Annie said.

I breathed a guilty sigh of relief—it really was a "family emergency."

"He was married to my mother's sister. Remember, I told you about him? He's the cop who arrested me when I was seventeen for drunk driving. Threw me in jail overnight." Annie smiled at the memory.

I did remember. Annie had told me how she was driving home after having a few beers with friends. Uncle Jack pulled her over, shined a flashlight in her face, and made her recite the alphabet. She couldn't even sing it past H.

"Anyway, he's always been a little odd, but not cuckoo or anything. He's a collector, one of those guys who can't throw anything away. Since Aunt Felicia died it's gotten worse."

"Uh-oh," my mother said, giving me a meaningful look. "Uncle Louie." She put plates of pot roast and noodle pudding in front of me and Annie.

I only dimly remembered my parents making an emergency trip to Florida. I must have been about ten years old. They'd returned with an emaciated, vacant-looking soul who they told me had once been the most charming retiree on the boardwalk. Uncle Louie, my dad's older brother, had lived with us for a year before he had a stroke and went to the hospital. He'd died soon after that.

"Mom keeps an eye on Uncle Jack. Sees him about once a week. Day before yesterday she goes over there. Usually he won't let her in the apartment, meets her at the deli across the street. But now he lets her in.

"Turns out the place is a horrendous mess and Uncle Jack is in La La Land." Annie's words belied the seriousness of her tone. She was holding back tears. "I went over there that day after work. That's why I couldn't meet you at the restaurant. It was . . . pretty awful. I was over there again today, trying to make a dent in the mess.

"That's not the worst part, though. It's Uncle Jack. I don't know how to describe it—it's as if he's gone flat. He'll be there, then all of a sudden he's not. And he's stooped over and moving around like an old man."

None of it sounded good. Flat demeanor. Shuffling gait. Suggested some kind of dementia.

"How old is he?"

"Not even seventy."

"Has he been ill?"

"Not really. Though my mother says she noticed that he's been more confused the last month or two. And he's lost a lot of weight."

"Do you think he's okay alone?"

"We've got a visiting nurse checking on him. And the people in the downstairs apartment. He should be okay for a night or two, but after that . . ."

"Good thing he's got family nearby," my mother said. "By the time your father and I got down to Florida, Uncle Louie was beyond help and the apartment—it was atrocious. I don't think it had been cleaned since your Aunt Gertie died." She wiped her hands on a napkin, as if some of the filth in Uncle Louie's apartment was still on them. "He had extension cords strung all over that house, draped over everything. Had to, of course. You couldn't get near the walls to plug anything in." She blew on her tea. "Don't know why I remember that."

"Why does this have to happen now?" Annie asked. "Mom has plane tickets for Ireland—leaving next week. She's never been. Her relatives are planning a family reunion and everything. Now she says she doesn't see how she can go. I don't know what to tell her."

I had my datebook out. At least this was something I knew a great deal about and could help with. "Why don't I go over with you and see him tomorrow morning? I haven't got anything scheduled until eleven."

Relief flooded Annie's face. Then she looked down at her plate, as if she were embarrassed by the emotion.

The pot roast was falling-apart tender, and the noodle pudding was dense and chewy with a crisp outer layer, savory—not sweet the way some people make it. Annie picked at hers. We both turned down seconds.

As we were leaving, my mother handed Annie a plastic container with her leftovers, reached up, and put her hands firmly on Annie's shoulders. "You listen to me. If there's anything I can do to help, you just ask." Annie gave a mute nod. "I've been there. Alone with this is not where you want to be."

Annie gave my mother a hug.

To me, my mother muttered loud enough for anyone three blocks away to hear, "Her you stand up for a date with a brain?"

. . .

On the porch, I watched as Annie rummaged in her backpack.

"So what *did* happen to you?" she asked.

"That woman who works on the unit—the one who I helped out with a flat the other night at the Pearce?"

"The one who was being stalked." Annie narrowed her eyes. "It happened again?"

"Not exactly. She's the one who arranged for me to watch a functional MRI. When she pulled out of the garage after—"

"You walked her to her car?"

"Uh-huh. I noticed her taillights were out. They weren't out the other night, and it's a new car. I thought . . ." What had I thought? Why did I have to go rushing out after her, follow her home? "I thought her car had been tampered with. Maybe there was a gas leak, too."

"So you followed her home." Annie had a bemused expression. In retrospect, it hadn't been the most rational thing to do.

"Her ex-boyfriend was waiting at her apartment."

"So he thought you were the stalker and you thought he was," she said, putting it together. "Two protectors stalking the stalker." She shook her head. "She must be something else."

"She's—" I did a double-take. "She's a post-doc."

"You're a good guy, Peter," Annie said, giving me a patronizing pat on the back. She pulled out her car keys and gazed up at me. "You know, I kind of like you with that shiner. Remember Marlon Brando in *On the Waterfront*?"

"I coulda been a contender," I snarled.

"He was a pretty sexy guy, you know." Annie slid me a smile.

"He was, was he?"

I took her in my arms and nuzzled her neck. I loved her smell—it was sharp and sweet, like fresh-cut grass and watermelon. Usually Annie melts into me, but tonight she felt stiff.

"Yeah, he was."

"You don't have to go home, you know."

"Yeah, I do."

"Annie?"

She held my gaze for a few moments, then looked away. "I'm sorry, Peter. I wouldn't be much company. I'm a complete basket case from worrying about my uncle, and I hate it that there's not a damned thing I can do. And I hate having to come running to someone for help."

Before I could say, "But I'm not *someone*," Annie was walking out to the street. She turned and blew me a kiss. Then she got into her car, started the engine, and took off.

Damn. I unlocked the door to my house and switched off the porch light. I turned and gazed up the street where Annie had driven off. "I'm sorry I wasn't here for you tonight."

7

THE SMELL was what you noticed first. Burnt food, mothballs, and the sharp, dried sweat smell of old age. There was a whiff of it in the entryway. It got stronger as we climbed to Uncle Jack's second-floor apartment. The stairs of the Somerville triple-decker were stacked with newspapers.

"It didn't used to be like this," Annie said.

In the upstairs hallway were more newspapers, paint cans from decades of home repair, bags piled on top of bags. I peered into one of them. There were dozens of cardboard toilet-paper tubes, paper napkins that looked as if they might have been used and refolded, a road map, and an empty plastic spray bottle of Windex.

Annie knocked at the door.

From what I could see, bags in the lower levels and further in were less of a hodgepodge—there were paperbacks in one, Styrofoam packing and nested plastic deli containers in another.

Annie knocked again. "Hey, Uncle Jack, it's me, Annie."

Still no response. Annie unlocked the door. Inside it was dark, and the air felt thick and musty. There were more shopping bags, stacks of newspaper and boxes in the entryway, and the smell was stronger.

"Uncle Jack!" Annie called.

Looking one way I could see the kitchen, its sink stacked with dirty dishes. The other way was the living room. Dark green drapes were drawn across tall windows. A fat gray tabby jumped down off the back of the couch, came over, and rubbed up against Annie's leg. Annie bent down and scratched the cat behind the ears. He got up on his hind legs, put his front paws on her shoulder, and gave a strident "Yeow."

"Hey, Columbo," Annie said, picking up the cat. "How you doin'?"

Columbo rubbed one side of his jaw against Annie's face, then the other, marking his territory. Smart cat.

A man appeared in the kitchen doorway. He was tall and stooped. His dark cardigan seemed a few sizes too large.

"Annie?" he said in a flat voice, his face slack and without expression. His belt was tied to keep his pants up.

"Did you get my message?"

Uncle Jack blinked back at her. "Message?"

"Yeah, I called to say we were coming." Annie gave me an anxious look. "This is my friend Peter."

We worked our way through the dining room. There on a credenza was a black-and-white wedding photo. The man, presumably Uncle Jack, was about a foot taller than Annie's radiant young Aunt Felicia. I could see a little of Annie in her eyes. He looked like a prizefighter, the way the lapels of his jacket bowed away from a broad chest. Uncle Jack had undergone quite a transformation since then.

"Friend of Annie's?" Uncle Jack gave me a direct look, his face suddenly alive and wary. Made me feel like a kid who'd showed up unannounced to take out his daughter. He still had a firm handshake.

Annie set Columbo down on the floor. He went over and sniffed one of three open tins of cat food, turned up his nose, and stalked off.

Some of the kitchen cabinets were open. One was filled with cat food—cans of Friskies beef and liver dinner, Friskies seafood entrée, boxes of chicken liver treats. Another cabinet held more than a dozen boxes of Jell-O, spaghetti, and more cat food.

Uncle Jack shuffled over to the kitchen table, his gait stiff, his movements jerky. There were metal chairs with padded red vinyl seats, like the set my mother had. Mail, magazines, newspapers, and crusty placemats covered the table. Only an area at the near end was cleared.

"Mr. O'Neill?" I said. He was nodding at the table. I wondered if he was waiting for me to sit. I put my hand on his arm. "Annie tells me your wife passed on? I'm sorry to hear that."

He didn't respond. He moved to the sink with little jerking steps. Then back to the table. He lowered himself into a chair. His body pulsed and his eyes were going all over the room.

"Felicia vacuum holder thing . . ." he said, addressing his words to one of the other chairs. "Leave the table—" He paused. "—Stop and Shop." It was word salad.

Annie pressed herself against the door jamb and put her hand to her forehead.

Uncle Jack became agitated when I started to sit in the chair he'd been talking to. He put out his arm to stop me. I looked at the chair seat, thinking maybe there'd be something on it, but there wasn't.

No sooner had I taken one of the other chairs than he rose to his feet and shuffled out of the kitchen and down the hall to the back of the apartment.

"Hey, Uncle Jack!" Annie said. "Where you going? You can't take a nap. We just got here."

Uncle Jack chuckled and waved a hand like he was brushing away a swarm of gnats.

I followed him into a bedroom. This room was as cluttered as the rest of the house. There were two television sets, neither of them plugged in, a vacuum cleaner, several old electric fans, more newspapers, piles of bedding and clothing. Long strips of yellowing Scotch Tape ran along cracks in the plaster walls — Uncle Jack's version of home repair.

"How are you doing?" I asked, touching his shoulder again, trying to draw his attention. He looked at me, as if seeing me for the first time. "I'm Peter. Annie's friend?"

"Annie," he said, and gazed around the room.

Annie appeared in the doorway. "You rang?" She went over and took his hand. "Hey, buddy. How are you feeling today, anyway?"

"Anyway, anyway," he said. "Been worse, that's for sure." It was a direct answer to a direct question. He was with us, for the moment at least.

"Can I get you anything?" I asked as he shuffled his way back out into the hallway.

"One of those things out there," Uncle Jack said.

"What things?"

"On the steps. On the steps."

Uncle Jack sat at the kitchen table.

"Newspaper?" I said, guessing.

"I'll get it," Annie said. "I saw one outside."

While Annie was gone I fished a quarter out of my pocket. I

held it out in the palm of my hand. I needed a quick test to gauge the extent of Uncle Jack's confusion.

"I've got a little game—can I try it out on you?"

Uncle Jack looked at the quarter. "Double or nothin'," he said.

"You're on. See this quarter?" I closed the quarter into my fist, put my hands behind my back like I was passing it from hand to hand. Then I held out both fists. "Which hand is it in now?" This time it would be a simple guessing game.

Uncle Jack cocked his head and stared at the back of one hand, then the other. He jabbed a finger at my left hand. I opened the hand and showed him. He'd guessed right. He tried to swipe the quarter.

"Hang on. Now I'm going to switch the coin to my other hand." I said it slowly, with careful emphasis on the word *other*. I put my hands behind my back and transferred the coin. Then I held out my fists.

Once again Uncle Jack's eyes darted from one hand to the other. I waited. He pointed to the same hand he'd guessed the first time. Wrong. Not a good sign.

The simple game was a test of flexible thinking—one of the first things to go at the onset of dementia. It had been nothing more than a spot-check, but it confirmed what I suspected and what I knew Annie was dreading.

I could hear the front door shut and Annie's footsteps on the stairs. "You win," I said, and handed him the quarter.

Annie slid the morning paper out of its plastic bag and handed it to Uncle Jack. He took the paper and also the plastic bag. Carefully he pressed the bag on the table and folded it in quarters. Then he went over and shoved it into the cabinet under the sink, which was already bulging with bags. He returned to the table, opened the newspaper, and seemed to pore over it.

"Red Sox won again," Annie said.

"Pshaw," Uncle Jack said. "It's spring." He was with us again.

Uncle Jack was working his lips and brushing the fingers and thumb of one hand together, a pill-rolling tremor. "Nixon's a crook," he said.

· · ·

"There was mold growing in the bottom of the kitchen sink," Annie said later as we sat at a table at the back of a Dunkin Donuts.

We'd stayed at Uncle Jack's for a couple of hours. I'd washed down the kitchen floor, counters, and table while Annie did the sink and stove top, and gave the bathroom the once-over. We'd thrown out the open cans of cat food. Uncle Jack got upset when I tried to get rid of some of the newspapers.

I inhaled the coffee and donut smells, trying to flush out the smell of the cramped apartment. The counter person gave me an odd look—reminding me that my face looked like I'd run into a door. It only hurt when I smiled.

"So?" Annie asked. "What do you think? I mean, he's there some of the time. And then other times he's not." Her voice was brisk, like she was trying to hold this at arm's length.

Automatically I catalogued the rest of what I'd observed. There were word-finding problems. Parkinsonian symptoms—tremors and a shuffling gait. Social withdrawal. Poor hygiene. Hoarding. Taken together, that was a collection of symptoms for which we had a name, though not a precise diagnosis: Diogenes syndrome. Diogenes of Sinope had been a philosopher in ancient Greece who supposedly showed his contempt for material things by living in a barrel. He wandered about Athens with a lantern in the daytime looking for an "honest man" but never finding one. Diogenes syndrome often marked the boundary between eccentricity and a dementia such as Alzheimer's or Lewy body. Without intervention, half of the patients with Diogenes syndrome die within a year.

Added to the Diogenes syndrome I noted the rapid onset of symptoms, high energy, waxing and waning consciousness. And I wondered if he'd seen someone or something in that chair that he wouldn't let me sit in. Maybe he was hallucinating.

If I'd had to give a diagnosis then and there, I'd have said Lewy body dementia. The usual treatment options were palliative at best. I didn't want to get Annie's hopes up, but I wondered if Dr. Shands would be willing to evaluate her uncle. Maybe enroll him in their research study and qualify for experimental treatment.

"He needs to be evaluated," I said. "We probably won't get a definitive answer, but it may indicate what kind of treatment—"

"It's treatable?" Annie asked, pouncing on the possibility.

"There are drugs that may lessen the symptoms, plus some experimental treatments that are showing promise."

Annie dug her thumbnail into the Styrofoam of the cup. "So what are you saying? Diagnosis is iffy and the only treatment is experimental?"

It pained me to admit she was right. Welcome to my world—modern mental health, house of smoke and mirrors.

"Do people with this always end up living like that?" Annie asked.

"You and your mom caught this early. Much earlier than usually happens when someone's living alone."

"Maybe if I come over more often . . ."

"Annie," I said, leaning across the table and putting my hand on her arm, "we can get the place cleaned up. Get him a geriatric care manager to help day to day. That will buy time. But he needs a thorough evaluation so we know what we're up against."

Annie pushed away the coffee. "You think I'm in denial."

"You're not the first person to have a hard time coming to terms with something like this."

"I suppose that should reassure me."

Denial, anger—both were perfectly normal. "Listen," I said, "I was in deep denial when my father started showing unmistakable symptoms of Alzheimer's, and I was an expert on the disease."

Some of the tension ebbed out of Annie's face. "I guess I'm not ready to lose him."

"Let me see about getting him admitted to my unit. We can do some tests, try to figure out what's going on. Maybe there are some medications that will help. And there is something you can do now. Get him to sign a health-care proxy and give you power of attorney. That way you'll be able to make the decisions you think he'd make himself."

"When he's unable to?" Annie asked, reading between the lines. "It's that bad?"

Sadly, I couldn't disagree.

"THE TREMORS are somewhat better but he's still having hallucinations," Gloria said. Uncle Jack had been with us on the unit for
a couple of days. We were discussing his case at morning meeting.
"He keeps picking things out of the air and talking to someone
named Felicia."

"That was his dead wife," I said.

Kwan had Uncle Jack's file open. "Rapid onset, Parkinsonian
symptoms, visual hallucinations . . . Hmm, what do we have here?"
he said, looking at Emily.

"Dementia. Maybe Alzheimer's. Possibly Lewy body."

"When do we ever get a definitive diagnosis?" Kwan asked.

"There's a new test," Emily said. "They're doing research on it
at University Medical Imaging where I'm a research fellow. Dr.
Shands's whole focus is on Lewy body dementia."

"James Shands?" Kwan said.

"You know him?" I asked.

Kwan pursed his lips. "By reputation."

I'd known Kwan long enough to read his expression. He had reservations about the great Dr. Shands.

"If the test isn't going to change the treatment, why do it?" Kwan continued. "We've already got Mr. O'Neill on medication to mitigate the symptoms."

"There's a research study that he might qualify for," Emily said.

"Experimental protocol?" Kwan asked.

"Early results are promising. We're looking at whether increasing the permeability of cell membranes in the brain may counteract some of the effects of Lewy body dementia. We're using a cholesterol-lowering drug."

"Not a whole lot on the risk side," I said. "They do the tests on a new imaging system. Four point five tesla."

Kwan's eyebrows went up a few microns. Now he seemed impressed. "Maybe it would be a good idea. If it works out, a closer connection with them wouldn't hurt. They provide the funding, we provide the patients. It's a win-win."

• • •

I caught up with Kwan after the meeting. "So you know Dr. Shands?"

"Sure. He's the go-to guy on functional magnetic resonance imaging."

"And . . . ?"

Kwan sat there like the Buddha who knows all and tells squat.

"Listen, if there's anything off about him I don't want to be bringing our patients over there. We don't need a connection like that. There's plenty of other experts—"

"As an expert he's in a class by himself. You won't find anyone who knows more. Groundbreaking papers. Of course, he's a narcissist."

So what else was new? Every researcher who did groundbreaking work had to have a healthy dose of narcissism or he'd never survive the skeptics and naysayers.

"And?"

"I've heard he's a rogue. A womanizer."

Alpha male. Alpha geek. I remembered the argument I'd overheard between Shands and Dr. Estelle Pullaski. That level of anger rarely arose out of professional differences.

"Likes 'em young," Kwan added.

"He's into his research assistants?"

"There may have been a few ugly situations in the past that got hushed up."

My antennae went up. I was loath to swallow a rumor without questioning it first. Not too long ago, one manager's primary weapons for encouraging attrition at the Pearce were rumor and innuendo. I'd had a good friend, a psychiatrist, whose reputation got shredded by an ugly rumor campaign. When she was killed before she could defend herself, I did it for her.

I must have looked skeptical because Kwan put up his hands. "That's his reputation. I'm just telling you what I hear." He cleared his throat and glanced about. No one was within hearing distance. "I have no idea if he and Dr. Ryan are, you know. . . ."

I thought about Shands, that supernova presence of his that lit up a room. Had Emily been as seduced by the man's charisma as she'd been mesmerized by his intellectual brilliance? And what about Shands? What would he assume about Emily coming in one day wearing a suit jacket with nothing underneath? What about the way she touched him when she talked to him? Shands would probably assume *she* was coming on to *him*. It was his due, after all. He'd given her credit on a paper, something Philbrick confessed had taken him three years to achieve. Was that a bribe for future favors, or a reward for services rendered? It was entirely too easy for someone like Shands to take advantage of his position. Junior staff were ambitious, eager to please, and the power equation was stacked against them.

• • •

At first I thought Uncle Jack was playing with a piece of string, holding it in both hands, pulling it one way, then the other. Then I realized there was no string.

We'd put him in a sunny corner room and he'd made himself right at home. Magazine and newspaper clippings already littered the chair, the bed, and the bedside table. On the windowsill he'd started a collection of sugar packets. And that wasn't all. There was a silvery key ring with car keys on it, four Pearce Psychiatric Institute pens, and a pair of ladies' sunglasses. Apparently he was a magpie who helped himself to shiny things. I slipped the keys into my pocket, intending to bring them to our Lost and Found, and I made a mental note that we'd need to keep an eye on Uncle Jack.

"Good morning, Mr. O'Neill," I said. My voice distracted him only for a moment. Now he held up the phantom string and examined it. At least the medication Kwan had put him on had calmed the tremors.

"What do you have there?" I asked. "Can I see?"

"At a theater near you," he said, offering me his hands. "Felicia gorth fribbins."

Suddenly his eyes opened wide and he reared back as if someone had struck him in the face. He let out a holler and his shoulders twitched. Then he stood there wide-eyed and gasping, the breath knocked out of him. There were benign hallucinations with which you could play cat's cradle, and then there was this other kind that knocked the stuffing out of you.

I called Annie and told her about the troubling hallucinations. "Still, overall, he's adjusting well. Even seems to like the food. As soon as we get a more definitive diagnosis, we'll have a better idea about the best treatment. We're trying to get him scheduled for a functional MRI."

"You're going to slide him into one of those contraptions? Won't that upset him?"

"It might. But hopefully it will give us a diagnosis. We can always sedate him — "

"Sedate him?" Annie sounded horrified.

"Something short-acting. There wouldn't be any lasting effects."

There was silence on the other end. Then, "Can I be there, at least."

"I'll ask." Already I was marshaling my arguments for getting around their "no visitors" policy. "How's it going with the apartment?"

"We're making progress. Slowly. We're talking years of accumulation. How did this get so bad without us knowing?"

"You told me your uncle was a little obsessive to begin with. He was always collecting things, right?"

"Sure, but not like this."

"When you begin to dement, often you try to hang on by focusing all your remaining energy on a single thing that you can still control. Psychologists have a fancy word for it: hypercathexis. Collecting turns into hoarding, and pretty soon you're reluctant to throw out anything because hey, you never know when you're going to need it. It's all about trying to keep your internal world from spiraling out of control."

Annie gave a weak laugh. "Is he ever going to be upset when he gets home and finds the place cleaned out."

She wasn't ready to hear it, but it wasn't likely that Uncle Jack would be returning home.

• • •

There was hardly an empty seat in the waiting room. There'd been a cancellation and Emily had been able to slip Uncle Jack in for a nine o'clock appointment. I'd ridden over in the ambulance with Uncle Jack. Annie had convinced her mother not to postpone her trip to Ireland, and had delivered her to Logan before dawn. Emily had helped me convince Dr. Shands to let me and Annie observe.

Uncle Jack wore new sneakers and creased khaki pants that looked freshly laundered. His face was clean shaven, the skin nearly translucent. Comb marks lined his hair. Now he was poring over an article titled "Golf Mania." He tore a page from the magazine, then another. Carefully he folded the two and stuffed them into his pants pocket. Now he tore out a discount coupon for eighteen holes at a country club in Myrtle Beach and added that to his stash.

By the time the receptionist came for him, Uncle Jack's pocket was bulging. She told us they'd be doing a brief physical exam. When Uncle Jack had been prepped, someone would come get us.

Annie stood as Uncle Jack shuffled off. "He's okay in there alone?"

"They deal with dementia patients all the time. It's like a hospital," I said.

Annie looked at the door through which Uncle Jack had disappeared, as if some force were tugging her. With a sigh, she went over to a table of magazines and picked up *Time*. She sat and riffled through the pages, then set it open on her lap and gazed off into space.

She leaned over and whispered into my ear, "Did you know that an MRI magnet is four times as powerful as the ones they use to lift cars in junkyards? In Rochester a while back, an MRI magnet yanked a .45-caliber gun out of a police officer's hand. The gun discharged a round that ended up in the wall."

"You don't say? I had no idea," I said, suppressing a smile. It was a relief to find some of the old Annie in there. "I gather you decided not to pack a pistol?"

"Thought I'd err on the side of caution."

"Wise move."

When Leonard Philbrick came out to get us, he had on what looked like the same rumpled lab coat. Today the inner office hummed with activity. A man and two women in white coats with plastic name tags clipped to the pockets were working at the counter in the central area. A man with a stethoscope around his neck strode through, carrying a large file folder. A nurse darted down one of the corridors. Phones were ringing, and in a corner the wall lit up as the receptionist used a copier.

Annie left her leather backpack and the folding knife she kept in her pocket at the desk. I emptied my pockets.

Philbrick took us to the control room. Annie looked through the window into the scan room next door where Emily was showing Uncle Jack the machine. He was dressed in a white-and-blue hospital gown and looked even more frail and uncertain.

"Mr. O'Neill," Emily said, bringing her face near his. Her voice sounded slightly distorted and tinny as it broadcast through the speaker. "We're going to ask you to get up onto this table"—she put Uncle Jack's hand on the cushioned platform—"and then we'll raise the table and slide you in there." Uncle Jack gazed at the hole in the massive white metal cube.

She continued with a simple explanation of the procedure. "There will be a lot of noise, but that's perfectly normal." She showed Uncle Jack a pair of shiny black earphones. She put them on Uncle Jack's head and adjusted them. Now Uncle Jack looked like an insect with enormous compound eyes on either side of his head.

She helped him get up on the table and lie back, his head pointing into the tube. He lay there, blinking up at the fluorescent light boxes, his head cradled in a foam pillow. The only hint of agitation was the way his hands wavered restlessly at his sides.

Emily overlapped the ends of Velcro straps across his forehead and pressed them in place. Then she took what looked like a plastic birdcage and set it over his head. She picked up a microphone from a side table and spoke into it.

"Can you hear me?" she asked. Uncle Jack jumped at the sound of her voice. "Good. I'll be asking you to do some things. Let's try a few."

She asked Uncle Jack to open and close his eyes. Asked him to say his name. Tap his fingers. It was a simplified version of the protocol she'd run through with Mr. Black, minus the balls to squeeze and without the pictures. Uncle Jack managed to do most of what she asked.

"Now I'm going to slide you into the scanner," she said. "Then I'll go into the room next door. Ready?"

She pressed a button and the table began to slide until Uncle Jack's head was in the center of the tube. His feet in paper slippers stuck out the end toward us.

"God, already I hate this," Annie whispered to me.

Emily returned to the control room. Philbrick sat at the computer monitor alongside the window overlooking the scan room. He typed something and a dark window came up.

Emily picked up a microphone from alongside the control panel and began speaking into it. "Just relax, Mr. O'Neill. I'm right here. We're about to begin. When we turn on the machine it's going to be noisy. Don't worry, that's perfectly normal."

Buzzing noises started and a gray, three-dimensional image took shape in a corner of the computer monitor. Philbrick clicked to enlarge it.

"That's your Uncle Jack's brain," I told Annie.

Annie's mouth fell open. "Wow."

I felt an unexpected surge of relief. I hadn't realized how much it mattered to me that Annie found this awe-inspiring.

Philbrick leaned forward and rubbed his cheek while he stared at the image. I noticed a bruise there, and the remains of blood at the corner of his eye. Looked as if he'd been in a fistfight. He hardly seemed like that kind of guy, but then neither did I. It had been a week since my run-in with Kyle, Emily's ex. All that remained was a yellowish smudge and a slight tenderness.

Annie put her elbows on the desk and watched intently. Now the machine began thumping.

"What's that?" Annie asked. Then the image went fuzzy for a moment. "What happened?" she asked, her voice taut with panic. She stood and pressed her face to the window into the next room.

"He just moved is all," Philbrick said. "Here it comes." The brain reappeared.

"You sure he's okay?" Annie asked.

"It's absolutely painless," Philbrick said.

The brain shimmied again.

"Mr. O'Neill, please, try to hold your head still," Emily said.

This was nothing like the baseline data I'd observed when Mr. Black had had his MRI. I could feel my heart starting to race as I watched the activity increase. There were little explosions of green and yellow, then flashes of orange and red behind the forehead in the frontal system, more at the center of the brain in the limbic system.

"He's having a panic attack," I said, rising to my feet and overturning my chair.

"Please, try to hold still," Emily said into the microphone. Now the image went out of focus again. "Mr. O'Neill!" Emily tried.

Uncle Jack's feet were flailing. One of the slippers had come off and was floating to the ground. I felt as if I were watching someone being tortured.

"Get him out of there," Annie said, her voice strident. She reached for a panel of red buttons marked EMERGENCY. "How the hell do you shut this thing off?"

"Don't touch those!" Philbrick bellowed. Annie backed off. "Christ almighty, before you wreck the system, let me take care of this."

Above the din of the machinery I could hear Uncle Jack's weak voice. "Help! Help!"

Philbrick pressed a button marked STOP SCAN and the machine fell silent. The thumping that we now heard was Uncle Jack inside the tube.

Annie and I started to follow Philbrick and Emily into the scan room but he stopped us. "Please, let us take care of this. It won't help to have the four us crowding around him."

Annie and I watched through the window. It seemed to take forever for the table to slide out. "I'm not dead," Uncle Jack said. He was whimpering.

Philbrick adjusted a lever and the table rolled away from the machine. He released the Velcro holding Uncle Jack's head in place.

"Coffin stop. Let me go!" Then a string of unintelligible syllables as Uncle Jack strained against the straps that were still holding him. He'd soiled himself and urine dripped off the table and onto the floor.

Philbrick stooped so his face was level with Uncle Jack's. He placed his hand on the old man's heaving chest. "Mr. O'Neill, it's all right," his voice came through the speaker. "Take it easy. Try to relax."

Annie was breathing in time with Uncle Jack's labored breathing, and she had her hand clamped on my arm.

Philbrick loosened the straps as he continued talking in a soothing voice. "It's going to be okay. I'm right here with you."

I was dumbfounded. Philbrick was acting nothing like the slightly prissy fellow who'd spoken in jargon and avoided eye contact. I'd never have guessed it, but clearly his bedside manner was as useful to Shands as his technical expertise.

Now Uncle Jack's breath was coming in wheezes. Emily went around to the other side of the table and held one of his hands, which had been fluttering like a moth caught between windowpanes.

"Don't bury me yet," he said, his voice weak and quavery.

Not a shred of word salad. A strong emotional shock can do that sometimes, clear the synapses like a good sneeze.

"Call Dr. Shands." Philbrick flung the order at Emily. Then he turned his attention back to Uncle Jack. He helped him to a seated position. Uncle Jack looked down into his lap and moaned.

It was Dr. Pullaski who steamed in moments later. Uncle Jack drew back as she scrutinized his face. Gently she picked up his wrist and took his pulse.

"We should have sedated him beforehand, but we had no idea he was so volatile," she said.

"Mr. O'Neill hasn't been volatile," Emily said. "Not until just now."

Dr. Pullaski barely acknowledged that Emily had spoken. She'd taken out a hypodermic syringe. Efficiently she pushed up the arm of Uncle Jack's gown, swabbed the flesh, and jabbed. Slowly she depressed the plunger. In moments, Uncle Jack's shoulders and face had relaxed as any residual agitation smoothed over.

Dr. Pullaski put a stethoscope to Uncle Jack's chest and listened. She sent Emily off for oxygen.

Philbrick crossed to the sink and ran water into a basin. He snapped on some latex gloves. Gently, he washed Uncle Jack's legs and in between with a sponge, then took a towel and dried. He helped Uncle Jack into a fresh hospital gown. While he was wiping the table Emily returned pushing a handcart holding a cylinder of oxygen.

"This will help you breathe," Philbrick said, showing Uncle Jack the face mask. Uncle Jack recoiled. Philbrick held the mask an inch from his own mouth and breathed, showing Uncle Jack how it worked. Then gently, he held the mask over Uncle Jack's mouth.

"Just breathe and try to relax," he said. "That's right, deep breaths." Philbrick strapped the mask around Uncle Jack's head.

Dr. Pullaski and Philbrick talked quietly. They both looked toward the window at Annie and me. Then they left Emily with Uncle Jack and came through into the control room.

"Dr. Zak, isn't this your patient?" Dr. Pullaski asked. "You should have warned us. I'm sure I don't have to tell you how much better it is when we can anticipate these things."

It had been a judgment call. Kwan and I had discussed it, and we both felt sedation unnecessary. Plus, a sedative might have made Uncle Jack less responsive to the test protocol. Though I didn't like to admit it, Annie's aversion to Uncle Jack being sedated had weighed in. With twenty-twenty hindsight, it was clear that I'd made an error.

"We're ready to try again," Philbrick said.

"You're kidding," Annie said, looking incredulous.

"With the sedation your uncle will be fine," Dr. Pullaski said.

"Are you nuts?" Annie said.

Uncle Jack's head jerked around. Philbrick put his hand over the microphone.

I knew it was standard operating procedure *not* to let family observe these kinds of procedures for this very reason. It hadn't gone smoothly, and now Annie's concern for her uncle was swamping her judgment about what was best for him.

Philbrick gave me a look that said, *This was your idea. Now fix it.*

"Annie, think about why you're here," I said. "This machine is the only one that can do this kind of testing. We may get a diagnosis. Maybe even a treatment."

"And what if he has a heart attack or a stroke in there?"

"We'll be monitoring him. If he becomes upset again, we'll stop," Philbrick said.

"It'll be over before you know it," I added.

"But—" Annie started, tears building behind her wall of anger.

"Miss Squires," Dr. Pullaski said gently, "Dr. Shands and I have been doing this work for more than a decade. We test patients like your uncle every day of the week. This is very routine. Your uncle is going to be fine. Just let us do our jobs."

We had her surrounded—three against one. It wasn't fair, but it was the right thing to do. Finally she agreed.

Philbrick went back into the scan room and listened to Uncle Jack's chest. He removed the oxygen mask and Emily wheeled away the tank. Uncle Jack's color was approaching normal and his back had straightened. Now he was smiling and scooping nonexistent dust balls off the floor.

This time Philbrick took charge. We watched as he helped Uncle Jack up onto the table. The computer monitor was flickering salt and pepper where Uncle Jack's brain had been. I glanced at the red panel where Annie had almost pushed a button. Could she really have wrecked the system by pressing one? Another good reason not to have visitors.

Philbrick placed the plastic cage in place over Uncle Jack's head, then slid the table into the tube.

"Peter, you're sure this is going to help my uncle?" Annie said under her breath. "Tell me this isn't a stupid useless procedure."

"It's not." I squeezed her hand and hoped to hell I was right.

• • •

Through the rest of the testing Annie sat with her hands gripping the chair arms, her jaw locked. She hadn't relaxed, even after Uncle Jack was back in his street clothes and on his way to the Pearce and we were waiting in the control room for Shands to see us.

We could see Philbrick wiping down the MRI system and the table again as Emily backed into the room. She was carrying a mop and pail of water. She turned around, her eyes wide and her mouth open in protest. The front of her lab coat was pulling away from her as if some creature in the pocket were fighting to escape. She dropped the bucket and water spilled all over the floor as she strained to pull back.

"Watch out!" Emily cried as the pocket ripped and something blasted across the room and crashed into the MRI scanner less than a foot from Philbrick.

He recoiled, arms over his head. Then he turned slowly and stared at it—the big magnet that Emily had used to check me out was now stuck to the side of the scanner. Emily must have used it to test the metal pail and then, without thinking, stashed it in the pocket of her lab coat. Philbrick seemed to grow larger, his anger filling the room as he glowered at Emily.

"What in the hell is wrong with you? The scanner is a magnet. A great *big* magnet. Right? We don't bring magnetic objects into this because, repeat . . . after . . . me," he thundered at Emily, "the magnetic field is never off!"

"I'm sorry," Emily squeaked.

"Say it!"

"The magnetic field is never off."

I squirmed as I felt Annie looking at me. I knew what she was thinking. *And you trust these people?*

WE SAT around a small table in a small meeting room with Shands. Philbrick was pointedly turned away from Emily. He'd ignored her repeated attempts to apologize. Annie was too tense and anxious to notice.

Shands said he'd taken a look at Uncle Jack's MRI. "Preliminarily, I'd say Mr. O'Neill has those changes in his brain that we look for. They're the early markers we've identified for Lewy body dementia." He said this as if he were delivering a weather report. A *fine day, a few high clouds* . . . "I'm confident that analysis will confirm."

I wanted to kick the asshole. He was completely oblivious to the impact of this news on Annie. She'd gone pale and her jaw was quivering.

"We'd like to sign your—" Shands paused, looking through a file folder.

"Uncle." Annie shot the word at him.

He looked up, momentarily stung. "Yes, we'd like to sign your uncle up for our study." Shands gave Annie an understanding smile. "As I'm sure Peter has told you, we're testing a new treatment for Lewy body dementia. Results so far are promising, though of course there's never any guarantee. And even we won't know if your uncle is getting the treatment or the placebo."

Annie was looking at him but I wasn't sure she was processing his words.

"It's a clinical trial," I said. "They assign half the patients to treatment, half get a sugar-pill. Even the doctors here won't know what Uncle Jack is getting."

"And if he gets nothing?"

I swallowed. "He'll still be getting other treatment — something for the tremors, something for hallucinations."

Shands leaned back in his chair and tented his fingers. "There's evidence that the treatment increases brain-cell membrane permeability," he said, talking to his fingertips.

"Meaning what exactly?" Annie asked.

Couldn't he just say it in English? I thought I caught the shadow of a smile on Philbrick's face.

Shands laced his fingers. "It may slow the progress of the disease, ameliorate the symptoms . . . perhaps more. Taken early enough, it may even provide a cure," Shands explained, talking more slowly now. "That's the hope. Of course, your uncle is already showing clear symptoms of dementia." Annie flinched at the words. He plowed on. "The trials are designed to help us find out exactly what the treatment effects are."

I doubted Shands was making the impression on Annie that he usually made on patients' family members. "And the drug he'd be taking?" she asked.

"Cimvicor," Shands said. "It's already FDA-approved for treatment of high cholesterol. Generally well tolerated. We're administering it at a somewhat higher dosage. Of course, there may be side effects. In some, it can cause adverse reactions."

He handed Annie a piece of paper. I read over her shoulder. Though the risk of most of these nightmares was low, the list was daunting. Starting with dyspepsia and ringing of the ears, it moved on to photosensitivity, impaired vision, muscle weakness, and liver dysfunction. Doctors were required to disclose worst-case whenever discussing treatment. But even for me, it was impossible to know what to make of this laundry list of afflictions. Basically it was a big fat CYA, just in case anyone decided to sue.

"We'd like to put him on the treatment regimen and see how he responds. With permission of course. Then retest him every few weeks," Shands said.

"More MRIs?" Annie groaned.

"It's important to monitor his progress."

"If it was me, I wouldn't want to come back here. That's for sure," Annie said.

"He'll probably have forgotten all about it by lunch time," Shands said complacently.

It wasn't the right thing to say. "*I* won't have forgotten," Annie said, her voice cold.

Shands recoiled, blinked. "I'm sorry," he said. For the first time, he seemed to really look at Annie and to take a moment to think before he spoke. "I realize that sometimes I sound insensitive. I don't mean to. Maybe if I explain." Now he lowered his voice and spoke as if he and Annie were the only ones in the room. "Medicine has been wonderful in helping people live their full allotment of years, but sadly deficient in attending to the quality of life during those last years. Over four million Americans suffer from dementia. We're at the edge of a major breakthrough here." There was a passion in his voice and his eyes were alive. "And while it's true, your uncle only has a fifty percent chance of getting our new treatment, he has a one hundred percent chance of helping save countless others from this devastation, not to mention saving families from going through what you're going through now."

Annie sat back, mollified. He slid some more papers across the table. "This is just the paperwork we need to start the process. Unfortunately, research entails a lot of bureaucracy."

Annie fingered the pages but she wasn't reading. The shock of the diagnosis. The uncertainties of treatment. I knew what it was like. Shands held out a pen and Annie stared at it.

"She doesn't have to decide this minute," I said. Annie gave me a grateful look.

"Of course not. This is an awful lot to digest," Shands said, sliding the pen back into his own pocket. "I really couldn't let you sign the consent forms now. Take them with you. Think it over. There are only a few slots left in the research protocol. If not this study, I'm sure there will be another one at a later date. But keep in mind, the earlier we get started, the better the chances are that treatment will be effective."

• • •

Annie and I walked with Emily to the elevator in the lobby. Annie seemed exhausted, wrung out.

"I know Dr. Shands seems a bit aloof," Emily said. That was just the beginning as far as I was concerned. A windbag, a narcissist, a guy with the sensitivity of sandpaper. Still, I had to admire his intensity and single-mindedness—clearly a man who believed in his own work.

"He's a brilliant researcher," she went on. "His work is light-years ahead of anyone else."

Under her breath so only I could hear, Annie said, "Wouldn't be the first time the genius is a jerk."

Sometimes they went hand in hand. Here was the golden boy who'd gotten in early on a new technology and run with it. At least he was self-aware enough to know his own weaknesses. He'd surrounded himself with people who could shore him up. He had Philbrick with his technical know-how and gentle touch with patients, Dr. Pullaski the efficient manager who seemed in charge of day-to-day operations. Apparently he'd attracted a string of bright, eager young researchers who, like Emily, stroked his ego and wrote up his results.

"Dr. Philbrick was wonderful with Uncle Jack," Annie said.

"Yeah, Lenny is something else," Emily said. "Great with patients, perhaps less good with people. And he doesn't tolerate fools. I'm afraid now he thinks I'm one. Can't believe I did something so stupid in there. I've been drilled over and over again on safety procedures."

We got to the elevator and I pushed the button.

"Thanks for walking me to my car," Emily said.

Annie gave Emily an appraising look. "I hope you don't mind— Peter told me about you being threatened. I'm an investigator. I've had some experience with stalkers."

The elevator arrived. Emily glanced over her shoulder before she stepped inside. "I didn't think it was getting to me, but it is."

"Have you thought about who might be doing this?" Annie asked as we rode down. "Most likely it's someone you know. That's how it usually works."

"Is it? I had something like this happen a few years ago and it turned out to be someone I'd never met before."

We got out at the parking level.

"You had this happen before?" Annie asked. She was probably

thinking what I was — that it was usually celebrities that got stalked by people they didn't know. Being the victim of two stalkers made Emily still more unusual. I wondered if she'd done something . . . then I stopped myself. That was the insidious thing about stalking — or any kind of abuse, for that matter. It was easy to blame the victim. So much less frightening when we can tell ourselves, she must've done something to deserve it.

"It happened back when I was in college. But it couldn't be him now. That guy died in a car accident. I have no idea who it is this time. The only thing I know for sure is that it's not Dr. Zak. He saved me from him." We'd reached her car. Emily stared down at her feet. "I'm not sure I thanked you properly for that."

"Don't worry about it," I said.

"Have there been any more incidents since Peter" — Annie paused and shot me a sideways look — "saved you? Wasn't that about a week ago?"

"A week and a half," Emily said. "Nothing since then. Maybe he got scared off."

"Maybe," Annie said. She didn't sound convinced.

"I don't know, though. I feel like he's still out there watching me."

Emily opened her car trunk and put her briefcase inside. I looked at my watch.

"See you at the Pearce," I said.

Annie and I walked to Annie's car. We got in and Annie started the engine.

"Stalking doesn't usually turn off like a faucet," Annie said. She backed out of the space and started to accelerate. "And don't you find it odd —"

Just then Emily darted out in front of us. Annie smashed down on the brakes and the car bucked to a halt just in time. Emily's scream echoed off the garage walls.

I tumbled out of the car on one side, Annie on the other. "What's the matter? Are you all right?"

Emily was holding her arms around herself, her face twisted in horror. "In my car," she managed to gasp between incoherent sobs.

Annie was looking in through the open door of the Miata, her face stony. I went over and peered in. Someone had put a white bra over the seat back and laid out a pair of white lace panties on the seat, making it look as if the seat was wearing Emily's underwear. That was disturbing enough, but the bra had heart-shaped holes cut in it, the dark seat back showing through at the center on each side. A heart had been cut from the crotch of the panties, too. I looked away. It felt obscene.

"Great. A stalker with a sense of humor," Annie muttered. "I'm calling the police."

This time Emily didn't protest.

Annie got out her cell phone out and punched in numbers. She waited, phone to her ear. Then looked at the readout. "Damn. There's never any signal when you need it." She went over to use the pay phone by the elevator.

Now Emily was crying quietly. I put my arm around her.

"Was the car locked?" I asked.

Emily nodded.

Annie returned. "They're on their way."

"I already changed the locks twice," Emily said. "I guess I'll have to change them again. Shit. You wouldn't believe what it costs. I can barely afford the payments as it is."

When two police officers arrived—a man and a woman—they questioned Emily. It was damned frustrating to see them shrug it off with nothing more than the appropriate *tut-tut* sounds. Tracking down someone who liked to cut hearts out of women's underwear wasn't going to be their top priority. After all, no one had been hurt, no property had been damaged—unless you counted the bra and panties. At least they took the underwear as evidence.

"Want us to follow you home?" I asked.

"Thanks. The police offered to do that." She gave me a hug, burying her face in my chest. I gave her a squeeze. I could feel her trembling as she kept holding on. "Sorry to be such a pain in the butt. You've been great."

Annie was watching us, a speculative look on her face. Gently, I peeled Emily away.

Annie gave one last look around the garage. "You sure you don't have any idea who . . . ?" she began.

"That's what the police kept asking me. Boyfriend? Ex-husband? Anyone I'd recently dumped? They even suggested that I might have done this to myself." Emily looked up, her eyes pooling with tears. "That would be so pathetic."

10

"IT'S SO hard seeing him suffer," Annie said as she drove me back to the Pearce.

"I know." I put my hand on her thigh. "I'm sorry — I should have realized how painful it would be for you to watch. When Emily told me about their new scanner and the research they were doing, I guess I got caught up in it and lost perspective."

Annie turned off the radio, which had been forecasting overcast skies and rain.

"It's not your fault," she said. "Really, I'm grateful for everything you're doing. Thanks for being there for me."

Gratitude. I groaned inwardly. That implied obligation, which wasn't what I wanted from Annie.

"My mother used to tell me how she hated to take me or my sister to the doctor because she couldn't stand it when he gave one of us a shot. She'd a million times rather have taken it herself than see us hurt. Now I know what she meant."

Annie was stopped at a light.

"You're doing everything you can," I said.

The light turned green and Annie accelerated. We drove the next few miles in silence.

"My elementary school was across the street from their apartment," Annie said. "I used to love to go over to their house after school. Uncle Jack would take me to the park. Taught me how to throw like a guy."

Now we were approaching the Stavros Diner. It was past lunchtime and neither of us had eaten.

I was about to ask Annie if she wanted to stop for a bite when she said, "You know she's coming on to you, don't you?" You could get whiplash talking to Annie.

"Who is?"

Annie shook her head. "Poor Peter. You can be so clueless at times. Emily Ryan. Don't you think she seems a tad"—Annie bit on her lip—"I don't know, manipulative maybe?" Annie swerved to avoid getting hit by a bus. "She's got that knack for getting people to rescue her."

"I just don't like to see someone bullied and threatened." I knew I sounded defensive.

"What is it, three times now?" Annie asked as she pulled onto the Pearce grounds.

I didn't say anything.

"She gives you puppy-dog eyes."

"She gives everyone puppy-dog eyes. Kwan. Even Gloria."

"I noticed you holding that embrace an awfully long time."

She was hugging *me*, I wanted to shout.

Annie drove slowly along the narrow winding lane through the grounds, up the hill to the Neuropsychiatric Unit. She cut the engine and we sat there, silence echoing around us.

I didn't want to get out, but I did. How long it had been since Annie and I had gone out together or made love—nearly two weeks? "When will I see you?"

"I'll be in to see Uncle Jack tomorrow."

I shut the car door.

Annie hesitated. She began rolling down the passenger side window, then changed her mind and rolled it up again. She turned the car around and drove off.

When I finished banging my fist into my palm, I took a deep breath. Annie was wrong about one thing. I wasn't "there" for her—she wasn't letting me be.

You can be so clueless sometimes. I couldn't just write off what Annie was suggesting. After all, she was trained to see what other people miss.

I knew Emily Ryan was attached to me, infatuated in the way that post-docs can become with a mentor. Sure I'd been flattered, but I thought I had it diagnosed it for what it was and set it aside. That's what *I* was trained to do.

✤   • • •

When I got back on the unit I wasn't hungry. I checked on Uncle Jack. He was lying on his bed asleep, his breathing regular but still a little wheezy. Insufficient oxygen getting to the brain would only worsen his dementia. I made a mental note to mention it to Kwan.

The pages Uncle Jack had torn out of the waiting-room magazines were on the bedside table. I looked through them. Golf vacations, cell phones, and Viagra. All of life's essentials.

I went up to my office and returned calls. Then I read the day's accumulated e-mail messages. After that, I found myself sitting, staring at my computer screen, unable to concentrate on work. I picked up the phone, wanting to call Annie. I hung up before dialing.

I went back down and walked the unit. Usually that helps get my mind back on track. Not today. I still felt only half plugged in, my mind churning. I could hear Emily Ryan's scream. The tires screech. *Manipulative.* That was Annie's take on her.

I felt claustrophobic, unable to think. I needed to get the hell out of there and out on the river. Rowing usually helped blow the dust balls from my brain and drain away tension. Not as well as sex, but that option wasn't on the table at the moment.

There was nothing on the afternoon's calendar that I couldn't skip. I checked in with Gloria and then I left.

• • •

The day had turned gray and drizzly. When I slammed the car door the speaker grill fell into my lap. Again. I felt a cold trickle down the back of my neck. The sunroof was leaking. Still. God-damned car was a Crackerjack toy. Car of the year, schmar of the year, as my mother would have said. Meaningless award, anyway — after all, the Pinto and the Escort had both been proud recipients. At least the radio worked. I turned it on and was immediately calmed to hear guitar virtuoso Richard Thompson playing.

I revved the engine, backed out of the parking spot, and took off. I crossed into Cambridge and headed for the river. There were parking spots near the boathouse. Small wonder. Only a fool would be out jogging or rowing in what had now turned into a steady rain. Didn't matter — my shirt was already soaked from the sunroof leak.

The new BU boathouse faintly echoed the original boathouse, a hundred-year-old structure that had been torn down a few years ago. I missed the scooped out steps, the ancient timbers and creaky boards. But for once, change had been in the right direction. The new boathouse was a showpiece with its gables, blue-green copper roof, and balcony overlooking the river. The high, barrel-vaulted ceiling and band of windows all around made it as light and airy on the inside as the old boathouse had been dark and dank.

I went into the locker room and changed. Then I trotted down the wide central stairway to dock level. Two of the double-doors were flung open to the river. The rain had stopped and with the clouds beginning to lift, sun slanted in from one side. Felt like a good omen.

I got a pair of oars and set them on the edge of the dock. From the overhead sling I lowered the single that belonged to my friend Rudi. He'd been letting me borrow it since mine got demolished by a speedboat that was aiming for me. When I got around to replacing mine, I'd get one like this. The Levator, its sleek carbon-fiber shell long and thin like a razor clam, looked as if it were made of a rich mahogany. I held it over my head and carried it out onto the dock.

Sunlight sparkled off the water. Soon I was stroking upriver. The water was mirror-smooth, only my puddles marring the surface, the air cool and clean-smelling from the rain.

Rowing requires complete concentration and exquisite precision, dipping the oars, then pushing off with the legs to propel the boat forward. I tried to relax, imagining that the oars were fixed and I was using them to lever the boat through the water. I checked over my shoulder every few strokes. Ripples feathered from the prow as the boat cut through the water.

As I approached the Weeks footbridge I broke a sweat. I ignored the growing ache in my legs, knowing that soon the endorphins would kick in and it would be just me and the rhythm of the river.

I slid through a band of darkness under the Anderson Bridge and continued toward Watertown Square. The landscape turned pastoral, the riverbanks wide. I could convince myself that I'd stepped back a century into a Thomas Eakins painting, long before anyone had conceived of highways or ten-wheelers. A great blue heron stood regal in tall grass not far from where a good-sized rat foraged along the edge of the bank. No other boats were on the water.

After about forty minutes, I'd reached the Newton Yacht Club. I stopped and hung there, oars out like dragonfly wings, looking upriver where the water met the sky, savoring the peace and solitude. Reluctantly, I spun the boat and headed back.

Rowing with the current was easier and my mind started to wander. Did I have feelings for Emily Ryan that were clouding my judgment? Was I being manipulated by her? And if so, why was I allowing it to happen? Why *did* I feel so protective toward her?

If I'd been my own therapist, I might have pointed out that it probably had more than a little to do with guilt over my wife's murder. Repetition compulsion. With Emily, here was a chance to get it right.

I had no trouble sizing up Emily's rose-colored version of Shands. A bad case of hero worship, probably combined with a powerful dose of physical attraction. Maybe he'd seduced her. Was she wearing those same rose-colored glasses when she looked at me?

And what about Annie's misgivings about University Medical Imaging? Based on little more than Emily's say-so, I'd allowed Annie's uncle to be evaluated there. I hadn't bothered to check the place out other than asking Kwan and then ignoring his reservations about Dr. Shands.

Had the accident with the test magnet been a one-off, or was it part of a pattern of lax safety procedures? And what about Cimvi-cor? Was taking it in such high doses as straightforward as Shands insisted?

A little due diligence was in order. When I got back, I'd check out the lab's safety record. I'd also find out more about the risks of taking Cimvicor.

I arrived back at the boathouse feeling my equilibrium somewhat restored. I had research to do, some psychic distance to install between myself and Emily, and more than a little sorting-out to do with Annie.

· · ·

Back in the office I logged into the medical school library system, where virtually every piece of medical research from the late eighties onward was online. I typed in "James Shands." There were dozens of hits.

The oldest record was from a paper published in 1981. "Functional Mapping of the Human Visual Cortex by Magnetic Resonance Imaging." Apparently Dr. Pullaski had outshone Shands early on, because she was listed as the paper's principal author. "James Shands, Jr., Ph.D., Assistant Professor of Neuroanatomy" was one of three coauthors. He must have started as a researcher and gotten the M.D. later.

Shands had coauthored several more papers that year with Dr. Pullaski as lead author. I read the abstracts. Lots about functional brain mapping. Nothing about Lewy body dementia.

There was a six-year gap. Then there was a paper, "Dementia with Lewy Bodies: Cognition, Neuropathology, and Cell Permeability" by James Shands—now with an M.D. and a Ph.D. In the preceding years he'd evidently finished a medical degree. No coauthors were listed.

The paper reported on functional MRIs and subsequent examinations of the brains of patients who had been diagnosed with Lewy body dementia. This must have been his breakthrough. Probably included the patient whose brain scan and cortical brain cells were proudly displayed on his office wall, the way a shopkeeper displays his first dollar bill.

Since then Shands had been prolific. Nine or ten papers a year, plus a few book chapters. On most he was sole author; some were coauthored with others, including Leonard Philbrick and Estelle Pullaski. Now he was listed as professor of neurology. It was an impressive body of work, especially given the short period of time.

I brought up the *Boston Globe* archives, curious to see if there had been any news articles about him. The first hits were in 1984—an engagement announcement and an obituary. In March, Dr. Estelle Pullaski's parents had announced her engagement to James Shands, Ph.D. I wasn't surprised that their relationship had been personal as well as professional.

A month later was the obituary: "Dr. James Shands, cardiologist and researcher, died on April 10 in Beth Israel Hospital after a long illness. He was 65." These days, that was awfully young to die. I skipped to the end. "Dr. Shands is survived by a son, James Shands, Jr., Ph.D." The obituary was several inches long. The senior Shands had to have been a brilliant researcher—he'd been a primary author of the Amherst Cardiology Report, the first longitudinal heart study that provided us with virtually everything we know today about heart disease.

I wondered if his father's death had precipitated a breakup with Dr. Pullaski. I noticed, too, that the start of the gap in his research output lined up approximately with his father's death. Maybe that's what had propelled him into med school.

Then there was a 1991 article on the opening of the Cambridge Brain Bank. "Researchers in Cambridge today opened a state-of-the-art repository for human brain tissue." I remembered the fanfare at the opening. I was finishing a post-doc at the Pearce at the time. Today, the Cambridge Brain Bank was still going strong.

I read on. "Dr. Estelle Pullaski, executive director, said the new brain bank is 'indispensable to our efforts to relate what happens at the cellular and molecular level to behavior.'" There Dr. Pullaski was in a photograph of the dedication ceremony at the center of a group, with Shands at her side. The article went on to mention Shands as one of an esteemed staff of researchers.

I looked at the others in the group. Most I knew by reputation. There, with his head half-turned away from the camera, was Dr. Nelson Rofstein, my first mentor. According to the article, he'd been on their board of directors.

There were other articles. One covered the hoo-hah at the opening of University Medical Imaging Center years later. There were numerous pieces about aging and dementia in which Shands was quoted as *the* expert. He'd been keynote speaker at a national conference on the brain. No mention of unpleasantness or scandal.

There was no simple way to check on the lab's safety record. I could at least check that it was accredited by the American College of Radiology. I quickly discovered that while 4.5 tesla scanners could be used for research, they were not yet FDA-approved for clinical use. Nevertheless, University Medical Imaging had met the standards set for lower-strength devices.

While I was at the Web site, I found a list of reported accidents. I scrolled through, drilling down to look at details. There was the incident Annie told me about in Rochester, a gun pulled out of a police officer's hand, hitting a wall and going off. In another incident, a woman in Minneapolis was killed when a metal oxygen canister got sucked into the machine.

Two technicians and a patient had suffered frostbite and ruptured eardrums in a San Diego lab when a magnet quenched — rapidly lost its magnetic field and the liquid helium within the chamber boiled off into the scan room. That didn't sound like fun. I hoped Annie hadn't read about that incident. And if she had, I hoped she'd gotten to the part where it said that accidents like that were "extremely rare" and that MRI systems had an "exceptionally high safety record."

No incidents had been reported at University Medical Imaging.

Finally, I hauled out my copy of the *Physician's Desk Reference* and looked up Cimvicor, the drug Shands was using to treat Lewy body dementia. The entry began, "Cimvicor is a synthetic, lipid-lowering agent . . ." I scanned the drug description and a lengthy section on how it worked. As I would have expected, its clinical trials had been for treatment of high cholesterol, not dementia. I read through the warnings, precautions, and finally adverse reactions. I looked through the symptoms of overdose. I could see nothing there that Shands hadn't disclosed, nothing that set off alarm bells.

I called Annie at work.

"What's wrong?" she said the minute she heard my voice.

That about summed up our relationship — I called and she immediately assumed the worst.

I told her Uncle Jack was up and about and had eaten lunch. "And I checked on the lab's safety record. It's clean."

"At least that's something."

"And Cimvicor, the treatment drug? I don't think there's a huge risk taking it, even at the higher dosage."

"So you'd give this experimental treatment a green light?"

"I think it's worth a shot."

"I talked to my mom this morning. That's what she says, too. Given the alternatives."

There were no good alternatives. The brutal truth was we had no way to treat this disease, no way to cure it or even slow it down. All we had were medications for the grosser symptoms.

"What he has — it's basically a death sentence, isn't it?" Annie asked.

I wished I could have seen her face to gauge whether she wanted me to just say it outright or soften the blow. "I'm afraid so," I said, my throat closing around the words. Knowing Annie, she probably wanted the facts. "A year, two at the outside. Even with the treat-ment we can give him, the visual and auditory hallucinations and the movement disorder will probably get worse."

There was a long pause.

"He'd be living a nightmare," she said, her voice calm and quiet. "I'll fax the consent forms over to the lab this afternoon. Though I have to tell you, I don't like that place. Do all research labs treat patients like crash-test dummies?"

It was the perfect image. Maybe it was inevitable. After all, re-searchers had to be dispassionate observers, and that required a certain sangfroid in the face of human suffering. They worked at the macro level looking for patterns — the occasional patient who beat the odds only muddied the picture.

"I'm glad you're not a researcher," she added.

11

FOR TWO weeks Uncle Jack became my proverbial watched pot. I knew improvement, if any, would come in imperceptible increments. But even in this short time there did seem to be some. His gait was more stride than shuffle. He seemed a bit more coherent and the hallucinations less frequent. The nurses reported that he was doing better caring for himself, and was sleeping without nightmares.

I tried to curb my enthusiasm when I gave Annie progress reports. It could just be a bubble. I looked forward to those daily phone calls, even though all we talked about was Uncle Jack. Whenever I suggested that we get together, Annie put me off.

That morning Uncle Jack had gone to the imaging lab for a follow-up MRI. This time, he'd made the trip with a mental health worker. Philbrick had given me a curt "absolutely not" and cited safety concerns when I'd asked if I could observe.

I checked on Uncle Jack when he got back. He was in the

common room watching TV. This time, the experience had left him somewhat subdued but otherwise unscathed.

I wondered if his test results would confirm the improvement, or if I was seeing what I wanted to see. It could be simply a result of the move to the Pearce, regular meals, combined with our trained staff and the meds we were giving him for the tremors and hallucinations. For all we knew, Uncle Jack could be getting the sugar pill.

"I finally got the analysis of Mr. Black's test results," Emily told me during our weekly supervisory one-on-one that afternoon. Her stalker had been dormant since the incident in the garage. "Usually it only takes about a week. Guess this wasn't anybody's top priority but mine." She reached for a tissue, discreetly removed the gum from her mouth, and threw it away.

"And?"

"Very disappointing. Differences left to right are pretty much the same for him as for the average person we've tested. If I'd been reporting results just based on observation, I'd have said for sure there was something there. I guess that's why research studies are always double-blind."

"We see what we want to see," I said. "Fortunately there's all that sophisticated equipment and data analysis to keep you honest. How's Mr. Black doing?"

"I've been thinking about what you said. That you never know what's right for your patient. Intellectually, I know you're right. I've heard it over and over—they drill it into you. But emotionally I can't quite wrap my arms around it." She gave me a hard look.

I didn't say anything.

"I know, I know, as a therapist, I'm supposed to keep telling myself that I can only try to control what goes on within the confines of the therapy room. To believe otherwise is a sure recipe for disaster."

I had to smile. "A sure recipe for disaster" had been one of the trademark phrases of Dr. Rofstein. That was how mentoring worked—hopefully we only bequeathed the good stuff.

"So how is this different from a patient who's suicidal?" Emily continued. "I'm not supposed to just sit there and nod and say, 'How interesting. Tell me more about how you're going to kill yourself.'" Today she wore a white blouse under her suit jacket, and there were no flashes of bare skin as she leaned forward. "Don't I have an obligation to act?"

"If you think a patient is serious about killing himself, then yes, you have an obligation to act. If he tells you he's going to hurt someone else, then by law you have to warn that person."

"So here's a man who says he's going to cut off his arm? What can I do to stop him?"

"If he's psychotic or demented, you can commit him. Do you think he is?"

"He's not."

"Do you think he's suicidal?"

"No. But he's got this obsession—"

"You can't hospitalize him unless what he's doing is life-threatening. We're talking self-mutilation. That's not necessarily even about wanting to die. It can be just the opposite. Some people crave pain in order to feel connected to the real world. While we all might have opinions about what Mr. Black should or shouldn't do, as his therapist you have to accept the fact that you can't control his actions."

"It's so frustrating," Emily said, her fists clenched. "So I just sit back and watch, engage in some intellectualized bullshit when a person is in desperate need of a kind of help that I'm not allowed to give?"

I admired her passion, her determination to help, but she was dead wrong. "It's not intellectualized bullshit."

Emily stared out the window. "Well, I can't do nothing. Can't I at least tell him that as an outside observer, I don't think this is such a good idea?"

"Sure you can, but what would be the consequences? Suppose you say, 'I don't think you should cut your arm off,' but that's what he wants to do? Why would he come back to you? By offering your opinion you run the risk of ruining the therapeutic relationship."

"So what *do* I do?"

"Think about it this way. It's like penicillin. If a patient has an infection, then the key to treating him is to make sure he takes the penicillin."

"So"—Emily paused, sitting up straighter—"you're saying that the key is to keep Mr. Black working in therapy before he takes action. Make sure he keeps working at understanding where this need comes from."

"Right," I said. "Explore other ways of dealing with these urges."

"So I was on the right track when I tried to help him understand the downside of doing this?" Now she didn't need to look to me for approbation. It was one of those "aha" moments that make supervision so gratifying.

"You could go even further," I said. "Encourage him to get the data he needs to make an informed decision."

"Data . . ." Emily murmured. She frowned and thought for a few moments. "So I could suggest that he talk to people who are amputees."

"Sure. That's the kind of thing that would give him a chance to experience vicariously before he acts."

Just then my phone rang.

"I wonder—" Emily said, her brows coming together over her eyes. The phone rang again. "Go ahead, take the call." She stood. "I gotta run anyway. Mr. Black is probably waiting for me and I've just had a brainstorm."

I picked up the phone. It was Gloria. "I thought you'd want to know," she said as Emily shut the door. "Mr. O'Neill isn't feeling well. Started vomiting after lunch. Now he's wheezing and feverish. We called his niece and let her know."

As if to underline Gloria's concern, the red message light on my phone had begun to blink. I ignored it. Whoever it was would beep me if it was important.

"But I was down there just a couple of hours ago and he was fine."

"Hey, I'm just the messenger. Could be a stomach bug. We're keeping an eye on him."

I checked my watch. My last patient of the day wasn't due for fifteen minutes. I hurried down to the unit. Uncle Jack's bed was cranked nearly vertical and an oxygen mask was strapped over his face. He looked pale but comfortable, his chest rising and falling with each breath. At the end of each exhale, I could hear a little whistle from his lungs. His eyelids fluttered when I touched his shoulder.

"How you feeling?" I asked, pulling up a chair and pushing the mask aside.

"Been better," he said.

"Heard you had another MRI this morning," I said.

He muttered something that sounded like "fool thing." Then his eyes drifted and he was focusing on a space over my right shoulder, a faint smile on his lips. I wondered if Felicia's ghost was back.

I turned around. Annie had come into the room. She must have had to testify in court today because she was wearing a dark suit and had her hair pinned up. She looked worried. I knew this wasn't the time or the place to notice her legs, but I couldn't help it. Uncle Jack blinked at her. She took his hand.

"Hey big guy, what's this about you getting sick?"

Uncle Jack managed a chuckle.

Later, in the hall, Annie asked me, "You don't think this has anything to do with that test he had today? I mean, both times he gets an MRI he ends up wheezing."

"MRIs don't cause breathing problems," I said. I didn't add that this time it was more than breathing problems. He couldn't keep food down and his temperature had spiked to over a hundred.

"But he was in that tube. Maybe the person in there before him was sick. Coughed all over the place. They don't bother to wipe it down—"

I didn't bother to point out that in fact they did. "Most bugs that make you sick like this have an incubation period that's more than a couple of hours."

Annie was having no part of it. "People pick up all kinds of infections in hospitals that they wouldn't if they just stayed home," she said. "Didn't I read about flesh-eating bacteria that some guy got after he was operated on for a hangnail?"

"Flesh-eating bacteria?"

"I'm not making this up."

"Annie, your uncle's probably got the flu, not a hangnail. It's the kind of thing he could have picked up anywhere. At least he's here, where can monitor him closely."

Annie was pacing up and back now in short rapid strides.

"Maybe I should take him out of here. Right now. He was fine at home."

"Annie!" I stopped her and put my hands on her shoulders. "You know as well as I do that he was not fine."

"But he wasn't sick like this." A tear started at the corner of her eye.

"I know, I know," I said gently, taking her in my arms. "But he is now." I rested my cheek against her and inhaled her fruity scent. "And he needs to be monitored. It could be a virus of some kind."

"Just flu?" She sounded hopeful.

With someone Uncle Jack's age it was never "just flu." Flu and pneumonia were among the leading causes of death in older people.

"We'll watch him round the clock. If there's any problem we'll get him admitted to the medical hospital immediately."

"Hospital?" Annie pulled back and gave me a horrified look.

• • •

It had been a long day. Administrative meetings had lasted until seven. After that I checked in again on Uncle Jack. The oxygen mask was on the table and he seemed to be breathing easily. He had the covers pulled up to his chin but seemed chilled. I got an extra blanket and tucked it around him.

I went up to my office, hauled my briefcase from under the desk and slid in some notes I'd taken. I was feeling tired and achy myself and wanted to get home. I reached for the phone, intending to give Annie a quick update before taking off. The red message light was still going.

I groaned, and considered leaving it until morning. I swallowed my impatience and dialed voicemail.

"You have four new messages. . . ."

I sank into my chair and scrounged for a pencil and a scrap of paper.

"Dr. Zak? This is Leonard Philbrick calling." I recognized his high-pitched voice. "I wanted to"—there was a pause, like he wasn't sure why he'd called—"I wanted to check on how Mr. O'Neill was doing. The procedure went smoothly this time, but he did have some breathing difficulty. I was concerned about . . ." His voice trailed off. "I wonder if you could give me a call. I'm at the lab." I made a note of the number and deleted the message.

The next one had come in at three. It began with a stretch of silence. At first I thought it was one of those automatic-dial phone solicitations. Then, "Damn." Sounded like Philbrick again. The third message came in at 3:26. It was my mother, wondering if I wanted to join her and her friend Mr. Kuppel for a seven o'clock screening of *The Collector* at the Brattle. Too late for that. Too bad, too. I remembered the film—a dweebie bank clerk adds a girl he's lusted after from afar to his meticulously catalogued collection of butterflies. It was a world-class creepy performance.

The last message. Six-twenty. I waited. The caller cleared his throat. "This is Dr. Philbrick again. Please give me a call this evening? I should be home after nine." He left his number.

He hadn't called all that long ago. Maybe he was still at the lab. I called. Their answering system picked up. I punched in Philbrick's extension. Six rings, then his voicemail. I left a message that I'd call him at home.

There was no answer at home either. Later that night I tried again after the ten o'clock news. Still nothing.

• • •

I got in early the next morning. First thing I went to check on Uncle Jack. His empty bed had been stripped. Was he up and about, a miracle overnight cure? I didn't want to think about the alternative. I wheeled around and ran smack into Kwan.

"We hospitalized him," he said.

"How come no one called me?" My voice came out louder than I intended.

"Peter, he just went off a couple of hours ago. I knew you were coming in and—"

"What happened?"

"If you'll stop interrupting me, I'll tell you."

A woman patient was hovering down the hall watching us. I pulled Kwan into Uncle Jack's room with me.

"His fever was worse and he had shaking chills," Kwan said. "Shortness of breath, chest pain. Not severe, but I didn't want to take a chance. Better he's in the hospital where they can treat him aggressively if it turns into pneumonia."

Pneumonia. Some called it "friend of the aged" because it was a relatively benign death. Certainly it was quicker and neater than dying of Lewy body dementia.

"Has anyone told the family?"

"I was just about to do that," Kwan said.

"I'll take care of it."

I rushed up two flights of stairs and down the corridor to my office. I barely noticed Mr. Black waiting outside Emily's office. I unlocked my door and went for the phone. Annie might still be at home or she might be on her way to work. Either way, her cell phone was the better bet.

One ring. Two. *Please pick up.*

When she did, I exhaled.

Before she could ask what was wrong I said, "Kwan doesn't think it's life-threatening, but as a precaution your Uncle Jack has been admitted to Beth Israel." I told her about the fever, the chills, chest pain.

She didn't say anything for a moment. Then, "This was just what

I was afraid was going to happen. I told you I didn't like that place."

"And I told you that MRIs can't cause upper respiratory ill-nesses."

"So why is he sick? That's it. No more tests. No more magnets. No more little pink pills. I don't care. That place is a death trap."

"Annie, I'm really sorry," I began, the words sounding lame and inadequate.

"It's not your fault. It's mine. I should have listened to my gut."

Instead she'd listened to me. I gave her the information about where Uncle Jack was and when she could visit. Then I hung up the phone and massaged my temples. It was too early for a head-ache, but I was developing a doozy.

I opened my drawer and took out a bottle of aspirin and what I thought was an empty mug—turned out it had a coating of pungent scum on the bottom. I headed for the bathroom to get some water.

Mr. Black was still out in the hall, waiting. "Have you seen Dr. Ryan?" he asked. "Her car wasn't in the parking lot when I got here."

Hadn't he just had an appointment with her the day before? She was his therapist, not his girlfriend. What she drove and where she parked was no business of his, and I was about to tell him so when I noticed his right shirtsleeve was empty. It was too late to keep my jaw from dropping.

Mr. Black glanced at his missing arm. Then he examined my face. He suppressed a grin. Then I noticed that his upper body seemed thicker on the armless side, and his shirt twitched. He must have taped his arm to his chest. Emily had said she had a brain-storm. I had to admire it. Here was an intervention, allowing Mr. Black to try out what it was like to live without an arm before actually doing it.

"I thought I had an eight-fifteen appointment with her," he said.

It was past 8:30. "Do you think she's all right?" He seemed genuinely concerned. "I'm sure I don't have the date wrong. I just saw her yesterday afternoon and we made a special appointment for first thing today. She wanted me to come in and report on my, uh" — he paused, glancing at his arm — "progress."

I went downstairs. Gloria was at the nurses' station. She checked the notebook she keeps with all our schedules. "She's supposed to be here." She cocked her head and looked up at the ceiling, as if she were looking up at Emily's empty office. "It's not like her to keep a patient waiting."

I picked up the desk phone and called Emily's beeper. I punched in the number for the unit. While I waited for a call back, I washed out my cup, filled it with fresh coffee and knocked back a couple of aspirin. I sifted through the mail, and Gloria hovered over the phone.

After ten minutes, Emily hadn't called. Gloria had already looked up her home number. She tried there. The answering machine picked up.

"Maybe she's at the lab where she works," I suggested. I looked up their number and called. The phone rang and kept on ringing.

That was odd. It was after nine. Where was Amanda, the receptionist? If the office wasn't open, wouldn't they have calls forwarded to an answering service? I was about to give up when someone picked up.

"Hello?" It was a man's voice, a little breathless. For a moment, I thought I'd gotten the wrong number. Then I recognized the voice. It was Dr. Shands.

"This is Peter Zak," I said. "I'm sorry to bother you, but I was looking for Dr. Ryan."

"She" — there was a pause — "she's unavailable right now."

"She has a patient —" I started. That's when I heard a woman scream. At first it was loud, then muffled, as if Shands put his hand over the receiver. "Dr. Shands? Is everything all right?"

There was scuffling sound. Then, "I'm sorry." His voice was emotionless. "Something's happened. We have an emergency situation here."

"I just need to talk to her for a moment. . . ."

The line had gone dead.

12

"WHAT? WHAT?" Gloria said, leaning over me.

I stared at the receiver. "I talked to the guy who runs the place. Emily can't come to the phone. He says there's an emergency situation."

"Emergency situation—what's that supposed to mean?" Gloria demanded, echoing my own question.

"And I heard a woman scream."

"Do you think it was Emily?" Gloria asked, her voice taut. "One of us needs to get over there." She gave a quick glance at the clock. "I can't leave, so it's got to be you." I'd always known which one of us was more dispensable. "You and I have a meeting with the head of plant and operations at ten, but that can wait. I'll send someone up to apologize to the patient."

I didn't even bother to go up for my jacket. Without thinking what I'd do when I got there, I raced out. As I drove toward Central Square, I ran the brief phone conversation through my head. Why wasn't the receptionist answering the phone? Did "emergency" mean there'd been an accident—*another* accident, this one with graver consequences than a flying hockey puck? Who was screaming? And what was Emily doing at the MRI lab when she had an appointment with Mr. Black at the Pearce?

Traffic backed up on Mass. Ave. as I approached Sidney Street. At the corner, I could see flashing lights reflecting off the building. Several police cruisers, a fire truck, and an ambulance were parked in front. Traffic was taking forever to crawl past. I stayed on Mass. Ave. and parked at a meter. Then I sprinted back.

I approached the building. There was a crowd of gawkers gathered outside. Firefighters were getting back into their truck.

I edged up to the cop at the entrance. "I need to go inside," I told him.

"Sorry, no one goes in," he said, his face impassive, his eyes in shadow under the visor of his cap.

"What happened?"

"We need to keep this area clear, sir," he said. "Please move along."

Through the glass doors I could see the lobby. The doors to the MRI lab were propped open and another officer was stationed there. An EMT came out through the lobby and into the street. I followed her to the ambulance.

"Is anyone hurt?"

She didn't answer, her face impassive. She grabbed for a metal suitcase from the back of the ambulance.

"I have a friend who works in there," I said. She paused. "A good friend."

She gave me a quick glance and shook her head. "Sorry."

I watched her disappear into the building. If someone had been hurt, they'd have been rushed to the hospital already. Police and

EMTs still there meant something worse had happened. Had Emily's stalker followed her and finally struck?

I had to get inside. But short of tackling the officer at the door, there was no way I was going to get past him. I walked around the corner. They hadn't blocked off the garage entrance. I ducked inside and trotted down the ramp.

Taking the elevator up wasn't going to help. I'd just end up being turned away again at the lobby entrance. Then I remembered the stairway exits in the MRI lab. Did any of them end down here?

I tried to orient myself. I moved to the part of the garage under the lab. There was a sign on the door to the stairwell: NOT AN ENTRANCE. In smaller print below, it directed people to the elevator. I tried the door. It opened. Someone had taped the latch over to keep it from engaging.

I took the stairs two at a time and stopped at the exit door painted with a big numeral one. The handle on the door creaked as I pushed down on it and pulled the door open a crack. I listened. There were voices, but not nearby. I slipped into the corridor.

I hadn't been in this part of the place before. There was what looked like a pathology lab—a large room with a couple of stainless steel tables, sinks. There were plastic buckets and containers stacked on the floor, plus all kinds of lab equipment including oversized microscopes jury-rigged with lights and cameras. Shelves held hundreds of jars with paper labels. Probably stains and fixatives for making slides.

I continued along the hall to a pair of fire doors. I looked through a window in the door. There was Shands's office. As I pushed through, Shands came out into the hall.

"How the hell did you get in here? I thought they had this place—"

"What happened? Is Emily all right?" I asked, cutting him off.

"Dr. Ryan?" His eyebrows came together in a question. "Dr. Ryan—" His voice hardened.

Just then two police officers came striding up the hallway. "Dr. Shands?" the taller one said, ignoring me. "I have a few questions. Is there somewhere we could talk?"

Shands hung there. He looked at me, then back at the police officers. Then, like a light switch, he turned on the charm. "Sure," he said with a benign smile. "Be happy to answer any questions you have." He took them into his office.

I continued down the hall into the central area with its warning signs and desk. Amanda the receptionist was sitting there, looking pale and in shock. The double doors to the inner areas were propped open. The sawhorse barriers had been overturned. The door to the scanning room was open, too. The EMT I'd seen outside strode past me and into the room. I moved closer.

I barely noticed the swarm of police officers and medical technicians. I was riveted by the blood on the white linoleum floor.

A man, probably a medical examiner, stood with his back to me, hunched over the table. I knew there was a person on the table, the same person whose blood had pooled beneath the system and been tracked across the floor.

I took a step into the room. A dented oxygen tank lay on the floor near the machine. I felt sick to my stomach, remembering how the magnet had hurtled toward the machine. An oxygen tank would be just as lethal.

I was pressing forward. I needed to see. A police officer came at me. He put his hands up. "Sorry, sir. I'm going to have to ask you to wait in another room."

"Who is it?" I asked.

Now the medical examiner was turning. He was stepping aside.

As he reached into his bag for something, the victim's arm slipped and dangled off the edge of the table. The armpit of the white lab coat was stained with sweat.

"Dr. Zak?" said a woman's voice behind me, uncertain and tremulous. It was Emily. I turned and exhaled a huge sigh of relief.

Emily moved toward me hesitantly, her face streaked with tears. Then she paused, wobbled, looking as if she might collapse. When I took her in my arms, her muscles went limp.

"Poor Lenny," she said. "It's so awful." She gave a deep, wracking sob. She hugged me tighter, her breathing quickening. "Thanks for being here." Then she righted herself, struggling to regain control before pulling away and giving me an odd look. "Why *are* you here?"

She wasn't alone in that thought.

"What the hell are *you* doing here?" It was Detective Sergeant Joseph MacRae.

• • •

I wasn't surprised to see MacRae standing there in his rumpled brown suit. After all, he was a homicide detective.

"Christ almighty," he said, rubbing his hand back and forth across the side of his red buzz cut and eyeing me with distaste. His ears burned with annoyance. I'd ended up in the middle of far too many investigations for his taste . . . or mine.

When I'd first met MacRae, he'd been smitten with a crime victim who claimed to remember who shot her in the head. I liked to think that over time we'd developed a grudging respect for one another. Maybe. It didn't help that he and Annie were old friends, and at one time may have been more than that.

"Hey, Mac," I said.

He eyed me suspiciously. "I didn't know you worked here too."

I barely missed a beat. "I'm involved in a research project with these guys."

"Uh-huh," he said. He sounded less than convinced. "Ms. Ryan seems to have found the victim," MacRae said, his tone implying something more than his words. Emily stood there trembling.

"*Dr.* Ryan," I said stiffly. "She works here." I knew she'd have been badly overmatched against MacRae.

Emily took another look at Philbrick's body and her lower lip quivered. She bit on a knuckle.

"How about I take Dr. Ryan somewhere she can calm down a little?" I offered.

"Just don't take her too far," MacRae said. "We're going to want to talk to her. And you too."

I took one last look at Leonard Philbrick. Even from across the room, I could see that his skull had been crushed. His personal belongings had been laid out on a rolling stainless steel table. Shattered eyeglasses. A couple of pencils. Wallet.

As I put my arm around Emily and shepherded her to the control room, I wondered why Philbrick had called me yesterday—three times. *Damn.* I could hear his voice. Had the call just been a routine follow-up on Annie's uncle? That made no sense. Why not just call the floor nurse and get it? Had he been reluctant to say why he was calling because he'd been calling from here and didn't want to be overheard? He hadn't answered his phone when I called him back—had he ended up staying here all night?

Through the glass panel we could see the police and the medical personnel working. We sat at one of the tables. Emily's face was swollen, her eyes bleary. She winced as a camera flashed next door.

"You want to talk about it?" I asked.

Emily hiccupped. "Lenny called me last night to tell me—"

"When?" I asked, cutting her off.

She gave me a surprised look. "At around eight, I think."

"He called me too. Three times yesterday afternoon. When I tried to call him back he didn't answer his phone. Here or at home."

"That's odd. He called me to say that Dr. Pullaski found my beeper," Emily said. "I was sure I had it with me but when I went to look, it wasn't in my bag. I told him I'd have to come in early because I had an appointment with Mr. Black at . . ." Her eyes widened. "Oh my gosh. Mr. Black." She rose to her feet.

"Don't worry. We sent him home, told him you were held up by an emergency."

Emily groaned. "I hope he's okay."

"So you found Dr. Philbrick?"

She nodded. "I heard the scanner going. Seemed odd, that early in the morning. I came in to see what was up." Emily's gazed through the window. They were shifting Philbrick's body from the table. "I saw the blood."

Emily looked down at her feet. I wondered if she had blood on her shoes.

"I could barely breathe." She swallowed. "I knew someone was inside."

"So you stopped the scan and slid the table out?"

"I tried to. But it was stuck." She started to cry again. "I tried and tried, but I couldn't get it to budge. Finally I shut everything down and turned off the magnetic field. Quenched the magnet." She pointed to a red button, marked EMERGENCY RUNDOWN, set apart from the others on the control panel. "I'd been drilled, over and over, never to do that except in a dire emergency when someone's pinned in the machine."

"You came in here to shut it down?"

"No. There's another panel on the wall beside the scanner. There was this loud noise, like a jet plane. Scared me half to death. Then the thing shut down. The helium vented to the outside. No explosion, thank God."

I looked into the scanner room. There was a sort of aluminum smokestack connecting the scanner to the outside wall. That must have been how the cryogenic gasses vented.

"The table still wouldn't move. The tank was wedged in there." Emily looked at back of her hand. The nail on her index finger was broken down to the quick. She put it in her mouth and sucked. "That's when Dr. Shands came in. He called the police. They managed to pry the tank out of there."

"Wait a minute," I said. "I thought you bring oxygen tanks into the scanner room all the time. You brought a tank in for Mr. O'Neill."

"That one was MRI-compatible. It's the only kind we use to avoid just this kind of accident. I don't know where that tank came from." Her eyes widened as she realized the implications.

"If that oxygen tank got here by mistake," I said, "and you happened to be the one who brought it into the scan room, no one would—"

"That's not what happened. Besides, we never assume—we always test before bringing one into the scan room." Her eyes beseeched me. "You don't believe me, do you?"

I didn't say anything. I was thinking about how careful Philbrick was. He'd been working around powerful magnets for years. Emily had been working around them for only a few months.

MacRae came to the window. He looked at Emily and jerked his thumb in the direction of the hall. Behind him a technician was dusting the MRI system for fingerprints. They'd find Emily's prints on top. Now he moved on to the oxygen tank. He'd find her prints on that, too.

"It doesn't matter what I think. What matters is what the police believe. You shouldn't be talking to them without an attorney."

"If I get a lawyer then they'll think I have something to hide." She reached for the door.

"That's the kind of thinking that gets innocent people in trouble. I know an excellent criminal attorney."

"I don't think so," she said quietly, and pulled the door open. "I'll just tell them the truth."

MacRae was waiting. "Don't you go anywhere, either," he growled at me, and led Emily away.

I leaned against the door. Blood on her shoes. Her fingerprints everywhere. She was a novice at working with these big magnets. She'd brought a dangerous metal object into the scan room before. The only person who might have been able to vouch for her was dead.

It wouldn't be long before the police understood how the system worked—that the magnetic field was never off even when the machine wasn't scanning, even if you pulled the plug and cut the electricity. They'd quickly grasp the implications. This "accident" couldn't have been caused by someone accidentally leaving an oxygen tank in the scan room. If Philbrick had carried it in himself, then it would have been drawn into the system before he could get in it.

No, the oxygen canister had to have been brought into the room while Philbrick was in the machine. While he was giving himself an MRI. Poor devil probably never even knew what hit him.

13

TWENTY MINUTES later Emily hadn't returned. My head felt like a jackhammer was going after my prefrontal cortex.

I wandered until I found a small room with a refrigerator, a sink, and a Formica table with some folding chairs. There wasn't any aspirin, but on the counter there was a coffeemaker. In one of the wall cabinets I found packets of coffee. I started a fresh pot, then sat down to wait.

The pot was sizzling as the last drops of water dripped through when I heard footsteps in the hall. Dr. Pullaski came in and reached into the cabinet for a coffee mug. No blood on those cream-colored high-heeled pumps. She nearly jumped out of her skin when she saw me.

"Peter Zak, Dr. Peter Zak," I said, in case she didn't remember. "I started a pot."

With an unsteady hand, she poured herself some coffee. "What a horrendous day. I still can't believe it. It's too awful."

"Looks like a terrible accident."

She leaned against the counter, held the mug in cupped hands and inhaled the coffee aroma, then took a sip. "I called Leonard's sister to let her know. I would have gone over there to tell her but the police want me to stay here. I didn't want her to hear it on the news. He's been with us since the beginning. I never thought—" Her voice broke off. She closed her eyes and leaned back, her lips trembling. Then she gave me a sharp look, a combination of suspicion and maybe a little fear.

"What are you doing here?" she asked. Her look turned speculative and before I could come up with an answer she said, "Were you meeting Dr. Ryan? Poor thing. I'm sure she didn't mean to."

"Mean to what?"

"Isn't it obvious?" She took a sip of the coffee. "She must have brought the oxygen canister into the scan room, not realizing that it was a ferrous container."

"Why would she do that?"

"Who knows."

"And why would there be a tank like that here in the first place? One that could be drawn into the magnet?"

"Sometimes the suppliers slip up. It's happened before. The tanks are usually labeled but we always check. At least that's standard operating procedure"—she pursed her lips—"which everyone is supposed to follow. And why was she here? She's not scheduled to be here this morning."

"She said Dr. Philbrick called her, said you'd found her beeper. She came in before work to get it."

"Me? She must have misheard him. Of course I'm not surprised. She's a bit scattered."

"Did you make those calls?" Shands asked, sticking his head into the room. His voice was steady and even, a man used to giving orders.

"I'm taking care of it." Dr. Pullaski gave a nudge of her head in my direction.

"Damage control," Shands told me. "I'm sure you understand."

"Of course we'll mount a full investigation," Dr. Pullaski said. "We've never had a serious incident. Shouldn't affect our funding. After all, with our track record, and the services we provide —" She was practicing some of that "damage control" on me. "It's a one-in-a-million accident. Of course, we'll reassess our training procedures."

"Poor Leonard," Shands said. For a moment his eyes went empty and his face sagged. Then he shook himself out of it. "The regulators are going to be all over us."

Dr. Pullaski took out a container of cream from the refrigerator and added some to her coffee, licking a drop that fell on a manicured fingernail. "We'll deal with it."

• • •

MacRae closed the door of the office where he'd set up shop. He'd finished with Emily and now he was ready for the next course. He had his pad open, pen poised.

"So when did you get here?" His look said, *And don't bullshit me.*

"A little after nine."

"A little after . . ." he repeated, his face impassive except for a little twitch in the jaw muscle. "That's after we got here — you must have broken the sound barrier getting over here."

"Busted my ass."

"And how the hell did you get in?"

"I came up the stairs from the garage." He raised his eyebrows at me. "The lock on one of the doors was taped open."

"Damn," he said, making a note. I suspected the officers securing the scene were going to get reamed. He finished writing and slowly looked up at me. "Taped open?"

"Go look for yourselves."

"We will. So Dr. Ryan doesn't show up for an appointment, and you rush over here to investigate. You go this protective on all your post-docs?" I reminded myself he wasn't being obnoxious just for the hell of it—it was his job to find chinks in people's stories.

"Look, someone's been stalking Dr. Ryan," I said. "She's had several incidents, one of them here. If you don't believe me, look it up—the police responded. Naturally we were concerned that she might be the one who was hurt."

"So *we* rushed over to save the day?"

I knew he was jerking my chain, but that was about the size of it. I folded my arms across my chest.

"You knew Dr. Philbrick?" he asked.

"A little. I'd met him twice. Both times here." I told MacRae about the scan Philbrick had done on one of our patients. Reluctantly, I gave him the patient's name. "Jack O'Neill."

MacRae's eyebrows went up. "Annie's uncle?"

I nodded.

"Great guy. One of the best beat cops in Somerville. Worked with juveniles better than anyone I've ever seen. Used to have kids actually come to the station asking for him. Kind of took over when Annie's dad died."

It bothered me a lot that MacRae knew all this. I reminded myself he and Annie had grown up together. They'd gone to the same high school; their families were close. Still, I wanted to be the one that knew what mattered to Annie, not MacRae.

"Is he sick?" MacRae asked.

"He's being evaluated."

"I'm sorry to hear that. Would you let Annie know I asked after him?"

I nodded, having not the slightest intention of doing so.

"What can you tell me about Dr. Philbrick?" he asked, getting back to the business at hand.

I rattled off what I knew. That he'd worked with Shands for a long time. That Dr. Pullaski said he had a sister. And he'd taken his own MRI before.

"Do-it-yourself MRI?" MacRae said, sounding incredulous.

"He was an expert on MRI technology."

"An expert." MacRae mulled the word. "So he knew it would be dangerous to bring that oxygen tank into the room?"

"The magnetic field is never turned off," I said, giving an oblique answer.

MacRae blinked at me. He knew this was important information, he just didn't know why.

I went on, "So you see, Dr. Philbrick couldn't have brought that oxygen tank into the scanning room himself."

I could almost see the wheels turning as MacRae grasped the implications. "So someone else had to have brought in the tank while Dr. Philbrick was in the machine," he said. He made another note. "And what was the victim's relationship to Dr. Ryan?"

"Professional." I felt a bit uncomfortable adding, "And they sometimes went out after work."

I could tell this was something he hadn't expected.

"Dr. Philbrick called me three times yesterday," I told him.

"He did? What for?"

"I don't know. We never talked."

"Had he ever called you before?"

"No."

"Did it seem odd to you, his calling you like that?"

"Not until now."

MacRae scratched his head. "Did you like him?"

It was such a bizarre question, it took me a moment to find my answer. I could hear Emily's take on Philbrick: *He's not so weird, once you get used to him.* I remembered him with Uncle Jack, how gentle and compassionate he'd been.

"Actually, I did."

• • •

I drove back to the hospital in a fog, barely aware of anything outside my head. My mind kept flashing pictures of Philbrick's body and the blood on the floor. I turned on the radio loud and tried to flood my head with music.

When I got back I checked in with Gloria. When she heard the news, she glanced uneasily about the nurses' station. "The minute you let your guard down, that's when accidents happen." She got up and checked that the door to the med room was locked. "I'm glad you went over there. Poor Emily. I hope you sent her home."

"I tried to. But she insisted on coming here when they finished with her. Said work was better than staying home alone."

"Now where have I heard that before?"

In the weeks after Kate died, I'd stalked the unit like a zombie. Gloria and Kwan had tried to get me to go home, but alone was the last place I wanted to be.

"How about you? You okay?" Gloria asked.

"I'm fine," I said. I actually thought I was.

I went up to my office. A few weeks ago I would have grabbed the phone and called Annie. Now I hesitated. This news would only confirm Annie's conviction that University Medical Imaging was an evil place where basic safety procedures were ignored, where patients came out sicker than they went in. And I'd been the one who'd recommended it.

I dialed her number. When she didn't pick up, I left a message for her to call me back.

At least I had plenty of work to bury myself in. I opened a spreadsheet and started on a budget revision. The room felt stuffy. I got up and opened the window, sat down again, and tried to concentrate. We'd be increasing our patient count by two, and decreasing staff by one. Welcome to the new millennium. I adjusted the numbers. Then I had to upload the new reimbursement schedule from the main computer and generate a forecast. I knew the results were going to be depressing.

The window shade flapped in the breeze. I got up and half-closed the window. I'd just gotten back to work again when the *beep-beep-beep* of a truck distracted me again. I watched out the window as it backed up to the side of the building.

I gave up and went downstairs. I found Kwan making himself a pot of tea.

"I can't get any work done," I told him.

"Work? You do work?" he asked, in mock amazement. He must have seen something in my look because his sardonic grin vanished. "Something's getting to you."

"Feels like all the stars are out of alignment," I said, and told him about what had happened that morning.

"She was the only one there when it happened?" he asked.

"She says she came in after."

"You mean someone caused a horrendous accident and then cleared out, leaving her there holding the bag? I'm not sure we should send any more patients over there for testing."

Of course this was exactly what Shands and Pullaski had been concerned about. For a medical lab, an unblemished safety record was an asset as important as any state-of-the-art machine.

Kwan urged me to go to the caf with him for an early lunch. I had a salad and an omelet that could have been made from recycled Silly Putty. When I got back, I checked to see if Annie had called. She hadn't.

I couldn't face the spreadsheet, so I went back down to the unit. I walked the corridors, checking in on patients as I went. There was a reassuring familiarity to the routine.

Emily was in one of the rooms working with a new patient. I caught her eye. She gave a little nod.

I wandered down the hall and into what had been Uncle Jack's room. We couldn't afford to keep beds empty. A new patient would be moved in there tomorrow. The only vestiges of Uncle Jack were a suitcase into which the staff had packed his belongings, and a stack of clippings from magazines and newspapers. I suspected Gloria was responsible for saving them. The sugar-packet collection, pens, and assorted other items that he'd amassed were gone.

The suitcase was an old leather one, good quality, plastered with peeling travel decals. Yosemite. Mount Rushmore. It occurred to me how little I knew about Uncle Jack. Only that he was Annie's uncle, a widower, and that he'd been a cop. A good cop. I thought about all the things he'd saved in his apartment and here. Hoarding. It was like trying to keep your footprints from washing away.

I leafed through the clippings. There was an odd assortment of stuff. He seemed to like ads with sailboats, beaches, or golfers in them. Why not? He'd just reached that point in his life when he and his wife should have been able to finally enjoy all the things they'd never had time for before. She wasn't supposed to die, and he wasn't supposed to come down with dementia.

I carried the suitcase and the clippings up to my office. When

I opened the door the phone was ringing. It was Annie.

Quickly I told her Leonard Philbrick was dead, and that I'd been at the MRI lab. "Looks like he was alone, operating the machine himself."

"Doing what?"

"Giving himself an MRI. They've got a remote control rigged up." I knew that sounded pretty strange. "Hey, he's a researcher. These guys are a little nuts."

"So who brought the oxygen tank into the room?"

"Emily says it wasn't her."

"Emily Ryan?"

I realized I'd managed to tell my story without mentioning that Emily was the reason I'd gone over to the MRI lab in the first place.

"We were worried when Emily didn't show up to meet with one of her patients. Then when I called . . ." My voice trailed off. "Gloria thought one of us should go over and see what was up."

"Gloria made you do it," Annie said. "Test magnet. Oxygen tank. Isn't it basically the same accident?"

"Except this time it wasn't her."

"You believe her?"

The question hung there in the air. I didn't want to admit the truth—that I was having a hard time believing Emily's story. There was the errant beeper that Dr. Pullaski insisted she hadn't found. That beeper was starting to feel like a flimsy excuse for coming in early so she could "find" the body. And now with Philbrick dead, there wasn't anyone to back up her story. Maybe there'd been some other reason that she'd gone over there so early in the morning, someone she was meeting and was now trying to protect?

"They're not getting their hands on Uncle Jack again. Assuming he survives," Annie said.

"How is he?"

"He's really weak. This afternoon they had him on a respirator. I talked to his doctor."

"And?"

"Hang on. I had to write it down." There was silence on the line. "Here it is. Something about an opacity in the left lower lung. Bacterial infection. Elevated white blood count."

None of that sounded good. "At least we caught it early," I said, trying to keep my voice upbeat. "A bacterial infection should respond to antibiotics."

"That's what the doctor said."

"Nothing to do now but wait."

"Doctor said that, too. Waiting. Now that's something I suck at." Annie gave a tired laugh. "Listen, I've got to go. I'm way behind on work and—"

"Annie, don't hang up yet." There was silence on the other end of the line. "You still there?"

"Uh-huh."

"I know you're just barely hanging on right now, between Uncle Jack being so sick and work and all"—I took a breath—"but you're shutting me out."

I heard a heavy sigh. Then, "Listen, I'm beat. And I've got eight million things to do. I probably won't even have time for lunch—"

"At least let me take you to dinner."

"The last thing I want to do is drive anywhere."

"I'll pick you up, drive you home. You have to eat anyway, right?"

"All I've got with me is jeans."

"Jeans are fine. It's very informal. A little place in the North End."

"I'm so tired. I just want to go home."

This time I wasn't going to take no for an answer. "You'll see. It feels like home."

· · ·

We stepped through the gate under a glowing red neon sign: IDA'S ITALIAN CUISINE.

"Wow," Annie said, looking over the fence at the back of the little alley in the North End.

Fifty feet below us, cars streamed out of the mouth of the Sumner Tunnel like water gushing from a storm drain. Behind us Hanover Street pulsed with pedestrians in this neighborhood that still boasted Boston's best Italian restaurants. The air was thick with the smell of garlic.

It felt wonderful to be somewhere with Annie other than a hospital. I held the restaurant door open. The tiny place really did feel like someone's North End apartment with its linoleum floor and red-checked tablecloths. On the walls hung framed mirrors flecked with gold, and on high shelves there were basketed wine bottles alongside piles of plastic grapes.

"Dr. Peter," an older man said coming to greet us, his arms outstretched. He patted me on the back and seated us in the corner at the only empty table.

"How on earth did you find this place?" Annie asked, fingering the plastic-covered menu, her gaze shifting from what looked like a pair of well-coiffed Back Bay matrons in designer suits at one table, to a pair of scruffy older men wearing zip-up jackets and talking animatedly in Italian at another. An older couple had gotten up to leave and was getting hugged good-bye by the waitress.

"Actually, Kate found it." Now I had Annie's attention. "She read that Caroline Kennedy had a party here, so she had to try it. That was about ten years ago. We came the first time, loved the food—"

"The funky atmosphere."

"The food," I said. The waitress, a smiling blond woman whom I knew was the owner's sister, brought us a basket of bread and a chipped earthenware carafe filled with homemade red wine. I poured some into the thick wine glasses that were on the table. I lifted my glass.

"To Uncle Jack."

Annie smiled. "To Kate."

Over the kind of antipasto and soup my mother would have made if she were Italian, Annie told me about her work. She and Chip had struggled for the first year and a half after they left the public defender's office. Now they had more work than they could handle.

"This is unbelievably good," Annie said after her first bite of Ida's famous chicken—a roll of breast meat, browned and glistening in a rich sauce, stuffed with pine nuts, spinach, prosciutto, and cheese. She took another bite, leaned back, closed her eyes, and chewed. "You were right. I needed this."

"I needed this, too," I said, and looked up at her. She knew I wasn't referring to the food.

I told Annie about the budget I had to balance and how I was trying to convince administrators at the Pearce to let us expand some of our outpatient services. She talked about the great resumes they'd gotten for the office staff they were adding. Neither of us wanted to talk about Uncle Jack's dementia or Leonard Philbrick's death.

Annie was picking the last pine nut off her plate when the waitress came and cleared.

"I'm sorry I've been so distracted and crabby," Annie said. "Everything feels so . . ."

"Chaotic?"

"Uh-huh."

The waitress brought us some coffee.

"You don't like it when things get out of control, do you?"

Annie sat back and gave me a wry smile. "You going to analyze me?"

"No, just making an observation," I said, taking a sip of my coffee. "Holding me at arm's length isn't going to make everything else fall into line."

"You think that's what I'm doing?" She thought about it for a moment. "Maybe. It's just that I'm feeling so overwhelmed. Uncle Jack was there for me when my father died, and the years before that, too, when my father had given up on life. Now I'm losing him."

Annie picked up her coffee and blew on it.

"It hurts to lose someone you care about," I said. "But keeping yourself from caring isn't the answer."

The cup hovered an inch from Annie's mouth. She put it down.

"Believe me. I know what I'm talking about," I added, reaching under the table to touch Annie's leg.

"I know you do," Annie said, squeezing my hand.

Too soon, dinner was over. It felt like it had been weeks ago that I'd raced over to the MRI lab to find Philbrick dead, not just that morning.

The waitress brought the bill. I glanced at it. I fished out my wallet and slid out my credit card. But instead of putting it on the little tray, I just hung there, staring at it. It reminded me of something. Something I'd seen that morning but couldn't put my finger on.

I closed my eyes and tried to picture the room. The medical examiner was standing in front of the body. He stepped aside. There was Philbrick on the table wearing his lab coat, his skull crushed, his arm hanging off the edge. On a table were Philbrick's belongings, his shattered eyeglasses . . .

"I'll take that for you," the waitress said, offering to take my credit card.

Suddenly I knew what I'd noticed but failed to register.

• • •

That night I stayed at Annie's. We made love, and then I held her until we both fell asleep.

"So?" MacRae growled when I called him from my office the next morning. "Every man I know carries a wallet in his pants pocket."

"And credit cards in his wallet? Were there any in Dr. Philbrick's wallet?"

MacRae grunted that there were.

"He wouldn't have gone near that MRI system with those in his pocket. The magnets would have wiped them clean."

There was silence as MacRae chewed on that.

"Dr. Philbrick was a fastidiously careful technician," I said.

"We're waiting for the results of a tox screen," MacRae said.

Sounded as if he was a step ahead of me. If Philbrick had been drugged or drunk, that could explain why he'd forgotten to remove his wallet before he went into the scan room.

"Lab's got a perfect safety record. You think they're reporting every incident?" He dangled the question like a piece of bait. From his tone, seemed as if he already knew the answer.

"I witnessed an incident. A near miss. Someone brought a good-sized test magnet into the scan room. Dr. Philbrick went ballistic."

"Him and the magnet," MacRae said.

A comedian. Now he was waiting for the punch line. Reluctantly I gave it to him.

"It was Dr. Ryan who brought in the test magnet."

"Uh-huh," MacRae said. "You'll call me if you think of anything else I should know," he added with more than a touch of irony. "By the way, when we checked the exit doors in the garage, none of them were taped open."

"But that's how I got up. I'm sure—"

"Oh, we're not doubting your story. We found residual evidence that one of the locks had been taped open. If you hadn't gotten in that way, we never would have known."

It was the closest I was ever going to get to "thank you" from MacRae. And the implications were enormous. It meant that someone, anyone, could have been there before Emily, come and gone without passing through the lobby security.

I'd barely put down the phone when it rang. "Dr. Zak?" I didn't recognize the woman's voice. "I'm just calling to remind you. You have an MRI scheduled tomorrow at two? We've sent you a packet of information"—I gazed at the pile of unopened mail on my desk; I'd probably assumed it was junk—"with directions for getting here and instructions about what to expect."

I flipped open my date book. There it was, at 2:00 tomorrow, "MRI." I'd completely forgotten. Seemed like years, not weeks ago that Emily had scheduled the appointment for me. Now I was a whole lot less enthusiastic about getting up on that table and sliding into the narrow tube where Leonard Philbrick had died. Would I lie there wondering if someone was about to walk in the scan room with a tire iron? Was I going to pick up a smallpox or dengue fever? Annie's paranoia about the place was catching.

"Dr. Zak? We'll expect to see you?"

I thought about canceling. Then I began to rationalize. How could I pass up the opportunity? There wasn't another other system in the country as powerful as theirs. After the accident, surely the staff would be even more vigilant than usual. Worst case, I'd pick up a cold. Seemed unlikely, but even if it happened, hey, I was young, in good shape. I'd survive.

．．．

"So did you see this?" my mother asked. I was in her kitchen that evening having a piece of pound cake, some coffee, and a long-overdue chat. She pushed a newspaper across the table to me. It was folded back, and in red marker on the inside front page she'd circled "RESEARCHER KILLED IN FREAK MRI ACCIDENT."

I nearly choked on my mouthful of cake. I'd read the article that morning and knew it didn't mention me.

"More?" she asked, standing and moving to the counter.

"No, really, I've had enough."

"Enough" is not in my mother's vocabulary. She was eyeing me like maybe I was sick. "You sure?"

I held up my hands.

"I want Minnie to see that," she said poking a bony finger at the paper and sniffing.

Minnie Sadowsky was my mother's longtime friend. Minnie was okay, though still a cheek pincher. It was Dr. Geoffrey—her paragon of a son, an MD, married with three kids—who was the bane of my existence.

I pretended to read the article.

"Why do you want her to see this?"

"Geoffrey gave her a body scan for her birthday." From my mother's expression I could see that she didn't think much of this gift. "Completely safe, he tells her. If there's cancer, we'll know, he tells her." My mother shook her head. "At our age, better not to know."

"This accident was at an MRI lab," I said. "He probably gave her a CT scan."

I'd been noticing ads cropping up all over the place enticing people to "give your loved one a full-body scan." It was entirely predictable. Every hospital had gotten itself a CT scanner when computerized tomography was the hot new technology. Along comes magnetic resonance imaging, and yesterday's latest invention becomes today's white elephant. All that excess equipment lying around still needed to be paid off so *voilà*, enter the physician/entrepreneur.

"CT, schmee-T. That's like an X ray?" she asked. I nodded. "I could go to Chernobyl if I wanted radiation. And you know I love Minnie, but this is not such a good gift for her. Already every bunion she's got is skin cancer; she's tired, it's fibromyalgia or Epstein-Whozits syndrome."

"Maybe he thinks she'll stop worrying when they don't find anything."

My mother looked at me like I had the IQ of a frog. "To find, there's always something."

This wasn't so farfetched. Body scans could easily pick up false positives or harmless anomalies, sending patients off for more unnecessary tests, surgery even.

"It's some racket," my mother continued. "You don't think these guys are hooked up with the surgeons?"

As usual, my mother's conspiracy theory was entirely plausible. She'd never bought margarine, either.

A while later when I was leaving she asked, "Busy day tomorrow?"

"Every day is busy," I said. She didn't need to know that I was as nutty as her friend Minnie.

14

IT WAS a little before two and the chairs in the reception area at University Medical Imaging were empty. Apparently business had taken a dive. Probably only temporary. They were still the only show in town—even Mass General didn't have a machine as powerful as theirs.

I checked in. The young woman at the reception desk was short and chubby with dark hair and tinted glasses. She gave me a clipboard with forms to fill out.

I sat down and began. I scribbled in my name, address. Checked male. Height and weight. Was I pregnant? I scanned the rest of the questions. Right- or left-handed? On any medications? Any metal implants? Neurological disorders? Not, not, not.

There were several more pages of questions. I sighed and started to fill in the blanks. This was going to take a while, but it was par for the course for any research study.

The final two pages were a consent form. I scrawled my signature at the bottom.

I brought the forms back to the receptionist. She looked them over, then hesitated for a moment as if unsure what to do next. I wondered if tall, blond Amanda had jumped ship and Dr. Pullaski had hired this replacement.

I'd barely sat down with a magazine when the door opened.

"Dr. Zak?" It was Emily. She was smiling, but she had dark circles under her eyes and her skin was almost as pale as her lab coat.

She ushered me into the now-familiar central area with its warning signs and introduced me to the man in a lab coat who was working at the counter. I knew the drill. I shed my wallet and keys. I followed her to an examining room.

Emily shut the door behind her and leaned against it.

"I don't know how long I can keep this up," she said. "They're all looking at me like it was my fault. Dr. Pullaski told the police that I used the lab without her authority. She says she never found my beeper or asked Lenny to call me. I'm sure she would have fired me if it weren't for Dr. Shands. He's been the only one sticking up for me. And the police —"

"They questioned you again?"

"They showed up here yesterday afternoon, asking about safety procedures, and why we didn't report the accident with the test magnet. I told them no one was hurt. There was no accident."

Interesting rationalization. I wondered if she'd really convinced herself of that.

Emily sank down onto a stool. "Honest to God, I've told them everything I know." She started to cry. "Now they're questioning my neighbors." She hiccupped, the tears flowing freely. I put my hand on her shoulder. "Wanted to know when I left the apartment that morning. How many times"—she took a ragged breath—"do I have to explain, he was dead when I got here?" She looked miserable, like a wounded animal.

I raised her off the stool and put my arms around her. "I'm sure the police are casting a wide net."

"Now they want to talk to Kyle. I'm not even seeing him anymore," she said, snuffling into my shoulder.

Her hair smelled gingery and I could feel her breasts pressing against me, reminding me that this was a woman I held in my arms. The air in the confined space around us seemed charged like a magnetic field.

"The police are probably questioning them because you were here," I said, trying to move Emily to arm's length and ward off my own increasing feeling of discomfort. I reached for a tissue and handed it to her.

"They'll probably check your background," I went on. "See if there's anything in your past."

"Oh, God. You think so?"

Emily held the crumpled tissue over her mouth. Her pupils had dilated. She'd panicked at the mere thought of exposing whatever skeleton was in her closet. I realized how little I knew about her.

"Is there something you're afraid they'll find out?"

Red streaks had appeared on Emily's throat. She fiddled with the top button of her lab coat, buttoning and unbuttoning it.

"In college I did something really stupid. I needed money. I didn't realize what was going to happen. Kyle helped me through it. He protected me."

"You mentioned another stalking." She'd said it had been a stranger who'd since died in a car accident.

She nodded. "That was part of it. I hope the police don't drag that out again. I thought I'd finally left it behind me."

Before I could ask what, there was a tap at the door. Emily leaped away as it pushed open.

"Oh, I'm sorry," Shands said when he saw me, then Emily. Emily tucked the tissue into her pocket. "I see you're not ready yet." His gaze lingered for a moment too long on Emily. Then Shands gave me a speculative look. "I'll be back in a few minutes," he said and left.

"I'd better go," Emily said, handing me a hospital gown. She backed out of the room.

As I changed into the hospital gown, I wondered what had happened to Emily that was so shameful she could barely speak of it. Was that the reason she hadn't wanted the police to investigate her vandalized car?

I put my feet into paper slippers, and tried not to think about how ridiculous I looked. Health care could be humiliating.

• • •

"Peter!" Shands said when he returned, giving me his 150-watt smile. "You're going to enjoy this." *Said the spider to the fly.*

Lighten up, I told myself. They've got to be on their best behavior.

Shands looked over my medical history for at least ten seconds. He did the standard touchstones—pulse, blood pressure, reflexes—and then he jotted some notes in a file. As if out of thin air, he brandished a hypodermic syringe and came at me with it.

The vehemence with which I jerked away my arm surprised even me. Hadn't realized I was so jumpy. Still, he should have known better—something you learn early on, don't come at a patient unexpectedly unless you're prepared to get kicked in the groin.

"Take it easy," Shands said. "I was just going to inject a contrast agent. Gives us a clearer picture—"

"I know what a contrast agent does. It's just that I wasn't ex-pecting it."

I wondered if it ever occurred to him to say, "This will only take a moment," or "This might sting," or . . . No, he was a researcher. Annie had been right. He did treat patients like crash-test dummies.

I offered up my arm. He wiped a spot with alcohol. I watched the needle slide in. It burned a little as he depressed the plunger. I was glad Annie didn't know I was doing this.

• • •

"That's good. Keep your head very still." I heard Emily's voice coming through the headphones as I lay in the MRI tube.

Uncle Jack had been right. It felt exactly like being slid into a coffin. I needn't have worried about feeling spooked by Philbrick's ghost—the deafening buzzing and thumping pretty much over-whelmed anything that might have gone on in my head. Might as well be inside an engine block. At least they'd given me a pair of prism glasses so that when I looked up, I saw the reflection of my feet hanging out the end of the tube. It was better than staring at the inside of the scanner, inches beyond my nose. Still, I found it easier to take with my eyes closed.

I hoped the contrast agent was making my brain light up in Technicolor. The spot where Shands had injected the contrast agent felt cold.

"Excellent," Emily said. "We've got a good baseline. Now, take your time with this. I'd like you to slowly blink your eyes twenty times."

The test took about a half hour. Not too bad, and I survived it unscathed. Afterward I sat in the control room with Emily looking at my own brain scan. My "baseline" didn't seem particularly rest-ful. Like a percussion section, there were pulses on either side in the temporo-parietal region, probably synchronized with the machine's thumping. Only the visual cortex was quiet. Taking into account that I'd been listening to the Anvil Chorus with my eyes shut, it was about what I'd have expected.

As I watched, I realized that my mouth tasted funny. I mentioned it to Emily.

"Metallic?"

That was it. Emily said it was one of the side effects of the contrast agent and would go away in a few hours.

"Here's where you were blinking your eyes," she said. Now the visual cortex at the back and the motor strip were lighting up.

Shands came in and watched over Emily's shoulder, his arms crossed.

"Here's where you said your name."

Shands leaned forward, his chest grazing Emily's head, staring intently and touching his finger to his mouth.

"Your mother's maiden name," Emily said.

He gave me a surreptitious look and straightened. He'd seen something in the scan that he hadn't been expecting. It reminded me of the evasive look the evaluator gave my mother when we'd had my dad worked up. He'd just shown Dad a pen and asked him what it was. "Ink spreader," said my father, the same man who'd once read four newspapers a day, every day, including the *Daily Forward* in Yiddish. I leaned forward, examining the image, wondering what Shands had seen and not wanting to ask.

I heard the door to the room open. When I turned around, Shands had left and the new receptionist was handing a slip of pink paper to Emily. Emily read it. She swallowed.

"Something wrong?" I asked.

"Oh, no," she said, the smile forced. She picked up the test protocol and consent form from the table. "Just a call I need to return. Won't be a minute. You mind?"

"Of course not."

"You can run this some more while I'm gone. Do you need me to show you—"

"It's okay. I remember from last time."

When she turned to go, she dropped the papers she was holding. "Damn." She started to bend over.

"Go ahead," I said, and began to pick up the papers. Emily left.

I sorted the pages. Each task I'd done was listed on the test protocol. The beginning and ending times were noted. I set the forms aside.

As I sat there staring at the frozen image, trying to assume the perspective of an unbiased investigator, I felt anxiety gnawing at the pit of my stomach. This was *my* brain, not some stranger's, and something in it had caught Shands's attention.

I checked the test protocol. According to the time stamp, I was in the middle of tapping my fingers. I backed up the animation to the part where I'd been blinking my eyes. There was activity on either side near the temples and more activity in the limbic system—perhaps evidence that I was hearing sounds and feeling some degree of anxiety. There were pulses near the center as I processed information. But beyond that I saw nothing. It was like reading words written in another language—I could sound them out, but I couldn't extract meaning, never mind nuance. I watched my brain being put through its paces, not knowing what the hell I was looking for.

Frustrated, I sat back. I folded and unfolded the corner of the consent form. I felt a little queasy. Perhaps nausea was another side effect of the dye Shands injected.

Maybe if I looked at other people's scans, other "normals," I'd be able to see what was different about mine. I knew Emily's and Philbrick's had been taken. Shands's, too. I was just about to try to find other scans in the system when Emily returned.

She sat down beside me. "You were able to run it?"

"Pretty mind-blowing."

"Literally."

I clicked the mouse and my brain started to animate again, pulses of green, a flash of yellow. "How do you analyze it? I mean, if something were anomalous, how would you know?"

"It's not something most people can see. It's all in the statistics. Basically that baby in there"—she pointed to the computer in the adjacent glassed-in room—"separates signal from background noise. That's why we take a baseline, so we can ignore what your brain does just to cope with being in the scanner. Then the program compares your data to all the data we have on file. It's a sort of massive regression analysis. If there are anomalies, they get picked up and isolated. Lenny could look at a scan and tell you if it was going to come back with something. I can't."

"Can Shands?" I asked.

She gave me an odd look. "Sometimes."

She wiped dust from the monitor screen with the back of her hand.

"I think Lenny spent more time right here in the lab than he did just about anywhere else in the world." Emily spread the fingers of one hand and ran them lightly over the keyboard like it was a Ouija board. She took a long inhale and sat back.

"Do you think it would be okay to pull up other scans?" I asked. "Another normal? I'm just curious—"

"Sure." She pressed some keys and a new window came up, a

· 156 ·

dark background with a list of files. "A bunch of mine are in here." She scrolled through the list. The file names were all combinations of letters and numbers. "Question is, where."

She stood and went over to a shelf. There were software manuals and three-ring binders.

"The file names are coded to protect patients' privacy. Lenny kept a little black notebook . . ." She bent over and opened up a cabinet under the counter, then another. "He kept it out during the day. Which reminds me, when I find it I need to add you to the list."

I pulled open the drawer in the table where we were sitting and where Philbrick liked to work.

"This it?" I asked, indicating a black pad with a spiral binding across the top.

"The very thing," Emily said. She reached in and took it out. "Here we go." Emily had turned her attention to the keyboard and begun to type. "Here's one of me . . ."

But I wasn't listening. Folded up in the bottom of the drawer was a magazine clipping. It was a page from a girlie magazine. I took it out and opened it. Typical *Playboy* spread — there were pictures of young women in various states of undress. The settings were a bit unusual. One looked out coyly from a sedate office lined with books, another lay seductively on what looked like a bed in a dormitory room with a Dartmouth pennant on the wall behind her. The article was titled "University Playmates," and the issue was dated three years earlier.

"Here we go," Emily said. She was opening a new window on the screen with another brain floating in it.

I was about to put the clipping back when I noticed the woman in one of the photos was Emily. She'd posed up on her haunches with her chest thrust forward and behind thrust back, wearing nothing but a lab coat. So this was the "stupid thing" Emily said she'd done in college because she needed the money.

"We can run them side by side and—" Emily's voice died out. She stood there frozen when she saw what I was holding.

The sidebar next to the picture quoted her: " 'I think it's important that women not be seen as sex objects but as sexual beings. Nudity is normal. If a woman wants to show her body off, what's the harm?' says coed Emily Ryan, who is completing her degree in psychology at Harvard."

But there she'd been wrong. When the magazine had hit the stands, she'd undoubtedly had to fend off unwelcome advances from men who saw her posing for *Playboy* as a welcome mat. It explained how she'd achieved the kind of celebrity—in this case, notoriety—that it took to win the obsessive attentions of a stranger. No wonder she'd needed Kyle to protect her.

"Lenny?" Emily said, staring into the still-open drawer. There were about a half-dozen chewed-on pencils still in the drawer. From the back she pulled out a small piece of white fabric in the shape of a heart. "Lenny." This time the name came out as a moan. She sat and put her head in her hands.

I like to think I'm a pretty perceptive observer, a good judge of people. But I was batting zero with Philbrick. First I'd written him off as completely lacking in bedside manner. Now I was having a hard time casting him as a stalker. Odd, yes. Repressed geek, for sure. But a sexual predator? I looked at the heart, at the *Playboy* layout. Maybe he was.

"You didn't suspect it was him?" I asked.

"Lenny?" Emily gazed at me wide-eyed. "I knew he liked me. He used to walk me to my car. We went out for a beer across the street after work. But it never occurred to me that—"

"That he might be interested in you?" I couldn't keep the incredulity out of my voice.

Emily must have heard it, because she said, "He was lonely. Lots of guys are interested. Doesn't mean we couldn't be friends."

"So you had drinks a few times?"

"Well . . . more than that, I guess. It became a kind of regular thing. We'd go every Thursday after work, sometimes grab a bite."

"So you were dating him."

"No, no." She looked horrified. "I made it very clear to Lenny that I really admired his intellect and drive, and that I wanted to learn all I could from him. But I wasn't interested in him, not in that way."

"You didn't take him seriously."

"I did. I just didn't want to hurt his feelings."

I know men can be myopic about certain things, but this was the quintessential woman's blind spot. I wondered what awkward, geeky Leonard Philbrick had made of this bright, vivacious young woman who was sending him all those mixed signals. One minute she tells him she enjoys his company and adores his intellect. The next, she rejects his manhood. I could picture Philbrick prolonging the contact with Emily, savoring their "dates," enjoying what it felt like to be seen in public with an attractive woman. Self-esteem by association.

Then he discovers she's posed naked. Maybe his view of her changes—now she's nothing but a slut. He fantasizes about her, follows her. Infatuation turns to obsession. Not so farfetched.

I looked at the fabric heart. Sweet, really, like an elementary-school valentine—but sinister all the same.

"We were friends. At least that's what I thought we were," Emily said.

"The police will have to be told."

"The police? You think this has something to do with—?" It was hard to believe she could be so obtuse.

"Maybe nothing. Maybe everything. I'm not a homicide detective, but I do know that understanding the victim is the key to solving a crime."

"Crime," Emily echoed the word. She pressed her lips together. "I keep hoping they're going to tell us it was an accident. We'll figure out who brought in the tank. How it got delivered by mistake."

"Maybe," I said, "but Lenny's wallet and credit cards were in his pocket when he died."

Emily sagged at the news. "He'd never have gone near the scanner with his wallet in his pocket."

I agreed.

"So someone put him in the scanner? Staged the accident?" she said.

"That would be one explanation."

"But why? Why would anyone want to kill him?"

"That's why the police need to know about this stuff in his desk. If he was stalking you, that suggests all sorts of avenues to explore. Maybe you weren't his only victim." When had Amanda the receptionist left, I wondered, and what reason had she given?

"You think I . . . or one of them could have done it?" Emily bit her lower lip. "Do the police have to know everything?"

I picked up the phone. When I got through to the police, MacRae wasn't there. I'd just begun to leave him a message when I heard the door behind me open and felt a little breeze. I glanced over my shoulder. There was Shands.

"If you have a few minutes—" he was saying as he strode in.

"The police were called here a few weeks ago," I told MacRae's voicemail. "Someone had been following Dr. Ryan, vandalizing her car. The officers came and took some evidence, underwear of Dr. Ryan's with pieces cut out. We may have just found one of those pieces in Dr. Leonard Philbrick's desk. He's the man who was killed in the scanner here." I repeated the lab name and address twice. Gave him the phone number and extension. Then I hung up.

"What's this all about?" Shands demanded.

The *Playboy* picture had disappeared and Emily had her hand behind her back.

"We just found some evidence that suggests that Dr. Philbrick was stalking Emily." I explained, and showed him the piece of fabric.

Shands went pale. "Where did you find that?"

"Right here," Emily said indicating the drawer.

"Leonard?" He sounded even more incredulous than Emily had been. He reached into the drawer and took out one of the pencils. He ran his thumb up and down the bitten shaft. "Poor devil. Of course he was in love with you."

That was a quick turnabout. First reaction, Shands couldn't believe was Philbrick was a stalker. Now suddenly it made perfect sense.

"Sure he liked me. But in love?"

"I've known Leonard for years. From time to time, he became besotted. Always with someone young, pretty. Unattainable . . . for him." Shands said. Emily winced. "Oh yes, he adored you. Used to watch you when you worked. We all knew." The unsaid question hung in the air: How could you *not* know? "Of course I never thought he'd do anything like"—his gaze fell on the white fabric heart. He picked it up delicately between thumb and forefinger—"this." He closed his fist around it and turned to leave.

"Jim," I said.

"Not now, Peter. I need time to review your scan. Run a few statistical analyses." He was heading toward the door. "Then let's talk. Yes, we *will* need to talk. I'll call you." He pulled the door open.

"Sorry," I said, pressing the door shut. "You shouldn't be taking that."

He turned red. He wasn't used to confrontation, never mind being told what he could and couldn't do.

"Maybe it's nothing," I said, shrugging it off like this was no big deal, but I held my ground. "On the other hand, it could be important. I know the police will be concerned about chain of custody."

"Chain of custody?" The words exploded. "You think this is evidence of a crime?"

"Stalking is a crime," I said. "So is murder."

"I hardly think . . ." Shands started. He looked down at his clenched fist, then up at me. "Is this really necessary? Why tarnish Leonard's reputation? For God's sake, hasn't he suffered enough already?" He glared past me at Emily.

I held out my hand. Reluctantly he gave me the piece of cloth and then stormed out.

"I've never seen him come unglued like that," Emily said after Shands had left. She seemed shaken herself. "He's usually so sure of himself."

I would have said so well defended. Maybe the loss of Philbrick had weakened his armor, temporarily at least.

Emily seemed pretty unglued herself. Her hand trembled as she brushed a strand of hair from her face. "Thanks," she said, "for not showing him the *Playboy* picture. I'd die if he found out."

"You know the police are going to have to be told about it. Now, more than ever, you need a lawyer. Someone experienced with criminal cases to protect you from saying or doing anything that's not in your own best interest. Call this guy," I said, and wrote out Chip Ferguson's name and number on a slip of paper and gave it to her. She didn't argue.

The phone rang. I picked up. It was MacRae, and he was on his way over.

I went to tell Shands that the police were coming. I found him charging out of the door marked PRIVATE like he was late to an important meeting. When he saw me he jerked to a halt.

He just nodded when I told him a detective was on the way over. Then he made a U-turn and went back inside, leaving a wake of frigid, formalin-scented air dissipating in the hallway. Here was the stereotypical scientist. With shoes dropping left and right around him, the rest of us would have circled the wagons and huddled with coworkers. Shands apparently preferred to bury his head in his lab.

"YOU MIGHT at least have had the decency to inform me before taking matters into your own hands," Dr. Pullaski said to me, steely voiced. She'd found me and Emily in the control room waiting for MacRae to arrive. "I would have handled it."

I muttered something that I hoped sounded like an apology. I hadn't gone looking for her because I was afraid she might have taken matters into *her* own hands, as Shands had tried to do. Whatever else their relationship had become, they were partners in protecting the lab's reputation.

I showed her what had turned up in Philbrick's desk. "I should have known there'd be something like this," Dr. Pullaski said when she saw the *Playboy* picture. "I warned him." Emily wilted under her disapproving stare. "Just what we need to keep the press yapping at our heels." She smoothed her skirt and adjusted her pearls.

When MacRae arrived Dr. Pullaski was oozing helpfulness. "Let me know what you need," she said with a tight smile.

"You must hang out here a lot," MacRae said to me.

"Actually, no. I was here to have my brain scanned."

"You were what?"

"I had an MRI," I explained. He was looking at me like I had a screw loose. "I'm a 'normal.'"

"Sure you are," MacRae said, smiling and shaking his head. "And Ted Bundy was a misunderstood kid from a broken home."

Quickly he got to work. After questioning Emily and me, he moved on to Shands and other staff members. MacRae was still there when Gloria beeped me. Turned out Uncle Jack had worsened overnight. He was in toxic shock and on life support in the ICU. As soon as MacRae said it was okay to leave, I headed over there.

• • •

I picked up the intercom phone at the door to the ICU. A nurse picked up on the other side and buzzed me in.

The sound of an ICU is unique—the occasional hushed voice, the squeak of rubber-soled shoes, and the steady hiss of ventilators and beeping of monitors. I'd only been in an ICU a couple of times, but I was reminded once again how much it felt like the eye of a hurricane.

Annie was sitting in a chair alongside Uncle Jack's bed. Uncle Jack looked frail and gray, his eyes closed. The bed was propped up and an assortment of tubes and cables snaked off his body. Annie was reading aloud to him from the *Boston Globe*.

I took his chart from the end of the bed and read. Uncle Jack was running a fever of 100.5°, and his white count was still up. He was getting antibiotics intravenously. They'd discontinued the experimental protocol. I wished I had Kwan with me to decipher the rest of the scrawls.

When Annie paused in her reading and looked over at me, Uncle Jack shifted slightly toward her. That he noticed the change was a good sign. Her eyes spoke volumes — equal parts anxiety and sadness.

I sat with them until the nurse made us leave.

"Your father needs his rest," she said. Annie didn't bother to correct her.

Annie put her hand on Uncle Jack's arm and leaned close.

"I'm going to have to go now. I'll be back tomorrow afternoon."

Annie bent closer and kissed his cheek. Then she turned to go. Uncle Jack's hand hovered as he tried to say something.

"Oh yeah, sorry," Annie said, tucking the newspaper into the cabinet by Uncle Jack's bed. "For later."

A shadow of a smile flickered on Uncle Jack's face.

We took the elevator down to the lobby in silence and sat in a corner on a turquoise vinyl sofa.

"Acute bacterial pneumonia," Annie said. "That's what they say he's got. He's incredibly weak, but at least he's more comfortable than when they first moved him into the ICU." Annie looked exhausted, her eyes bloodshot. "They tell me the next few days are critical."

I took Annie's hand and held it between mine. "I'm sorry. I was so sure I knew what the right thing was for your uncle."

"It's not your fault," Annie said. She rolled her shoulders around and rubbed the back of her neck. "You couldn't have known."

I went around to give her a proper shoulder rub.

"You sleep last night?" Her shoulders and upper back were in knots.

"Some." She turned her head and looked up at me, smiling. "Not as well as the night before." Then her brow creased and her eyebrows drew together. "Hey, you don't look so great yourself. What happened?"

"Nothing really. I got my head examined."

Annie laughed. "So you finally took Kwan's advice?"

I worked my thumbs up Annie's neck. That was exactly why I hadn't told him—I knew he'd rag me endlessly about getting my brain scanned.

"I had an MRI."

Annie jumped up. "At *that* place?" She put her hand on my forehead. "Watch you don't come down with something." I knew she was only half joking. "I appreciate your not telling tell me until it was over."

"I seem to be no worse for the wear," I said. "Though my arm's a little sore from where they injected the dye."

"They put dye in your arm to light up your head?"

"Weird, I know. But that's how it works."

"And was everyone suitably impressed?"

Now wasn't the time to tell her I was worried about what Shands had seen in my brain scan.

"Knocked their socks off," I said. "While I was over there, I discovered something that suggests Dr. Philbrick was Emily Ryan's stalker."

"You're kidding," Annie said. "Philbrick?"

I told her what we'd found.

"She posed for *Playboy*?" Annie laughed. "Bet she wishes she could take that one off her CV." Annie shook her head. "I ever tell you I once mooned a cop on my way through some little town between Las Vegas and Death Valley? Who knew youth and stupidity were synonyms?" Annie's look turned sober. "And who exactly made this discovery?"

I told her. "Emily seemed completely surprised. Stunned, in fact."

"I'll bet she did," Annie said. Her gray eyes searched my face.

"I gave her Chip's number. I just hope she calls him."

"Peter, have you noticed how much that girl enjoys being the center of attention? First she's stalked. Then she finds the body. Later she makes sure you find the evidence that suggests the dead guy stalked her." Annie stood. "You're sure she didn't make it all up — being stalked, I mean?"

It was true, I hadn't actually seen Emily's stalker. It would have been possible for her to have made it all up, planted the evidence herself. "But why would she do that?"

Annie had an answer ready. "Look, you're the shrink. But if you're wearing blinders for some reason, the answer is simple. To get attention. Your attention." Maybe she was right, and I had been blindsided. I was supposed to be able to call myself on that kind of thing. "Of course now she's gotten herself in quite a pickle. She had motive, opportunity. And you're sure as hell paying attention. So are the police. I suppose if there's a lesson in all this it's be careful what you wish for."

• • •

I sat in the observation room the next day, watching Emily and Mr. Black. I was more than a little troubled. A person who'd allow herself to be photographed by *Playboy*, even ostensibly for the money, had to be something of an exhibitionist. Emily did seem to crave center spotlight. It was exactly what she was doing in her sessions with Mr. Black, subtly shifting the focus of the therapeutic relationship to herself. It was a personality style that probably had its roots in Emily's childhood, when she'd sought and never managed to sustain the attentions of a father who abandoned the family but kept returning every few years just long enough to impregnate her mother. But would she go so far as to create her own stalker? That seemed a reach.

"It's damned uncomfortable," said Mr. Black. "The tape itches, and my arm gets numb. But when I've had the operation, I won't have to deal with that. Beyond that, it's just a lot of inconveniences. Minor, really."

"Like what?" Emily asked. Today she had on a discreet, dark pantsuit with a pink turtleneck.

"Like it takes twice as many trips to the car to unload my groceries. And it's a pain in the ass using my computer one-handed. Buttons are hard. Zippers are harder. Handling money—getting dollar bills into my wallet? It's all stuff I can learn to deal with."

"Anything else?"

"Yeah. People look at me." He paused. "They really seem to connect with me now. It's like I jump off the radar. That part I like."

"How do they look at you?"

"Well, they look at the arm, of course. The one that's not there. Then the other arm. Then they look at my face."

"So it's a way of connecting."

"At least they're not ignoring me."

"What do you imagine they're thinking?"

"Maybe they're wondering if I was born this way. Or did I lose it in an accident? Did I fight in the military? Maybe it makes some of them uncomfortable. I'm sure some of them get off on it. There was this one guy who followed me. I'm in Walgreens and he's half an aisle away from me the whole time."

"Did that bother you?"

"Why should it? It's his problem."

Emily looked at him without saying anything.

"You mean like, do I get off on it?" he asked. "I guess I kind of do. Do you think that's what this is about? Wanting to be looked at? Like a flasher?"

"Does it make you feel like a flasher?"

"You mean, do I get some sexual charge out of being an amputee? *I do not.*" The words came out like an oath. "I certainly don't want to be made into a dirty joke. That's not what this is about."

"What is it about?"

"It's about feeling normal."

That was interesting—equating "normal" with being stared at as opposed to being ignored, dismissed as inconsequential. Self-esteem did seem to be at the root of his issues, and maybe Emily's issues as well.

"But there are inconveniences. True?" Emily asked.

"Some. Like I said, it's itchy."

"If your phantom limb itches, you won't be able to untape it and scratch yourself."

Mr. Black put his hand over his mouth and looked away from her. "What else am I supposed to do?" I wondered if Emily saw the same yellow lights flashing that I did. Mr. Black was asking her to save him. Would she take the bait?

"We've discussed medication before—" Emily began.

He stiffened. "Would you want to take a pill that erased part of who you are?"

"Think about it. You're afraid to take a pill to erase part of who you are, but you're willing to have a piece of yourself cut off, erasing part of yourself surgically?"

It was painful to listen to her — being confrontational like that was only inviting a pissing contest.

He reared back. "You condemn me for being self-destructive. Take a look around before you pass judgment. People do all kinds of things that are self-destructive. Smoking. Drinking. Driving a motorcycle. Owning a pit bull. You don't medicate those poor slobs. Though I don't know why not. Seems like we've got pills for everything. You want to be thin? Here's a pill. You want to be happy? Have another. More virile?"

He gave Emily a sideways look. He was attracted to her. But now his attentions didn't cast a sinister shadow. He wasn't the stalker and the attraction wasn't obsessive — this was part of transference, one of the inevitables of therapy.

"What happened to an individual's right to choose?" he asked.

"So what do you wish for, right now?"

"To be taken seriously," he shot back at her.

"And I'll take you more seriously if you cut off your arm?"

"No. That's not what I mean. What I mean is that I want people like you to take me seriously when I say this arm doesn't belong here. And that I'm not acting out some adolescent sexual fantasy. And that I don't need medication to anesthetize myself and turn into another kind of zombie."

"Mr. Black, I do take you seriously. I want to help you."

The session continued to spiral downhill. What had began as an auspicious self-examination had disintegrated, first with Mr. Black feeling attacked and disapproved of, then rising to defend himself. Now it had detoured into whether or not Emily cared about him. It was the kind of thing you expected from a novice therapist, not an experienced post-doc.

. . .

I met Emily in the cafeteria a few hours later. It was nearly two, but the cavernous room was still about half-full of staff, visitors, and patients, all dressed in business or casual clothes. Emily was at a table writing in a notebook. She wore tight leggings, and her sleeveless top, molded to her body like a second skin, was cut low. Her hair had come loose. If she'd been leaning casually against the wall and added some eye makeup and red lipstick, she'd have looked like a hooker who'd set up a concession in the middle of the caf.

"Why don't we sit over there," I suggested, indicating a table in the corner where there weren't a lot of others sitting nearby.

She finished writing and moved while I got myself some coffee. When I returned, she was drinking from a bottle of water.

She looked at me expectantly. "I hope it's okay meeting you in these." She indicated her outfit. "I'm trying to get my running in during daylight."

"You're still feeling anxious?"

She didn't answer.

"Has something more happened?"

"I feel so foolish saying this, but I'm pretty sure someone's been in my apartment. There's nothing missing. But some things in my bathroom were definitely rearranged. And my bed. I usually don't make it in the morning, I'm in such a rush. It was made when I got home yesterday. It's got to be all in my head, right? Lenny's dead, so this shouldn't be happening."

"Maybe you should stay with someone for a while," I suggested.

"Maybe I will."

"Did you call that attorney?"

She nodded.

I considered holding back the feedback I needed to give her about her interaction with Mr. Black. She was obviously vulnerable.

But she was the one who'd insisted on continuing to work with patients. My first concern had to be their well-being, not hers.

"Do you think the stress is affecting your ability to do your job?"

Spots of pink appeared on her cheeks. "Do you?"

"Why don't you tell me how *you* think it went today with Mr. Black," I said, sidestepping the question.

At first she seemed flustered. "I think it went fine. I—" Then her look hardened and she slammed the notebook shut. "But obviously you don't. If you're going to criticize me, why don't you just come right out and say so instead playing games?" Her voice echoed in the large space. Emily looked around uneasily, noticing that people at tables halfway across the room were staring at her.

I waited. This wasn't a game; it was a test. Self-control and self-reflection were essentials for a therapist.

She took a breath and steadied herself. "Mr. Black. It's going okay." She looked at me. "Wrong answer, I know. Okay, it's not going okay. I was sure once he tried living without his arm he'd be convinced that amputation was a mistake. But a few minor inconveniences is all, according to him. Then he goes all defensive on me. Accuses me of not caring what happens to him. How can he even suggest that I don't care?"

"Listen to yourself. He disappointed *you*. He goes all defensive on *you*. How could he suggest that *you* don't care," I said. Emily's mouth dropped open. I'd never been confrontational with her before. Now I was deliberately pressing to see if she was going to break. "It sounds as if you think Mr. Black's therapy is about you."

"Of course that's not what I think," she snapped.

"Then you seem to have lost your clinical perspective."

She took another drink of water, held it in her mouth, and then swallowed.

"And since you asked," I added, scanning the remaining dozen or so people in the cafeteria, "no, I don't think those clothes are appropriate here."

"Then I guess I'd better go change." Emily sat still, blinking back tears. "Why are you being such a shit?"

She stood, gathered up her things, and left.

16

"Good question," I said to myself, crushing the Styrofoam cup and tossing it in the garbage.

I'd lost it. By attacking her personally, I'd only given her permission to write off the message. She could tell herself I was the one who was under stress, overreacting. And maybe she was right. For the first time in a very long time, I felt unsure of my internal compass.

Instead of heading back to my office, I found myself walking up the hill toward the administration building to Dr. Nelson Rofstein's office. It had been more than a decade since he'd been my clinical supervisor, but even now he served as a touchstone whenever I needed one.

"Peter?" he said, his shaggy eyebrows lifting and his face lighting up when he saw me at his door.

"Got a minute?"

He was up, shaking my hand and patting my shoulder. "Of

course, of course. It's good to see you." A robust man, his face was lined with character and his once brown hair was now fully gray. A sloping right shoulder and a squinty eye were the only evidence of the stroke he'd suffered a few years earlier.

"Sit, sit," he said, indicating one of cushioned chairs that faced his desk. He sat, too, leaning back in his chair and lacing his fingers over his middle. "So, tell me. To what do I owe the pleasure?" He knew me well enough to know this wasn't a social call.

"I'm afraid I'm losing my perspective," I said, getting right down to it. I told him about my observations of Emily Ryan and our last interaction. "I lost it, and I'm not sure why."

"Tell me about her."

"She's been with us for a few months," I said. I gave him a synopsis of the work Emily had done on the unit. "She's exceedingly bright but doesn't seem to be particularly self-aware. Like how she looks. Wearing running tights and a skimpy top in the cafeteria—so completely inappropriate."

"I seem to recall you were a bit clueless in that department once upon a time," Dr. Rofstein said with a wry smile.

I was still embarrassed, remembering how I'd washed up on Dr. Rofstein's doorstep, ready to save the world. I'd promptly found myself struggling with my first patient—a woman whose husband was dying of a brain tumor—and my increasing frustration because she'd only talk to me about how she was renovating the house and managing the night nurses. "She's not taking you seriously," Dr. Rofstein had said to me. And why the hell not, I'd wanted to know.

He'd shrugged and looked up at the sky, a mute prayer for patience. "You can cut your hair any way you want," he'd said, eyeing my three-inch Afro, "and you can wear anything you like"—he gave a nod to my open-necked sport shirt—"but your patients come in with their own *mishigas* and they're going to judge what they see.

First impressions. It's not enough to act professional, which you do," he assured me. "If you want to be taken seriously, look the part."

Now, a dozen years later, Dr. Rofstein was giving the same heavenward look as he unlaced and laced his fingers. "Yes, you were very green. But a fairly quick learner, as I recall." He noted my shorn hair and suit and tie. "What else are you concerned about?"

I told him I thought Emily was showing questionable judgment in her work with patients. "I'm worried that she's relying too much on her feelings and not enough on her intellect. I'm trying to keep my perspective. She has been under a lot of stress." I went on, hitting the high spots—the stalker, the death in the MRI lab that might or might not have been her fault, the police surveillance. "It feels as if she's been depending on me, clinging more than I'm comfortable with. I guess it's understandable given what she's going through."

"And you're sure it's not projective identification—that you're not doing something to provoke this dependency?"

I didn't think I was. Though maybe he had a point. Following her home to tell her about a broken taillight. Rushing over to the MRI lab and sneaking in. Maybe whatever Shands had seen in my brain scan was already eroding my judgment.

"I do seem to be constantly trying to rescue her."

"So you're wondering if there's something going on with you that you're reciprocating this woman's unconscious attentions."

"I guess I am," I admitted. Dr. Rofstein sat there, waiting for me to get to the point. "And now I find myself doubting her integrity, wondering if she's made up being stalked. Wondering if she's as innocent as she says she is in her colleague's death."

"You're worried that these doubts, even though they're unsubstantiated, are coloring your professional relationship with her.

Making you doubt her competence." He pondered for a few moments, peering at me from beneath his eyebrows. "Sounds as if for some reason your view of her has changed."

I sat up. Hearing him restate my own words gave them a different meaning. Parallax, I reminded myself. If your position shifts, the position of the object you're looking at *appears* to shift. It's why when you're riding along in your car, the moon seems to be moving along with you; when you stop, it appears to be stationary.

There's a similar problem in psychology—what you *expect* to see colors how you interpret your observations. If you think someone is a jerk, actions seem stupid that you might have called inspired if you'd prejudged the person a genius.

So what had changed my perception of Emily?

"I found out that a few years ago she posed for *Playboy*," I said, feeling a little sheepish.

"And that makes you see her differently. Is it just her judgment this has called into question, or maybe there's something more?"

I'd been at this long enough to know what he was getting at. I'd been attracted to Emily. Flattered by her rapt attention. I'd responded intellectually while suppressing the sexual part. The *Playboy* photos felt like a betrayal. Not unlike someone who finds his lover has been cheating.

Rofstein continued, "Peter, you've got a number of things going on here and it's not surprising that you're feeling confused. You need to pay attention to your gut. It's telling you something, though it may take you a while to figure out what. And from what you tell me, it sounds as if this young woman has got a few things going on as well. No doubt you're right to be concerned."

"I haven't felt this unsure in a very long time," I said.

Rofstein sat up and leaned across his desk. "Peter, as long as you remain self-reflective you'll do fine."

"I should have had better self-control," I said.

"Yes, you should. So you'll work on it?" He rose. "And in the meanwhile, wait and see." He walked me to the door.

"So this young woman also works at University Medical Imaging," he said. "That's the one over on Sidney Street?"

"Right. You know Dr. Shands, don't you? The guru in charge?"

"Guru," Rofstein said with a soft chuckle. "Dr. Lewy body dementia. Thank heavens for the supervisor who discouraged that young man from going into clinical psychiatry. Some of us are healers and some of us are watchers."

"Bedside manner is not his forte. Didn't you know him from the Cambridge Brain Bank?"

"He was one of the lead researchers."

"But no longer?"

"We should all have his drive," he said.

My ears pricked up. This was an evasion, not an answer. "He and the brain bank parted company?"

"He needed to pursue his own path. The brain bank wasn't founded to support *special* research."

"And how was his research special?"

Dr. Rofstein had opened his office door. Now he closed it. "He developed a way of looking at cell membrane permeability, but it was a destructive process. Brains were being lost at an alarming rate. He assumed that the brains, not to mention the funding, were at his personal disposal. It was never made public, but it was pretty clear that a percentage of each grant was being skimmed off and funneled into his personal research."

"How did he manage that?"

"Let's just say that he and the executive director had a very close relationship. They both resigned."

"Dr. Pullaski?"

He nodded. "But you didn't hear that from me. When they left, part of the agreement was that the details would never be made public."

Dr. Rofstein opened the door again. He shook my hand, looked me in the eye, and said the same thing he always said when we parted.

"Remember, no good deed goes unpunished—"

I finished saying it with him. "—but do good anyway."

• • •

Late that afternoon as I was leaving to head home, I noticed Gloria and Emily sitting on the side porch of the unit. They were in chairs facing each other, heads together. Emily took a drag on a cigarette and offered it to Gloria.

Please don't, I thought—Gloria had had a miserable time kicking the habit a few years back. For a long time she carried around an unlit cigarette that she used as a sort of pacifier whenever she felt the urge.

Gloria declined the cigarette. I wondered if Emily was complaining about me. I hadn't come right out and said I didn't want her working with patients until she sorted her head out, but I was sure she realized I was getting close.

Just then a black Range Rover pulled into the circular drive. It stopped. I recognized the large, dark-haired man who stepped out. It was Kyle, Emily's ex. She waved at him and stubbed out the cigarette. So the white knight was back in Emily's life.

Emily and Gloria stood. Gloria had her hand on Emily's shoulder and they talked, their faces close to one another. They hugged and held the embrace, which surprised me because Gloria wasn't a huggy kind of person. Then Emily pulled away, picked up her briefcase, and ran to the waiting Range Rover.

· · ·

The next evening I made my way up the wide steps and across the broad courtyard plaza of the Charles Hotel where lights twinkled in the trees. Shands had called and suggested that I meet him for a drink. He was heading over to the bar after work anyway, and he'd had a chance to look at my scan results.

By the time I got to the dim, leathery, cigar-scented bar, I was more in need of a Maalox than one of their exquisite, pricey martinis. I'd spent most of the night before trawling the Web for information on how to interpret functional MRIs. The basic idea was simple — an fMRI showed you how blood flow was changing the brain. Beyond that, nothing was simple. I'd finally given up, frustrated.

At least there had been encouraging news about Uncle Jack. His fever was down and his lungs were starting to clear. They were talking about moving him out of the ICU and back into a regular hospital room. He might even be back at the Pearce in a few days.

I spotted Shands at a table in the corner. Handsome in his dark suit, his silver hair lustrous, he sat there brooding over his drink. As I approached, I wondered about him wanting to talk to me here instead of at the lab. Maybe he preferred this setting — first anesthetize the patient, fill his head with smoke, then whammo, deliver really bad news.

He rose and shook my hand. "Peter. Thanks for meeting me here."

He gestured the waiter over. I ordered a club soda. He ordered another martini.

"I hope you don't mind coming here. Things at the lab are a little . . . tense," he said.

"I suppose that's not surprising."

"You know that detective who's in charge?"

"MacRae?"

"He's a pain in the ass."

I laughed. "Yeah well, that's his job."

"You think they're looking at this as murder?"

So was this why he'd wanted to meet me here—to get the inside scoop on the investigation? *How the hell did I know,* I wanted to yell at him. Of course he'd be clueless that I was tied up in knots about what he'd seen in my brain scan.

"If MacRae's still there, you can be sure they're considering it. If it was an accident, then why hasn't that person who carried the oxygen tank into the scan room come forward?"

"Fear. Immaturity," Shands suggested, his chin out. I was sure he wasn't the only one who wanted to find a convenient scapegoat. "They keep coming back and asking questions. It's taking a toll on everyone. Especially Emily."

Our drinks came. Shands stirred his martini.

"Not that she was that stable to begin with," he went on. "I never would have hired her if I'd known she posed for *Playboy*. Know what I mean?" He took out the olives, slid one from the toothpick into his mouth. "Now the board is breathing down my neck. Very bad timing. Just when we're on the brink of a major breakthrough." He squinted at me through the dark. "Well, none of this is your problem. Of course, you want to know about your test results."

Finally. Queasiness knotted in my stomach.

"You mentioned that your father had Alzheimer's. Anyone else in the family?" he asked. This wasn't an auspicious beginning.

"My uncle."

"Father's brother?"

I nodded.

He cleared his throat. "One of the difficulties is that there's so

• 184 •

much variance across the sample. There are only shades of difference between the lower end of the normal range and the slightly abnormal, indicating that there's a problem."

Slightly abnormal? Maybe I could get myself a baseball cap with SA sewn onto it. "But you think there's a problem."

"I need to confirm it with a rigorous statistical analysis. Leonard used to do all of that." For a moment he sounded like a petulant child who'd been asked to clean his room.

"But you think my scan shows some abnormality?" I wanted him to stop waffling.

"Your father. Was it a steady decline, or was it marked by a fluctuating state of consciousness?"

"My dad . . ." I began. I remembered the ride from Brooklyn to Cambridge after my father had been diagnosed with Alzheimer's and he and my mother had agreed to come live in the other side of my two-family. Dad seemed to know where we were going, that we were on the Pike. We were having what felt like a normal conversation and then, somewhere around 495, the window shade came down. He became agitated, terrified that we were going to run out of gas. He kept trying to grab the steering wheel. I stopped to fill up but that did nothing to quiet his fears. Finally, my mother had to take over the driving and I got in the back seat with Dad to keep him from causing an accident. Only now did it occur to me to wonder about his agitation. Had he been hallucinating?

When we got to the house, Dad sat in an aluminum chair on the lawn, watching the movers. With perfect clarity he'd asked my mother, "Did you remember to bring my pipe? I left it in the bathroom." Each week after that, the periods of lucidity had grown more sporadic.

Shands was waiting for my answer. "Both, really," I said. "A steady decline with occasional periods of lucidity." All that had been consistent with a diagnosis of Alzheimer's.

"Movement disorder?" Shands asked.

"Tremors," I said. "Periods of jerky movement."

"I'm not surprised. I think your scan shows the markers for Lewy body dementia. When I've finished crunching the numbers, you can come down to the lab and we'll go over the results in more detail. You'll find it fascinating."

Fascinating? What planet did this guy inhabit? I sat there, gaping at him, trying to absorb the verdict.

Belatedly he added, "I'm sorry, Peter." He even seemed to mean it.

Hey, everybody dies, I told myself; so now you know *how* you're going to do it. Could be another twenty years, could be forty. Could be you get hit by a bus. I was sure of one thing: This was one piece of information I really didn't need to know.

Shands had one leg crossed over the other, his foot jiggling. He knocked back the last of his drink.

"So you'll come to the lab and we can discuss treatment?"

My mouth dropped open, but I couldn't even respond. Shands didn't notice. He reached into his pocket and pulled out his beeper. He must have had it set on vibrate because I hadn't heard it go off.

"I'm afraid I have to run." He stood and pumped my arm. Then he was gone.

I felt as if I'd been hit by a tidal wave and bounced off the bottom of the sea. Only a minor part of it was the check that the waiter delivered as soon as Shands left, as if on cue. Twelve bucks apiece for martinis?

What a swell guy. 'Bye, Peter. *By the way, you probably have Lewy body dementia. Anyway, see ya later, buddy, and don't skimp on the tip.*

17

I DIDN'T remember deciding to drive over to Annie's, but twenty minutes later I found myself on her doorstep. Lights were on in the bay window on the top floor of the triple-decker. I was about to ring the bell when the lights went off. I waited. There was the sound of footsteps on the stairs. Annie opened the door. She had on her jacket, her backpack slung over her shoulder. Her face was streaked with tears and she was holding a fistful of Kleenex. For a moment, she seemed startled to see me. Then her face crumpled.

"You heard?" she said with a sob.

"Heard what?"

"Uncle Jack died."

"He what?" I was stunned. "But I thought he was doing so much better."

"That's what I thought." She wiped her nose and sniffed. "One minute they're telling me they're moving him back into a regular room, the next I get the call that he's gone." Annie swallowed. "Gone." She repeated the word in a whisper.

I took Annie in my arms and held her. "I'm so sorry," I said. I closed my eyes, feeling distraught, exhausted. If I'd only left Uncle Jack at home with his piles of old newspapers, decaying cat food, and moldy sink with its everyday garden-variety germs, he'd probably still be fine — or at least Uncle Jack's version of "fine."

"I'm going over there. I need to say good-bye."

"Can I come?" "You'll come?" we said simultaneously.

I kissed her head, overwhelmed with relief that she wanted me to be with her in this.

"He once told me he saw Ted Williams play at Fenway, the year he batted .406," Annie said, leaning her head against the car window as I drove. "I was going to get us tickets for September."

We passed through Union Square and took a right, heading toward the BU Bridge.

"I just saw him this morning and he was looking so much better," she said.

"Sometimes that's the way it is. People rally just before the end."

"But his fever was down. White count almost back to normal. I just bought him two new pairs of pajamas." Annie gripped a tissue in her fist as we came through the rotary into Boston. "I can't believe it. It's surreal."

I pulled into the hospital garage and parked. It seemed like a very long walk through the connecting tunnel to the lobby. We took the elevator up. At the ICU they directed us to the room where Uncle Jack had been laid out.

The door was ajar and a curtain was pulled across the opening. In the hall just outside, a man in a white uniform was arguing with the nurse. "But we have the order right here. Supposed to pick up a Mr. O'Neill? I just need a signature."

"You have to get a signature from his next of kin," the nurse said.

"What's this all about?" Annie asked. "I'm next of kin."

The man showed her a piece of paper. "We just need you to sign this."

" 'Postmortem Confirmation of Consent,' " I read over Annie's shoulder. "Consent for what?"

The man in the white suit looked uncomfortable. "Autopsy and . . . Mr. O'Neill agreed to donate his brain."

"He what?" Annie said.

"Let me see that," I said.

Sure enough, there were orders from University Medical Imaging to pick up Uncle Jack's body and transport him there. I remembered the room past Dr. Shands's office, the one with the stainless steel tables and shelves of fixatives. That was probably where the autopsy and brain harvesting took place.

"I just need you to sign—" the man started.

I began to say something but Annie was right there, perfectly capable of putting this guy in his place. She glared at him.

"You'll have to forgive me, sir, but my uncle just died. I haven't even had a chance to see him, to say good-bye." By the end, her voice was breaking up with emotion.

The man took a faltering step back. "Sorry, ma'am. It's just that they like us to transport the deceased as soon as possible after death."

"I'll let you know when that is."

"Want me to go in with you?" I asked Annie.

"Thanks," she said, facing the curtained opening, "but I'd rather go in myself. I want to be alone with him."

Annie put her fingers to her lips, squared her shoulders, and stepped inside. A moment later she burst out again through the curtains.

"Is this some kind of a joke?"

"Is there a problem?" the nurse asked.

"I don't know who that poor man is, but he's not my Uncle Jack."

• • •

"Bureaucratic bullshit," Annie said, giving a snort of disgust as we headed down a floor and to the opposite wing to find Uncle Jack. The body behind the curtain had been another elderly man who'd died in the ICU at the same time Uncle Jack was transferred to a regular room. Paperwork mixup.

"He's not dead. He just moved to the fourth floor." Annie was laughing and crying at the same time. Her voice had an edge of hysteria to it. "You ever read *The Stupids Die?*" she asked.

"I don't know how I missed that one."

"It's a hilarious children's book. It's about this family that think they've died and gone to heaven. Turns out they're in Cleveland." Annie was moving so quickly I had to run to keep up with her. "I got it for my niece a few Christmases ago. Don't know what made me think of it."

We'd reached the door of Uncle Jack's room. "Welcome to Cleveland," Annie said as she entered. Annie was ebullient, her mood like a big bunch of red balloons filling the little room.

Uncle Jack had been sitting up in bed watching television. His color was good, and he seemed to recognize Annie. I watched the two of them together, my uneasiness over Shands's diagnosis seeping back into my consciousness.

When Annie and I got back to her house an hour later, she was still elated. She sat in the car, her head tipped back against the headrest. Her curly hair was soft around her face, the edges tipped with light from the glow of an overhead street light. She reached for my hand, looking more relaxed than I'd seen her in weeks.

"Amazing, isn't it, how much better things look when you realize how much worse they could be." That was my mother's credo: Expect the worst and you'll never be disappointed.

Now Annie shifted over onto one hip and gazed at me. She ran a finger up my arm, sending a shiver down my back.

"You have to go home?"

Reluctantly I told her that I couldn't stay, making up an excuse about unfinished work. It wasn't so much unfinished work as unfinished business—I knew I'd be preoccupied with what Shands had said about my brain scan, and this wasn't the time to tell Annie about it. She had enough of her own shit to deal with.

I walked her to the door and we kissed under the porch light.

I slept lousy that night, wishing I were in bed with Annie, spooned together, breathing her scent. Instead I was alone with worst-case scenarios galloping through my brain. In one, I was a patient on my own unit sharing a room with Uncle Jack. Annie was feeding me chicken soup through a straw and wiping the dribbles off my chin. When I finally dropped off to sleep, it was only to wake up from a nightmare in which Emily Ryan, wearing nothing but an open lab coat, was giving me a shot from a hypodermic syringe filled with some murky green concoction. As I watched the poisonous stuff drain into me, I heard Dr. Rofstein intoning, "Listen to your gut."

I was awake when the phone rang at 6:30. "I can't believe I didn't read it more carefully," Annie said. She'd been going over the consent form that she'd signed for Uncle Jack. "Says right here, consent for post mortem and retention of human material for diagnosis and research. Would've been nice if they'd put it in English."

I pushed myself up in bed and shoved back the covers. I remembered the words that Emily had crossed out on Mr. Black's consent. Most likely it was that section. Mr. Black didn't have Lewy body dementia, so Shands wouldn't have been interested in his brain.

"Annie, the only widely accepted way to diagnose Lewy body dementia is by autopsy. Their research would be worthless unless they confirm the diagnoses."

"But don't you think he should have said something when I signed the form? I don't think a brain donation clause should be slipped into the fine print. Isn't that unethical? Maybe criminal, even?"

I thought Annie was overreacting but I didn't say anything. The same clause had probably been in the consent form I signed. I hadn't bothered to read the final paragraphs. When the white-coated medics arrived to collect my brain, I knew my mother would take it in stride—she'd shrug and mutter "typical."

• • •

"Peter, did you hear what I said?" Gloria asked at morning meeting two days later.

"Of course he did," Kwan said. "That's why he has that deer-in-the-headlights look in his eyes."

"I most certainly did," I protested. "You said Mr. O'Neill is coming back this afternoon. I was about to ask you where we're going to put him."

"I just *told* you," Gloria said, giving an exasperated look, "we're putting him in his old room. It's empty."

I had zoned out. We'd been discussing a new patient that Emily had been evaluating. The woman had come to us because she kept getting lost in her own neighborhood. Her husband would find her wandering in some backyard, two blocks away. Was that me ten years from now? Twenty? When would my memory start to go? Was it going yet? I tested myself. Who'd been my kindergarten teacher? Mrs. Dreiwitz. First grade was Mrs. Lowe. Second, Miss Goldsmith. Third? I couldn't remember, though I could picture the corner classroom on the second floor. When would I start to talk to my dead relatives?

"Wouldn't hurt to put his things back there," I said. "Make it feel more familiar."

I'd visited Uncle Jack again yesterday. He was doing well. Still weak, but eating and moving around on his own. He seemed to understand that he was getting out of the hospital, though he couldn't seem to grasp the fact that he was not going home.

"So his family wants to keep him off the experimental treatment," Kwan said. "Frankly, I think they're overreacting."

"What they don't want is to have to take him back for another MRI," I said. "Is there any way we can continue the treatment? It seems to be helping."

"They won't give him the protocol without the tests," Kwan said. "But he did seem to benefit from what he was taking. We can put him on another statin. Worst case, it won't do him any good cognitively and it'll lower his cholesterol. Best case, we'll see continued improvement, too. It's worth a shot."

After the meeting, I stood in the hall staring at my hand holding my coffee cup and wondering if there was a slight tremor.

"Earth to Peter. You all right?" It was Gloria.

"I've had something on my mind—" I began, and very nearly

spilled Shands's "tentative" diagnosis. "It's nothing, really. Sorry if I seem distracted."

"You run the meetings. You're not allowed to be distracted," Gloria said, giving me a concerned smile.

"So noted," I said, executing a little salute and turning to leave.

"Peter," she said. I turned back. She pulled me down the hallway and around the corner. Then she checked to see that there was no one within listening range. "You know I try not to butt into your business, but we've been friends a long time so I figure I've earned the right to say what I think." Uh oh. I'd heard this prelude before. "I think you're being a bully. With Emily. I mean, she's green, she's learning. You're always on her case."

Gloria didn't usually serve as a conduit for personnel issues. "Has she been complaining to you?"

Gloria stood her ground. "She didn't have to complain to me. I could see for myself. She's stalked. Her colleague dies and she finds the body. And on top of everything you start coming down on her like the world's come to an end if she doesn't look and act like a consummate professional twenty-four hours a day." There was a pause, as if Gloria were deciding whether or not to say more. "I recall a time when you were under a lot of stress and we cut you a fair amount of slack."

I felt my face grow hot. She was referring to the time after Kate was killed. Sure, I'd buried myself in my work. Been a surly son-ofabitch to my colleagues. But if I'd messed up with patients, I'd have expected Gloria and Kwan and anyone else on the unit who noticed to have taken me to task.

"She's been showing poor judgment, and I'm the one responsible if she screws up."

"But—" Gloria started.

"And why do you feel you have to protect her? Think about *that*, why don't you."

I turned on my heel, leaving Gloria with her mouth open. The satisfaction I felt at leaving her at a loss for words vanished as I marched up the stairs to my office. I muttered to myself as I gathered up Uncle Jack's battered leather suitcase and his pile of newspaper clippings. Why couldn't I just have kept my trap shut? Mouthing off at Gloria was only proving the case against me.

I rode down in the elevator and stepped out onto the unit. Emily was on the phone at the nurses' station. I'd be glad when her stint with us was over. There'd been a whole lot of drama ever since she'd arrived, all of it with her at the center.

"Oh, wait. Never mind. Here he is," Emily said into the receiver. Tentatively she offered me the phone, like she was afraid I'd bite off her hand. "It's Dr. Shands. For you."

"Shands?" I croaked. He'd probably finished the statistical analysis. The last thing I wanted was to get the bad news while I was standing in the middle of the unit. When I set down the suitcase the pile of clippings fell to the ground. I kicked at them in anger and took the phone.

"Zak here," I said. "I wonder if I could call you back—"

"Just called to ask how Mr. O'Neill is doing," boomed Shands.

It occurred to me that he didn't know Uncle Jack was dropping out of his research study. It was Annie's decision, really not my job to tell him.

"Well, he's not here yet," I said. "They're sending him back to us sometime today."

"I heard, I heard. Great news."

Emily was collecting the clippings.

Shands went on. "Awfully sorry about that mixup at the hospital.

I'm sure you know how important it is for brain tissue to be flash-frozen as soon after death as possible. Frankly, I'd rather make a dozen errors like that one than let a brain slip by us. I hope Ms. Squires wasn't too upset."

Now Emily was crouched, staring at one of the clippings.

"Right," I said.

"I also have the final analysis of your test results. We should talk about it. I've got some time tomorrow. Around five?"

I pushed down the dread that was backing up my throat. Get a grip, I told myself. Reality was always preferable to the nightmares the imagination could concoct. Usually, anyway.

"Peter, you there?"

"Five. Thursday. Sure." I hung up.

Emily was still holding a newspaper clipping. I went over to help her, my mind churning with what Shands might tell me.

"This is very weird." She looked up at me. "I wonder where on earth this—" Her voice broke off. "You okay?"

"I'm just fine," I said, biting off the words.

She gave me a searching look. "You don't seem like yourself." Then seemed to remember what she was holding. "Did you see this?"

I took it from her and read. It was an obituary. "Mr. O'Neill had this. Felicia. Same name as his wife. He probably got it from one of the newspapers on the unit."

"Look at the date."

The obituary was dated May, three months ago. Long before Uncle Jack joined us.

"Here's another one." Emily held up another newspaper clipping. It was an obituary for a Frank Mosticcio, and it was dated even earlier. "I wonder where he picked these up."

What the hell difference did it make? Uncle Jack picked up stuff everywhere he went. He'd have torn the coupons from the back of the cereal boxes at breakfast and walked off with the plastic cutlery if we'd let him.

I looked at my watch and did a quick computation. Thirty hours, approximately, and I'd be hearing the "final analysis." Did that mean that afterward I'd be ready for the "final solution"?

"Who knows, maybe there's a stack of these somewhere and he helped himself to a few," I said.

"Odd coincidence, don't you think? Both of these people were patients at the MRI lab. They both had Lewy body dementia."

Now she had my attention.

18

UNCLE JACK returned to the Pearce that afternoon. Sometimes a transfer can be exhausting, but he seemed energized. It was Annie who looked wiped out. She sat in the vinyl-cushioned easy chair alongside his bed, her head back, eyes closed.

She opened her eyes. "Hey, Uncle Jack, look who's here."

Uncle Jack was sitting up in bed. He looked at me without a spark of recognition.

"I'm Dr. Zak, Peter Zak," I said.

Then he surprised me. "Got a quarter?"

I grinned, reached into my pocket, pulled one out, and gave it to him. When he started to put it in his mouth, I took it back. One step forward, one step back.

A radio crackled static on the table. Staccato sentences with a lot of numbers. Then, "Ten-four. I'm en route."

"Police scanner," Annie said. "Uncle Jack used to keep one in his kitchen. I brought this in, thought he'd enjoy listening."

Another burst of static, then a bunch of number and the dispatcher gave an address. Uncle Jack sat up straighter.

"Domestic disturbance and a stolen car," Annie translated. "Not too far from Uncle Jack's house."

I gave Annie Uncle Jack's stack of clippings that I'd saved.

"You saved these for him? That was so sweet."

"Why don't you have a look at what's there," I said.

She gave me a questioning look. She knew I wanted her to notice something. She started looking through. "Golf. Mobile homes." She shook her head. "Who knew?" She paged through some more. "What's this?" She'd found one of the obituaries.

"Emily says she was a patient at the MRI lab. She had Lewy body dementia."

"What?" Now Annie was sitting up, alert.

"There's another one in there, too."

Annie found the other obituary. She looked up, flushed. "But this says he died after a short illness."

Now Annie was burrowing through the rest of the clippings.

"That's it?" she said, sounding disappointed. "Still, I wonder. I mean, don't you find this significant?" She waved the two obituaries at me. "And look, the edges are cut, not torn like the rest of his stuff."

"I wonder if someone at the lab cut them out and your uncle helped himself. Maybe the name on this one caught his attention. Felicia."

Annie flattened both obituaries on the table. "*After a short illness.*" She looked up at me. "That's what Uncle Jack's obituary would have said if he'd died. Wouldn't hurt to do a little checking."

She tucked the two obituaries into her backpack, then leaned over and kissed Uncle Jack on the forehead. "I'm going home now," she told him. "I'm beat. And Columbo needs to be fed."

She picked up her backpack and I walked her out into the hall.

"By the way, I talked to Mac," Annie said. "He called to ask about Uncle Jack. I guess he heard he was sick."

"He did?"

"Yeah, right. As if you didn't know. Anyway, I told him Uncle Jack got sick right after he had an MRI at the place where there was an accident and that doctor got killed. Funny I should mention that, he says. Tox screen came back on the victim. Blood alcohol level was .09. Also positive for diazepam."

I whistled. A couple of drinks and a dose of Valium could easily cloud your judgment. Knock the crap out of you, actually, depending on how much. At least it explained how Philbrick could have forgotten to take his wallet out of his pocket.

When we reached the lobby I heard footsteps behind me, someone running up the hall. I turned around as Emily Ryan bore down on us.

"They're holding Kyle for murder," she said, breathless. When she saw Annie, she backed away, tripping over her own feet. "Oh, I'm sorry. You weren't up in your office. I didn't realize you were . . . It's just that I don't know what to do. They took him in for questioning a few hours ago. Now they're holding him."

It was happening again. Why was this my problem? I was torn between tucking her under my wing and drop-kicking her into the middle of the parking lot.

I didn't have to make a decision. Annie nudged me aside. "Sounds like you'd better tell us what happened."

We went upstairs to my office. I pulled a bottle of bourbon out of the back of my desk drawer and poured some into a coffee mug. Emily took a sip and grimaced.

"I guess he was at the lab the morning Leonard was killed. Following me."

"He was there?" I said.

"He followed me from home that morning. Then he waited. He saw you. When the police arrived he took off." Emily took another sip of the bourbon. "He was just trying to protect me. He's an idiot, but he's not a murderer."

"What else?" Annie asked. She knew that wouldn't be enough to hold him.

"They found out that Kyle had threatened Lenny, followed him home one night a few weeks before. The neighbors saw them arguing in front of Lenny's apartment building. He knew Lenny went out with me occasionally, and that he'd been walking me to my car."

I wondered if that explained the bruise I'd noticed under Philbrick's eye the day Uncle Jack had gotten his MRI.

"Anything else?" Annie asked, picking up the bourbon bottle and getting ready to pour some more.

Emily put her hand over the top of the mug. "I guess Kyle called Philbrick. A few times. Left messages threatening to do I don't know what, slash his tires maybe, if he didn't stop following me. Lenny must've saved the tapes."

Annie sat there giving Emily an appraising look. "And what do you think about all this?"

I'd been pushed to the background but I didn't mind.

"Kyle would do just about anything to protect me. That's always been the problem. He's overbearing, controlling, and a major pain in the butt."

"Do you think he killed Leonard Philbrick?" Annie asked.

"God, no!" Emily said. "Why would he?" She looked from Annie to me and back. Her mouth fell open. "To protect me? I know how it looks. But think about it, whoever killed Lenny knew about

MRI scanners. Kyle majored in beer and sports. He's a PE teacher, for goodness sake. He could no more pull off Lenny's murder than I could coach a football team."

"Did you get yourself an attorney?" I asked.

"I'm not going to need one. I didn't do anything," she said stubbornly.

Annie and I exchanged a look.

"You just finished telling us that Kyle hasn't got the know-how to pull off the accident," Annie said. "The police are pretty smart. They're going to realize that, too, and they'll be thinking maybe Kyle didn't do it alone. Maybe someone helped him. Someone who knows all about those contraptions."

It wasn't hard to put this particular one and one together. Kyle had the strength, Emily had the knowledge. They work as a team. Maybe Emily and Philbrick have a couple of drinks. She laces his with Valium. Philbrick passes out and Kyle gets him up on the platform. Emily operates the scanner. Then it's just a matter of introducing the offending oxygen tank to the scan room. Kyle might even have been the one to procure it so there'd be no trail of evidence pointing to Emily.

"But I can explain—" Emily started.

"You shouldn't be doing any explaining to anyone unless you've got an attorney present," Annie said. "You tell the police half the stuff you've told us and they'll run with it. In about thirty seconds flat you'll find yourself arrested as an accessory—or worse."

• • •

"You actually think she did it?" Annie asked me later as we walked out to the parking lot.

"You don't?"

"Mysterious death at MRI lab. Stalking victim's revenge? I don't think so." She reached into her backpack and pulled out the two obituaries. "This is what I think it's all about."

"Mad scientists killing dementia patients?" I said. The red Miata beeped as Emily drove past us. That was where my money was.

When I got home I poured myself a glass of Zin and settled into the leather-cushioned Morris chair in my living room. I tried to read the paper, hoping it would keep my mind off tomorrow's appointment with Shands and what he might have to tell me about my brain. Instead I found my thoughts wandering to how I was going to deal with my suspicions—which were now hardening into a conviction—that Emily Ryan had something to do with Leonard Philbrick's death. Either she'd caused the accident and wasn't willing to admit her mistake, or worse, she and Kyle had conspired to kill him. The idea that I was supervising a murderer, allowing her to continue working with patients, felt damned uncomfortable.

19

I WAS cooling my heels in the waiting room at University Medical Imaging. I'd been dreading getting there. Now I wanted to get it over with. There were several other patients waiting. I picked up a newspaper and settled in. On a page inside the metro news section there was a short piece about Kyle being questioned and released.

Estelle Pullaski strode through. She barely acknowledged me, started through the door to the interior, then did a U-turn.

"Dr. Zak," she said, coming at me with a smile I didn't know she had in her. Today she wore a well-tailored suit and open back shoes that showed off shapely ankles. There was a dark intensity about her.

I stood and took her outstretched hand. She gave my hand a firm shake.

"He keeping you waiting?"

"Actually, I'm a tad early."

"Why don't you come in? There's usually coffee."

Immediately my antennae went up. Coffee was always welcome, but I knew there had to be a reason she was chatting me up. She said something to the receptionist and ushered me inside.

"So," she said as she poured coffee into two mugs and handed me one of them. The mug had UNIVERSITY MEDICAL IMAGING on it in red letters, and in deep blue PROACTIVE HEALTH CHOICES. Patriotism and health. "I understand the police have made an arrest. I'm so relieved."

I took a sip. The coffee was mediocre but tasted good nevertheless. If she thought I knew the inside scoop she'd be disappointed. "Actually, today's *Globe* says he was released."

"Released? But . . . the security guard tells me this young man was here just at the time of the accident. How could they have released him?"

She was still calling the event an "accident" even as she expressed relief over the police arresting a perpetrator. The best kind of perp, in fact. Not a disgruntled patient or family member. Someone with no formal connection to the lab.

"Come on, Peter," she said. So she remembered my first name, too. "Don't you have connections to the DA's office, to the police? I've heard you do forensic work. Surely you have an opinion at least."

"You probably know more than I do. Weren't you here that morning? You and Dr. Shands?"

"I . . . we . . . yes, of course," she said, stumbling over her words. "We got here after the accident. We work here. What I want to know is what this man was doing here." Now she'd regained her equilibrium. "Maybe it wasn't the first time. Is he going to be hanging around, hiding in the garage tonight when I go to get into my car? Are any of us safe?" Her eyes blazed. It occurred to me that any stalker who went after Estelle Pullaski would quickly discover he'd bitten off more than he could chew.

"He's—" I started. I honestly didn't know if Kyle was going to keep following Emily around like a lovesick puppy.

Dr. Pullaski's eyes widened. "You know this young man, don't you?"

"We've met. He's a friend of Dr. Ryan's."

"He is, is he? I can't say I'm surprised."

"He admits he was here. But says he didn't see anything," I said, paraphrasing what I'd read in the paper. "He says he followed Emily here. Stayed until the police arrived."

"Well, I certainly hope they find out what the hell is going on. We have important work to do, and I'm sure the last thing Leonard would have wanted is to have our research put on hold while the police dither about."

· · ·

Twin brains floated in fields of darkness—mine, and the one Shands kept referring to as a "normal brain." I adjusted my glasses and leaned closer.

He was going back and forth between the two, pointing out what he claimed were differences, anomalies which I was either too dumb to appreciate or too much in denial to recognize. I felt my eyes glaze over as he went on and on about volumetric analysis and coefficients of permeability.

I snapped to when he said, "Bottom line, you're on the cusp. Lower end of the range for normal, upper end of the range for Lewy body dementia." He fixed me with a grave look. "As I told you before, if I were you I'd start treatment as soon as possible."

"Upper end for Lewy body dementia," I said, repeating the words I hadn't quite absorbed. "On the cusp."

"You understand, only a brain autopsy allows us to see for sure. Of course we could do what they used to do back in the eighties. Drill a hole in your skull and scoop out a little piece of your brain. Count the plaques and tangles and look for proto-Lewy bodies." He watched me wince. It was probably the same look he gave worms he poured salt on when he was a kid. "Every once in a while it doesn't hurt to remind ourselves why magnetic resonance imaging was such a leap forward for medical research."

He probably wanted me to kiss his feet, but at that moment I didn't feel much like groveling.

"So you're saying I might get it? And I should take medication every day to stave off this . . . potentiality?"

"Or you might call it an eventuality. You said both your father and uncle had it?"

"Maybe. It was never diagnosed."

"Brothers. We know there can be a genetic component. In those cases, children have a fifty percent chance of inheriting." I wouldn't have placed a bet on myself with those odds.

"How soon?" I asked.

"You know I can't tell you that. The onset of the symptoms is so variable. We do know that the medication has been well tested. Plenty of people have taken it to reduce their cholesterol."

Was this what I was signing up for? Decades of popping a daily dose of pills I wasn't sure I needed? I could see from Shands's expression that he expected me to embrace this opportunity, to marvel at my good luck. Surely this was preferable to waking up one morning and finding that I'd lost my mind.

"Think about it. Here are the consent forms." I watched my hand reach for the papers, as if those fingers belonged to someone else. "You're fortunate to have this opportunity."

Yeah, lucky me. He stood. That was my cue to leave.

My legs felt like rubber. I rose and started out. When I reached the door I looked down at the papers I was holding, the words swimming into focus. I flipped to the back page.

I turned around. Shands had gone back to examining my MRI. He was tracing something with his finger, then writing in a file folder.

" 'Consent for postmortem and retention of human material for diagnosis and research,' " I read aloud. He blinked at me over his shoulder as if a chair had just spoken. "How come you don't point this out to patients?"

In a disconnected part of my brain I wondered why on earth, after just having received what amounted to a death sentence, I was focusing on this extraneous detail.

I wanted to go up to Shands, poke my finger into his chest and say, "How come, huh? Why don't you tell patients about this?" I was itching for a fight, even as I realized that what I wanted to fight him about was the news he'd just delivered.

Shands held up his hands. "Whoa! Take it easy. Peter, you're not about to die."

"Mr. O'Neill almost did. It came as an unpleasant surprise to his niece when they came to collect his corpse."

"Unfortunate mixup," Shands said, looking annoyed. "Hospital's fault."

"So why don't you tell patients like me that we're signing away our brains?"

He swiveled to face me, tilted his head and rubbed his chin.

"The autopsy is critical."

"That's not what I'm questioning. What happened to *informed* consent?"

"It's there. We tell them to read—"

"Your patients and their families are under stress," I said, cutting him off. "They've just received the worst possible news. And here you come, offering this one hope. But there's a string attached. You should be telling them, up front, explicitly. Not waiting for them to interpret the jargon in the fine print."

He sighed heavily. *Go ahead,* I thought, *humor me.*

"In the beginning we used to discuss this with patients. Explicitly. What we found was that it made them squeamish. Distracted them from where they should have been focusing—this opportunity to create new science. They'd delay enrolling in the treatment. The patient suffered unnecessarily. The research suffered."

I folded my arms across my chest.

He went on. "We're going to nail this disease, develop a definitive early diagnosis and effective treatment. Think of all the pain we'll be able to avert. All the lives we'll be able to save."

I had to admit, that promise was pretty intoxicating. "Still," I said, feeling my anger deflate, "seems like something you should be upfront about."

Shands shrugged, like he was tired of having to explain. "Being a research subject isn't like being a regular patient. Regular patients get tested and treated in order to get better. When you're a research subject, sure you may benefit personally. But the bigger goal is to help humanity, make your own illness count, contribute in a significant way to our understanding of the pathology of the disease so others will be saved. That's why people go into it willingly, knowing they may or may not get treatment. Knowing we're going to want to autopsy their brain when it's all over. Besides," he added, "we need the family to give their consent once again after death. So where's the harm?"

"Suppose a patient won't sign this, won't agree to donate his brain?"

"It's a showstopper. No autopsy, no treatment."

"Really?"

"Sure. If we were still under the thumb of the medical school I couldn't make it conditional, but we have our own institutional review board and they understand the importance of this component."

"But the family can rescind the decision after death?"

"They rarely do," he said. I wanted to push in his smug face.

• • •

I walked back to the reception area feeling like I was watching myself from one of the fluorescent light boxes recessed into the ceiling. The receptionist nodded to me as I passed.

"Do you need to schedule a follow-up?" she asked.

"I'll let you know," I said.

In the lobby I pressed the elevator button. A voice in one ear scoffed, "Forget about it. It's purely subjective. Herr Doktor sees what he wants to see because it confirms what he's expecting."

Where the hell was the elevator? I pressed the button again.

A voice in the other ear hectored, "You'll be sorry if you don't listen. Twenty years from now you'll be hoarding wine that's long since turned to vinegar. You'll have bought so much Mission furniture it'll be shoving you out the front door."

Then a calm voice from deep within me took over. "Listen, twenty years from now, who knows what new cures there will be? They'll probably be able to manipulate that gene you've got, *if* you've got it. And that's a big if."

Finally the elevator came. I stepped in. The doors started to slide shut when I heard footsteps and then, "Wait!" I put out my hand to hold the door. It was Emily, holding a large envelope. She got into the elevator with me.

"I wanted to catch you and show you this."

She pulled out a sheaf of newspaper clippings. "I found these — "

I meant to say *This isn't such a good time, can we talk later?* But what came out was a sharp, "Not now." Emily took a step backward. I knew a piece of this was displaced anger but I couldn't stop myself. "There are other people, other problems in the world that aren't about you."

I got out at the parking garage and stomped over to my car.

"But I found these hidden in the back of one of the drawers in Lenny's office," she said, trailing behind.

I unlocked the car door and got in.

She looked at me hollow-eyed, wordlessly accusing me of abandoning her. "You *asked* if anyone at the lab collected obituaries, remember?"

I'd asked her no such thing, I thought as I jammed the key into the ignition. But I didn't start the engine. Grudgingly I had to admit that Philbrick was the most likely person to have collected obituaries, the one who'd care enough to note the death of a patient as more than a clinical finding. I remembered those three phone calls Philbrick made to me right before he was killed. That had been the same night Uncle Jack became critically ill after having an MRI. If these were obituaries that Philbrick collected and kept hidden, I owed it to him to at least consider the implications. On top of that, I could see Annie waving the two obituaries in my face. *This is what I think it's about.*

I rolled down the window. "Sorry. Yes, of course I'd like to see those. Okay if I take them?"

Emily gave a grateful nod and passed me the envelope.

ANNIE AND I had the obituaries and death notices spread out on her kitchen table. She'd pushed away a pair of mismatched oak pressed-back chairs. An empty pizza box was on the counter.

In about twenty more years, Annie's kitchen would be considered vintage. There were Sears metal cabinets on the wall and the gas stove was avocado-green. The only modern anything was a microwave.

Annie had sorted the clippings in chronological order. Columbo leaped up, settled himself on the pile in front of Annie, and began to purr. He gave a complaining squeal when Annie scooped him up and dropped him unceremoniously on the floor. Undeterred, he rubbed up against her leg. She scratched him between the ears.

"Let's suppose for a moment that Dr. Philbrick was collecting obituaries and death notices for all the patients of the lab who died. Does this seem like a lot?" Annie asked.

"Over three years? Not really. The lab treats a lot of sick elderly patients. And I think it's fair to assume that most of these had Lewy body dementia."

"If that's what killed them."

" 'Died after a lengthy illness,' " I said, pointing to one of the early ones.

" 'Died of a blood infection at Brookline Hospital,' " Annie read, indicating one that was a few months old. "Or how about this one? 'Died suddenly at his home.' "

" 'Loved ballroom dancing,' " I said, reading from another. "Doesn't give a cause of death, or even where."

A lot of them were like that.

"Just because it isn't listed as the cause of death doesn't mean dementia isn't what killed them," I said. "There's a stigma. People feel reluctant to admit that their husband or mother had dementia. They'd rather put 'heart failure,' which is what kills most of us in the end anyway."

Annie folded her arms across her chest. "I don't see a whole lot of heart failures." I could feel her digging in her heels.

"Annie, I know you want there to be something sinister going on here, but are you sure you're being objective?"

She looked me in the eye. "You think I'm burned because Uncle Jack returned from the MRI lab and came down with an infection which Gloria says he couldn't have picked up at the Pearce. And I admit, maybe I am looking for someone to blame for the fact that Uncle Jack almost died. And yes, it's true that I'm more than a little miffed because five minutes after he's supposed to be dead they send around a team of ghouls to collect his brains.

"Call me paranoid if you like, but I'm just wondering if Mr. Martin Drogan"—she put her finger on one of the obituaries, a longtime clerk at the Middlesex courthouse who, according to the article, played hockey in his youth and continued to skate well into his seventies—"died of a bacterial infection." The obituary gave pneumonia as the cause of death. "What harm would it do if I checked into some of these?"

"We don't even know if these guys were all patients at the imaging lab," I said.

"We'll find out," Annie said, giving me an exasperated look. "Surely that's something Emily Ryan can find out for us."

"Okay, okay," I said, sighing. "Got any paper?"

Annie opened a drawer and pulled out a pad of yellow lined paper.

"If we're going to do this, at least let's be methodical about it." I ruled off some columns and put a heading at the top of the first three: *name*; *date of death*; *cause*.

Annie read me the names, one by one, and whatever other information was provided. A half hour later we stood back. There were six obituaries from three years ago. Ten in the last year. A dozen already this year and the year was only half up.

"Plus the two that your Uncle Jack snitched," I pointed out. Made a grand total of thirty.

"Pneumonia. Blood infection. After a *short* illness. Pneumonia again." Her finger hopscotched down the page.

I had to agree, it was decidedly odd.

"Though you'd think if all these deaths were suspicious, someone would have blown the whistle on them long ago," I pointed out. "When a healthy patient goes in for a medical test and then drops dead, you can be sure the authorities are going to hear about it. Lawsuits, complaints to the regulators."

"Maybe," Annie admitted. "But what happens when that patient is mentally unbalanced, draining away family energy and resources? When that person isn't that person anymore, sudden death can be the answer to a prayer." Annie's eyes pooled with angry tears. "They don't sue. They say, 'Such a shame. Oh well, it was for the best.' "

I couldn't argue with her logic.

"So when did each of these people have their last appointment at the MRI lab?" I said, writing a heading over the next empty column: *last appointment at UMI*. "Emily can find that out for us, too."

"And I'll look up death certificates for these people and get the missing causes of death," Annie said.

Over the next-to-last column I wrote: *death certificate?*

"I'll verify the causes given. Then we'll see what we have." She sat back. "Wish I could talk to them, ask them . . ." She looked up at me. "I'm going to find some of these families. See if I can figure out exactly what caused these deaths."

She took the pencil from me and wrote a heading over the last column: *family?*

From her look, I knew it was useless to try talking her out of it.

"You need to be discreet," I said. "We don't want to end up getting sued by the lab for defamation."

"I'm always discreet," Annie said, batting her eyes at me and giving me the biggest, wettest, most obscene kiss ever. "God, it feels great to be doing something instead of sitting around on my butt cursing the fates. I feel like dessert." She opened the freezer. "Let's see, what have we here? How about some Toscanini's?"

I came up behind her and put my arms around her. "Are you sure it's ice cream that you want for dessert?" I kissed her neck and inhaled her sweet fruity scent.

She'd reached in and pulled out a quart of vanilla. "Mmm. My favorite. And I wonder—" Annie opened the refrigerator. There in the door was a cardboard container of fudge sauce. "Ah. Just the thing."

She put the fudge sauce in the microwave and set the timer. I went back to nibbling on her neck. The microwave dinged. Annie got out a spoon and stirred the hot fudge and offered me the spoon. I took a lick. Warm, intense. Perfect.

Annie had the ice cream container open. She gouged out some ice cream. "Hard as a rock," she said.

The ice cream wasn't the only thing that was hard.

Annie put the spoon in her mouth and drew it out slowly, leaving some of the ice cream in the spoon. Then she fed me what was left. "You're in charge of the hot fudge," she said.

We took turns feeding and being fed spoonfuls of ice cream and spoonfuls of hot fudge sauce.

"Wait a minute," I said. "You've got some fudge over here." I licked a little bit from the corner of her mouth. "And here." I put down the fudge and gave her a long, lingering kiss. Annie slid her hands inside my shirt and ran her fingers up and down my back.

"You think there might be some more fudge sauce down there?" Annie asked as I unbuttoned her shirt.

"You never can tell. Gotta check to be sure."

• • •

Late the next afternoon, I was waiting in my office for Emily to show up for our regular conference. I was glad I hadn't acted on suspicion and suspended her from working with patients. After Annie and I had finished analyzing the obituaries and death notices, I'd found myself agreeing with Annie that maybe Leonard Philbrick's death wasn't an accident, and maybe it had nothing to do with Emily being stalked. At the very least I was feeling a reasonable doubt.

What I kept wondering was, Why had Leonard Philbrick saved all those obituaries and death notices? My first thought had been that he'd cared, and in some small way wanted to memorialize them. But I had to consider the possibility that Philbrick himself was the one responsible. Maybe collecting obituaries of those who'd died was the equivalent of carving notches in his belt. And it would explain why he kept them hidden. Following that line of reasoning, maybe someone had taken revenge for the untimely death of a loved one. Thirty potential victims, thirty sets of friends and family. It was possible that someone among them had the know-how to set up the MRI accident.

When Emily arrived she was visibly elated — tendrils of hair had escaped from her ponytail and curled around her face.

"I think I'm starting to get the hang of this therapy thing," she said. "You'll never guess what Mr. Black did."

"Let me guess. He didn't amputate his arm."

"He got it tattooed."

That was the last thing I'd expected.

"Got himself a fire-breathing dragon slithering from his wrist to his elbow. He tells me what the hell, he's going to have it cut off anyway. So now he's got this tattoo and he's enjoying putting it out there, watching people react, adjust their assessment of him."

"Makes him feel powerful?" I said.

"Says he feels great. And attractive. And interesting. And before he knows it, he meets this woman. She comments on his tattoo. She thinks it's cool. She thinks *he's* cool."

"And?"

"Just what you'd expect from two consenting adults."

"Goes to show, patients never fail to surprise."

"I do think I was able to help. He was saying that having his arm bound wasn't helpful. Made him feel more conspicuous, not less, and he couldn't stand the pity and disgust he saw in their eyes. It wasn't all that different from the way they looked at his arm. He said he might as well go around in short sleeves and flaunt it. So all I said was, 'Maybe you should.'

"He just sat there. Looked at me like I'd whacked him upside the head with a two-by-four. Didn't even tell me he was going to do it. Just shows up for the next session in a short-sleeved shirt and gets the biggest kick out of my reaction. Truly, I was stunned.

"He's dropped that mantra about his arm and how he needs to cut it off. Thank God for that at least. And he's starting to introspect in ways he couldn't before. I think he's ready to try to figure out who he really is."

"Congratulations. Now you can start on the real therapy."

"I know there's still a lot of work to be done. But thank *you*," Emily said. "This never would have happened if I'd kept pushing my own agenda on him. I'm so relieved that finally something is going right." Her elation was contagious. "I feel like celebrating. I'm going to buy myself a drink after work—want to join me?"

I wanted to say yes, but there was a momentary hesitation that wouldn't have been there with any other post-doc. I pushed away the uneasiness. Why not savor this clear-cut success—such things were rare in this profession.

"Let me know when you're leaving," I said. "I'm buying."

Emily checked her watch. "I've got a six o'clock with a new patient. He should be here any minute. Okay if I come get you when I finish with him?" She paused on her way out the door. "I forgot to ask. Did you get a chance to look at those obituaries?"

"Yeah. I wanted to ask you about them. But we can talk about that after."

I'd returned a half-dozen phone calls and was in the middle of editing a paper when Emily returned. "What happened? New patient get cold feet?" I asked.

"I guess. He never showed up." Emily was slightly out of breath. "I just ran down to the lobby to be sure no one was there waiting for me. Then I called the number outpatient services gave me. It's disconnected."

"That's odd," I said. "And damned annoying."

"Nothing can upset me today," Emily said. She looked at me expectantly. Then at the papers I had spread over my desk. "Oh. You're still working?"

"Just give me some time to finish up."

Twenty minutes later we took the elevator down to the basement and continued out through the tunnel.

"About the obituaries," I said, handing her back the envelope, "tell me again where you found them?"

"They were in one of Leonard's file cabinets. He had them in a folder marked 'invoices.'"

"That's odd."

"I thought it was odd, too. Lenny was super-organized. That's what made me think he was hiding them."

"From whom?"

"Dr. Shands? Dr. Pullaski? Me?" She thought for a minute more. "Patients? Obituaries of former patients would be last thing you'd want someone coming in for a medical test to see."

"Did you think Leonard was concerned? Did he think there was something suspicious about any of those deaths?" I asked, holding open the door to the outside.

"If he did, he didn't tell me," Emily said, pulling her jacket around her against the cool evening breeze.

"Could you look up when these patients had their last appointment at the MRI lab?"

"No problem. It would be in their files and—" Emily's voice died off. "What on earth?"

The parking lot below us was lit up like a stage set, the exits cordoned off. Pulsing lights reflected off the asphalt and surrounding tree branches.

"Maybe there's been an assault?" Emily said, hurrying over to the steps.

I followed her. Car accident seemed more likely. But there were too many emergency vehicles for a fender bender. An ambulance and a police cruiser were nose to nose in the parking lot. Between them, emergency personnel were huddled. A police officer moved aside and I could see what looked like a man in dark clothing lying on the ground.

Emily picked up a gym bag that had been left on the steps. "This is Kyle's," she said, her voice catching in her throat. "And isn't that Kyle's car?" A black Range Rover was one of a handful of cars still in the parking lot.

Emily's knees buckled under her and she sank down on the step.

I sat beside her. She had her face pressed into the gym bag.

"You go. I can't," she said. She looked so pale and she was shaking so hard I was afraid she was going to keel over. When I hesitated, she said, "Go! Please. Find out what happened."

I got up and started down the steps. As I moved closer, I could see that the victim was lying on his stomach, legs splayed. He was a big man, broad back, dark hair, and his face was turned away from me. One of the men standing beside him looked up at me — it was MacRae.

"Stay back!" one of the officers barked in my direction.

MacRae came over to me.

"What happened?" I asked.

"If we'd been able to hold him longer, he'd still be alive," MacRae said. "Poor bastard. Looks like he got hit."

I looked for skid marks near the body but didn't see any. About twenty feet away, a police photographer was taking pictures of the pavement. "You think it happened over there?" I asked.

MacRae shrugged, his usual noncommittal self. Now Emily was standing at the base of the steps, still clutching Kyle's gym bag to her chest.

The camera flashed two more times. It was a long way from those skid marks to where Kyle was now. Would've had to have been hit at high speed to have been catapulted that far. There was no way to build up that kind of speed in the parking lot. More likely he crawled to where he was now.

One of the officers who'd been working over the body came over to us. He handed MacRae something small. MacRae held it in his palm.

"Recognize this?" he asked, but he wasn't talking to me. He was showing it to Emily, who'd come up behind me. She was still pale, like she was in shock. She gasped when she saw what looked like a small piece of gold jewelry. Before it had been run over, it might have been a tiny pin or a ring in the shape of a woman.

I put my hand on Emily's shoulder and hoped she was getting the message. *Don't say anything.*

"What's that?" MacRae asked Emily, indicating the gym bag.

"I think it's Kyle's," Emily said. "I found it up there on one of the steps."

"I'll take it," MacRae said, and he took the bag from her. "I'd like you both to stick around, particularly you Dr. Ryan. I have some questions."

Emily gave a mute nod. She was staring at where her car was parked in the far corner of the lot. A man in a uniform was running a flashlight carefully over the body of the Miata and taking notes.

I remembered what Emily had said happened to that stranger who'd stalked her when she was in college. *He died in a car accident.* Hit by a car in a parking lot? I wondered.

21

WE WATCHED from the steps as the investigators methodically worked their way across the parking lot. Emily alternately wept and cursed. Kyle was dead, and whoever did it had used her car. After a while, she just sat there staring off into space as the gravity of her situation seemed to settle over her. I put my arm around her, but I felt the distance between us growing as I sat there thinking.

I wondered when the medical examiner would place the time of death. While Emily was — and the word *supposedly* slipped into my head — waiting for a new patient who'd never showed?

Now she was trembling, suppressing the sobs. It felt completely genuine. Still, I found myself wondering exactly how long it had been since Kyle was run down. Emily had been out of breath when she reappeared in my office, as if she'd been running. Said she'd gone downstairs to see if the patient was waiting for her in the lobby. If Kyle was killed at around six, she'd have had time to get to the parking lot and back. Outpatient services were usually very careful about making appointments for new patients. Standard procedure would have been for them to check that contact information was genuine. Had they really scheduled Emily an appointment with a nonexistent patient, or had Emily made that up in order to buy herself time? It was something I could check in the morning.

If you took as a starting point that Kyle helped Emily kill Philbrick, it all made sense. Emily enlists Kyle's help to eliminate the stalker who's been making life miserable for her. After they kill him things start to heat up. Kyle gets taken in for questioning. Maybe he begins to crack under pressure. Emily's afraid he's about to spill the truth.

She arranges for him to meet her in the parking lot at the time when she's supposedly waiting for a new patient. When Kyle shows up, she runs him down. But it's a little car and he's a big man. The initial impact isn't enough. He crawls across the parking lot, trying to get away. So she runs over him again. How many times did it take? Then she parks her car off in the corner of the lot and races back through the tunnel and up to the third floor. When she shows up in my office she's still out of breath.

All of that fit together. But there were pieces that didn't make sense. Why run Kyle down with her own car and in so doing make herself seem guilty? Why leave her car not fifty feet from the body where the police could so easily see the damaged fender? Why not wait a few minutes so she wasn't so out of breath when she came to my office? And why show up in the parking lot afterward, right in the middle of the police investigation?

I knew what Emily would say. She was being set up. Someone had stolen her keys again. I'd been there, witnessed how the stalker let the air out of her tire, unlocked her car and helped himself to her belongings—intimate items that were hers . . . and an earring.

Now I realized what the bit of gold jewelry was that the police had found on the pavement—it was the ear clip that Emily sometimes wore hooked over the top of her ear. Was that the earring she'd claimed had been stolen by her stalker? Did the word *stalker* belong in quotation marks?

A pair of tow trucks arrived—I assumed one was for Emily's car and one was for Kyle's. MacRae strode over to us.

"You don't have to tell me," Emily told me as she rose to meet him. She squared her shoulders and, before he could get a word out, announced, "I know you have questions, and I'd be happy to answer them. But first I'd like to call my attorney."

MacRae already had his pad out. "I'm not arresting you, just trying to help you out here," he said, giving us his I'm-just-a-poor-slob-trying-to-do-my-job look. "Just wondering when you last saw the victim?"

Emily shook her head.

MacRae gave me a cold look. "How about you, Dr. Zak? I'm sure you won't mind answering a few questions."

He clicked open his pen and launched into his questions. Most of them established that I couldn't vouch for Emily's whereabouts for the better part of the last hour. When he was done, MacRae stood there clicking his pen rapidly open and shut.

"I want to see you tomorrow, first thing," he told Emily. "With your attorney, of course."

• • •

I didn't take Emily home. I phoned Annie and she helped me locate Chip at the Harvard Club, where he was in the middle of a squash match and not thrilled about having been tracked down. He met us at his office.

Still wearing shorts and a sweaty T-shirt, Chip looked rather incongruous in the well-appointed, skylighted office in the building where he and Annie had opened their practice after they left the public defender's office. With its exposed brick walls and oversized windows, the building had been a stable back in the 1800s when horses and buggies clopped along the cobblestone streets in this part of East Cambridge, Boston's first industrial center. Perfect location for a criminal law practice—the courthouse and jail were just a few blocks away.

He had a mahogany desk, leather-seated desk chair, an abstract oil painting on the wall. The only hint of Chip's dubious past was a 1976 Fillmore East Grateful Dead poster hanging on the back of his office door—a red, white, and blue skeleton.

After an hour spent talking to Emily, Chip had covered six pages of a yellow pad with notes scrawled in a hand that only he could read. He leaned back in his chair.

"I'll be honest with you, Dr. Ryan. I fully expect the DA will want to charge you with murder. We'll talk to the police first thing tomorrow, offer to help their investigation in any way we can. You should be prepared for the possibility that they may want to hold you."

"Hold me? What about my jobs?" she asked. People did that, hung onto shreds of normal routine as a way of denying that the world was crumbling around them.

"It would probably be a good idea to request a leave of absence. Until this sorts itself out," Chip said. Emily swallowed a sob. "And when we do talk with the police," Chip went on, giving her his sternest voice, "you must do exactly what I tell you. Is that understood? My job is to protect you."

Emily stood and went through the motions of shaking Chip's hand and thanking him. I walked her to my car. All the way back to her apartment, Emily stared listlessly out the window. It was nearly ten when we got there.

I walked her to her door. "Damn," she said, punching the inside of her bag as she rummaged for her keys. There was a pool of light in the entryway. Her bag dropped and out spilled much of the contents, coins rolling every which way.

"Shit! Shit! Shit!" Emily shrieked, kicking and stomping, sending a tube of lipstick skittering into the grass. "Goddamn that fucking miserable sonofabitch!"

"Calm down," I said, putting my hands on her shoulders.

She wrenched herself free and gave me an accusing look. "You think I did it, don't you. You think I killed Lenny and then ran down Kyle." She placed her heel on a hand mirror and ground down on it until it shattered. "That's what everyone's going to think. Maybe I should just give up."

She squatted and picked up one of the shards of mirror. Light glinted off the glass, sending a sliver of light into the darkness. She grew very still, her skin glowing pale in the evening light.

She sighed and tossed the piece of glass into the bushes. She wiped away tears and picked out her keys, then gathered up the rest of her belongings and stuffed them back into the bag.

I offered her a hand. She took it and pulled herself to her feet. Before I knew what was happening, she was in my arms, pressing herself against me. For an instant, it felt as if I were holding Kate — Kate was about the same size, with that same combination of physical vulnerability and strength. My breath caught as the smell of cinnamon and clove invaded my head. Kate's smell. I knew it was a memory. I gave a long, shuddering inhale, willing the sensation to last. Then we were kissing, all the alarm bells I was hearing muffled by the moment.

Slowly, with more reluctance than I would have admitted, I pulled away.

"I don't think this is a good idea," I said.

She fiddled with her keys and stared down at them. "I suppose you're right." She straightened her jacket collar. "I'm sorry." Her mouth was pouting now, sulky.

I looked at her face, the long neck and delicate chin, dark lashes resting on flushed cheeks. Cinnamon and clove had vanished, replaced by a cold clarity as I wondered if I was looking into the face of a killer.

• • •

"Assholes are us," I thought as I sat in the car outside my house. Why had I allowed it to happen? One minute I'm thinking Emily could be a cold-blooded murderer who was now on her third victim. The next minute I'm holding her in my arms and kissing her. Worse still, enjoying it. Maybe Lewy body dementia was already affecting my judgment. If not, then what the hell was going on? The one thing I knew was I didn't want to go home. I needed ballast and a strong dark beer.

I called Annie and asked her to meet me at the Inman Lounge. When I got there the place was half full, and a pair of TVs over either end of the bar had on *Seinfeld* reruns.

"It doesn't look good for her," Annie said. "Woman takes matters into her own hands, gets her boyfriend to help her kill the man who stalked her, then kills her boyfriend before he can implicate her. That's how it's supposed to look, anyway."

"*Supposed* to look?"

Annie skimmed the head off her beer with her finger and licked it off. "Your friend Emily is a flake, and I'm sure she hasn't got the world's best judgment in people, but she's not stupid. I think it's been made to look as if she did it."

"Don't you think it's a bit of a coincidence that she says she had a stalker before, and he was killed in a car accident?"

"You think he got run over in a parking lot?"

"Well?"

"He didn't. I looked into that old stalking incident." I must have looked surprised because Annie added, "It's my job. Of course I checked her out. She took out an injunction against the guy, a college student. He was killed six months later when his car hit a Greyhound bus that had rolled over on a highway in freezing rain. Doesn't seem like the kind of thing Emily could pull off, despite her many talents."

"Just a coincidence," I said, trying once again to adjust my mental image of Emily.

"Sometimes that's all it is."

"You want this to be about those obituaries, don't you?" I said. Annie grinned and raised her eyebrows, allowing that I might have a point. "Okay. I can see where Philbrick's death might have had something to do with the lab and a rash of suspicious patient deaths. But Kyle's death? How does that fit in with dead patients?"

"He was there the morning Philbrick was killed. Maybe he saw something."

"What?"

"I don't know. I haven't figured that part out." Annie ran her finger slowly around the rim of her glass. "Too bad Emily will be in jail. Now she can't find out when all those patients had their last appointments at the MRI lab. We'll just have to find out for ourselves. Go to the families and ask. If they don't know, try to get at the lab records."

I didn't like where this was heading.

"I already contacted Frank Mosticcio's daughter," Annie said, rushing ahead full tilt.

"The guy who loved ballroom dancing?"

"No. Mosticcio's one of the obituaries that Uncle Jack snitched.

Died a couple of months ago. Lived in Brookline. You and I have an appointment tomorrow to see his daughter."

"We do?"

"Yeah. I said I'd come over with a psychologist who works with dementia patients and their families." My jaw dropped. "Well you do, don't you? I told her the truth — sort of. That I was looking for families who'd gone through what I'd been going through. I hand-waved a little about why."

"Hand-waved?"

"I may have suggested I'd be writing about it. I really didn't have to say much. She said she'd be glad to talk to us. Seemed eager to, in fact."

"Annie — " I started. All kinds of red flags were waving.

"Peter, you need to know if Emily is guilty or not and I want to nail the bastard that tried to hurt my uncle." Annie had a way of bringing things into focus. "You'll give me . . ." She searched for the word. . . . "legitimacy. I'll make you less intimidating."

"I'm not intimidating."

"Okay, you're not. I checked with Gloria, and you're not busy then either."

"How would she know? Tomorrow's Saturday."

"So are you? Busy, I mean?"

"I guess I am. Now."

• • •

Frank Mosticcio had lived in Brookline on the hill up behind Coolidge Corner. The rambling Victorian had long ago been divided into apartments. A wooden staircase had been slapped onto the side of the house to give the second-floor tenant direct access. When we pulled up, a middle-aged woman in a T-shirt and jeans was removing a sign that said YARD SALE TODAY from the tree in front of the house.

"Sorry, we're just putting things away," she told us as we got out of the car.

"I'm not a yard saler," Annie said. "I'm Annie Squires. I'm here to talk to Frank Mosticcio's daughter."

"That's me. Dorothy Stephanos. Please, call me Dottie."

Annie shook her hand and introduced me.

"I thought I'd have all this put away by now," Mrs. Stephanos said, raking manicured fingers through her short blond hair. "My son's supposed to be helping me out, but . . ." She looked around as if she expected he might be hiding behind a tree. "Sold a bunch of his own CDs and took off. Kids. Short attention span." She surveyed the unsold items that littered the lawn. "Now I'm stuck with this mess. Why does it always seem like there's more at the end of the sale than at the beginning?"

"I'm sure it demonstrates some principle about conservation of stuff," Annie said as she picked up one of the boxes. "Where do you want this?"

"You don't need to do that," Mrs. Stephanos protested.

I followed Annie's lead and picked up a pair of lamps that looked as if the bases were made from World War II shell casings — miniature bombs dangled from the pulls. Now there was something every household needed. Only fifty bucks for the pair. A bargain.

Mrs. Stephanos led us around the back to a garage where we stashed the unsold items. A half hour later, the three of us had cleared the lawn and were sitting on the porch drinking iced tea. Mrs. Stephanos had brought out a file folder where she kept documents about her father's illness.

"It's been a struggle, getting the estate settled. So many details.

Well, I'm sure you know what that's like," Mrs. Stephanos said, giving Annie a sympathetic look.

"I do, actually," Annie said, not bothering to correct Mrs. Stephanos's impression that Annie's uncle had died. "My uncle was a big hoarder."

"This is our third yard sale and there's still more stuff I haven't gotten to up in the attic. Packed into the eaves. My husband says I should just pay someone to come in and clear the place out. But I can't bring myself to do that. There could be family photographs and who knows what else." She sighed, the aluminum chair creaking as she leaned back in it. "Would you believe, I found about a dozen uncashed checks for stock dividends in his toaster oven?"

"I'd believe," Annie said.

I asked Mrs. Stephanos about her father—when he'd become ill, how the disease had progressed.

"I'd never even heard of it," Mrs. Stephanos said. "Lewy body dementia. My son says it sounds like a rock group." She went on to tell us that her father's physician had suggested he participate in the research study.

She spread the contents of the file folder on the table. There was the consent form she'd signed for her father.

"Do you mind if I look through?" I asked, indicating the other papers in the folder.

"Be my guest," she said.

Mrs. Stephanos went on, telling us how her father had gotten a series of MRIs—four or five, she thought—at University Medical Imaging. The last one had been a few days before he died.

"He came home from the test and went right to sleep," she said. "Next morning he was running a fever. I thought it was just a cold. By that night, he was having trouble breathing. I called his doctor but by the time we got him to the hospital it was too late. It was some kind of bacterial infection. Like the one that killed Jim Henson? Galloping pneumonia, one of the nurses called it."

While she talked, I sifted through the papers in the folder. Mrs. Stephanos had letters from her father's primary care physician, hospital bills, and medical reports. There was a full-color brochure extolling the virtues of University Medical Imaging, and another tri-fold from Cimgen Pharmaceuticals—that was the company that manufactured Cimvicor. On the front was a photograph of a vigorous older woman and man on a sun-drenched golf course. She was teeing off. In italics and halfway down the first page it said, "Lowering cholesterol reduces the risk of hardening of the arteries, and hardening of the arteries has been linked to heart disease and the onset of dementia."

Subtle. Doctors could *prescribe* a lipid-lowering drug like Cimvicor for an "off-label" use such as treatment for dementia, but the company was forbidden by the FDA to *advertise* an off-label use. They couldn't come right out and say the drug could be used to treat dementia—but the implication was clear.

"Just curious," I asked. "Do you recall where you picked this up?"

Mrs. Stephanos took the brochure from me. "I don't—" she began. She turned it over and noticed something written on the bottom of the back page. Looked like a name and phone number. "Oh yes, I do remember. I picked this up at a family support meeting."

Drug companies got away with distributing this kind of misleading information by slipping it in under the radar.

"Dr. Shands was treating your father with medication for Lewy body dementia?" I asked.

"Such a brilliant doctor," Mrs. Stephanos said. "He was the only one who gave us any hope."

"Was the treatment helping?"

"Maybe. I'm not sure. It was so hard to watch my father deteriorate the way he did. Over just a few months, he went from being completely independent to needing help getting out of bed. He'd once been a teacher and now he was talking gibberish. Near the end, we had to get someone to stay with him all day. Nights I slept here. I was so exhausted.

"It's been three months since he passed away and I'm feeling like I'm just now starting to feel normal. At least it's a comfort knowing that my father's brain is being used to help find a cure."

"Your dad's death was unexpected?" Annie asked.

"His primary care physician had told us that despite the dementia, his heart was strong."

"So his death came as a shock?" Annie pressed.

Mrs. Stephanos hesitated. "We thought he'd linger. Yes, it was a shock." There was a long pause as she and Annie locked eyes. "And a relief. I'm sure you know what I mean. In the end, he just slipped away in his sleep. Not twitching and shouting like he'd been doing. It was for the best."

Annie shot me a look.

22

BY THE end of the weekend, Annie and I had met or talked on the phone with a half-dozen more next of kin. It was turning out to be a mixed bag. Two patients had died more suddenly than expected. For another, it sounded as if death had been a long overdue coda to the final dehumanizing phase of a nasty disease. In another case, the surviving daughter had been estranged from her father and simply didn't know whether death had been sudden or not.

The key piece of information—when each of the deceased had their last appointment at University Medical Imaging—remained elusive. Family members often didn't know or didn't remember.

"If only we'd gotten started in this direction a few weeks ago it would have been so much easier," Annie pointed out. "Emily could have pulled this information out of their files for us."

Now Emily Ryan was in no position to get information for anyone. She'd been arrested and booked. In Kyle's gym bag the police found a "Freudian Slip" like the one she'd used to leave a note on my office. On it was written:

See you at 6.
XX
Emily

Annie still wasn't buying. "Are you telling me she sat on the steps to the parking lot for twenty minutes holding his gym bag, and never bothered to get rid of the incriminating note?" It was a damned good question.

Monday morning, I found Gloria and Kwan in the conference room. They stopped and gave me an odd look when I walked in.

"What?" I said, immediately.

"We were just talking about Emily," Kwan said.

"There must be some way we can help her," Gloria said, her face etched with concern.

I sank down in a chair and told them I wasn't feeling too optimistic. I'd called outpatient services and they had no record of handling the referral that Emily claimed she got. The administrator got all huffy at the suggestion that her office would be careless enough to make an appointment for a nonexistent patient. They always checked insurance, she said. And they always called to confirm appointments.

"They insist they'd never have given Emily the number of a disconnected phone."

"But—" Gloria said, looking crestfallen.

"Did either of you see her when she says she came down to look for the patient?"

"I'd gone home," Kwan said.

"I saw her," Gloria said. "She asked me if I'd seen anyone wandering around, looking lost." I could sense how torn Gloria was about revealing the next bit. "Then I think she went outside."

"Did you see her come back in?" I asked.

Gloria admitted that she hadn't. "But that doesn't mean anything. Don't you see? Someone's setting her up."

Gloria and Annie were pretty much on the same page with their conspiracy theories—Gloria thinking Emily had been framed, Annie sure it was all about untimely patient deaths. And me? Parallax. Something had shifted, and despite the fact that more and more evidence was mounting to incriminate Emily Ryan, I was starting to agree with the conspiracists. My gut said she wasn't a murderer.

• • •

Security at the Middlesex County Jail on the top floors of the Cambridge Courthouse was getting more and more extreme—this time it took almost forty minutes to get through their screening process. They confiscated my briefcase and even my Tic Tacs. At least they let me take in a pad of paper and a pen.

Emily was waiting in the cell-like examining room, standing and staring out the barred window. She seemed lost in the baggy gray jump suit that had MIDDLESEX COUNTY JAIL stenciled on the back. Her ponytail was tied low at the nape of her neck. Strands of hair hung loose at the sides. I knew she wasn't appreciating the spectacular view of the Boston Harbor with the Leonard Zakim Bunker Hill Bridge in the foreground, a fan of cables at either end splayed like a futuristic harp.

"I can't believe this is happening. How can they think I killed Kyle?"

She sat at the table and put her head down in her arms. I took the chair across from her.

"Outpatient services says that referral you got didn't come from them," I said.

Her head snapped up. "But a woman from there *called* me. That morning. Gave me a name, phone number, reason for referral. Why would I make that up?" She blinked at me. "Oh. I get it. I used it as an excuse. So I could sneak down and kill Kyle and then sneak back up without anyone seeing me."

"Gloria saw you go outside."

"Gloria—?" Emily cocked her head to one side, thinking. "Of course I went out. I thought the guy might be lost. I came right back in." There was a pause. "She didn't see me come right back in?"

"No, she didn't."

"Oh, God," Emily said. "Who is doing this to me? You heard about the note they found in Kyle's briefcase? On *my* notepaper? I have no idea where it came from, because I certainly didn't write him a note. I didn't *write* Kyle notes. I called him. I talked to him. He was a friend. Besides, I only use that notepaper at work."

She sank back, her gaze roving across the ceiling, from the window to the radiator. Then she gave me a direct look, her eyes bright and intense. "I know what you're thinking. This woman is out of her mind—who is she kidding?"

"Actually, that's not what I'm thinking," I said. "What I think is that someone's gone to a lot of trouble to make you look guilty."

Relief swept across Emily's face. "Will you help me?" She put her hand on my arm. "You've got to help me. You're my only hope."

"Actually, I'm not," I said, yanking my arm away and immediately regretting it. I hated the way Emily kept thrusting me into the role of savior, but I knew I was overreacting. The situation was grave, and Emily really did need all the help she could get.

"Maybe it's not just two murders," I said. "Maybe it's about a whole lot of patients who shouldn't have died when they did. I don't know if Dr. Philbrick was responsible for these deaths."

"He couldn't have been. If he'd known something like that was going on, he'd have blown the whistle."

"Or maybe that's it. He was ready to blow the whistle. Maybe that's why he called me the night he was killed. To ask me to watch Mr. O'Neill. Maybe he still wasn't absolutely sure."

"And that would mean—" Emily spoke slowly, putting together her thoughts as she went. "—maybe Kyle was killed because of something he saw that morning when he followed me to the lab?"

But Kyle had told the police he hadn't seen anything. Maybe he'd been lying. Or maybe . . . "Wait a minute. Who else was at the lab that morning when you got there?"

"No one."

"But didn't Dr. Shands call the police?"

"Jesus," Emily said, grasping the significance. "Why didn't Kyle see him park his car in the garage and come in?"

"Could he have walked over, or come by T?"

Emily scoffed at the suggestion.

"Do you remember if you saw Dr. Shands's car in the garage when you arrived?"

"Honestly, I don't remember."

Suppose Shands was already at the lab when Emily got there. Suppose Philbrick collected obituaries because patient deaths seemed suspicious. Suppose there'd been a string of accidents, or even murders, that were being covered up.

I stopped. All I had was a web of supposes. What we needed was evidence, not conjecture. "If this is all about covering up the deaths of patients, then we should back up and ask ourselves who had access to those patients."

"Anyone at the lab."

It could easily have been done any number of ways in such a closed system. Bacteria could have been added to the contrast agent Shands injected. It could have been in the sedative administered beforehand to keep patients calm. Doctored packs of the Cimvicor or placebo medication given to patients in the study would have done the trick.

Emily considered for a moment. "Old people with dementia being killed. Immediately makes you think 'mercy killing.' But you can be sure that if Dr. Shands or Dr. Pullaski had anything to do with it, it wasn't about mercy."

I had to agree. But I was surprised at the clarity of Emily's observation—up until now she'd spoken of Shands only in the most glowing terms. Maybe prison was fading her rose-colored glasses. Or maybe she'd finally realized that her own survival was at stake.

"He once drew me his grand plan," Emily said. "Showed me how he targeted different age groups, males and females, at different stages of the disease. Thing is, he does it in life, too—collects the people he needs."

I'd made a similar observation myself. Shands had Leonard Philbrick, who could handle patients and knew more about MRI technology than anyone. He had Dr. Pullaski, efficient administrator, willing to move funds and deal with unpleasantness.

"And he had you, didn't he?" I said gently. "What did he need from you?"

Emily seemed flustered. "I have no idea. He came to me out of the blue. Offered me a position at the lab. Said he'd heard about my Ph.D. thesis on cognition and dementia. I was so pleased." Emily's face reddened. "Flattered." She looked away. "I thought he needed a diligent researcher. But there's a million of us out there he could have picked. Why me?"

She shifted in her chair and picked at a thread in the pants of the jumpsuit. "From the first day I'm working there, he's telling me how nice I look, how nice I smell. He'd ask me to stay late, and then he'd have to work late, too. His passion and determination to find a cure for Lewy body dementia drew me in. I got this idea in my head, this fantasy, that I'd be able to help him in his quest. That maybe we'd even be partners.

"Then the post-doc at the Pearce came through and I thought I'd died and gone to heaven. I had not one but two fantastic opportunities. And at last I'd have enough money to get myself some decent clothes. I could finally afford a down payment on my dream car. I was euphoric.

"I'd been there a few weeks when he starts putting his hands where they don't belong. I tried to tell him nicely that I wasn't interested in him. Not in that way. When that didn't work, I was more direct."

"Must've shocked the hell out of him," I said. Emily smiled. "Did he stop coming on to you?"

"It got much more subtle. It was as if he began a campaign to win me over. There were gifts and kindnesses. Really just bribes. So he'd feel entitled to ask for something in return. I'm sure he thought, sooner or later, I'd come around."

"What did Dr. Pullaski make of your relationship with Dr. Shands?"

"I think she wrote me off, like I was just some kind of a bimbo. Nothing I did or said made any difference. She made it very clear that I was not the first, and I wouldn't be the last. I'm sure she thought we were sleeping together.

"Kyle wanted me to quit. I should have. But I guess, in a way, Dr. Shands did seduce me. More than anything, I wanted to be able to say I'd worked there, helped the great doctor with his research. I was thrilled when he gave me a credit on one of his papers. Not that I didn't deserve it. I wrote most of it. Still, everyone in the lab was shocked.

"He is a genius, you know. His work is brilliant. Patients who come to him see this great man whose work is going to save them. If there's any possibility that someone was killing his patients, then something has to be done about it."

Interesting, the way she'd phrased it: *someone* was killing *his* patients. The obvious suspect would be Shands himself. But why would he kill his own patients? Weren't they more valuable to him alive, as research subjects to test his experimental protocol? The only thing a corpse could do was confirm the diagnosis.

"Right now the police are taking the path of least resistance and building a case against you. If we can convince them that this is not just a single murder, or even two, but a pattern of suspicious deaths, then they'll have to investigate. I've got the list of patients from the obituaries and death notices you found. We want to show that each of them died soon after their last appointment at the MRI lab. How do we find out?"

"That's easy. The information is in the computer system, of course. It's also in the patient files. Those are in the records room."

"Show me where," I said, handing Emily pen and paper.

She drew a map of the imaging center. There was the building lobby, the outer waiting area, the reception area in the center hub. Off that, she drew the corridor with Shands's office and the neuropathology lab. Then she drew the corridor that led to the scan room. On one side was the storeroom. Across the hall she drew two rooms. One she marked PRIVATE, the other RECORDS.

"Here. They keep it locked. There's a keypad with a combination lock." She wrote down a series of six numbers: 0-4-0-1-5-5. "It's easy to remember. Dr. Shands's birthday." April Fool's Day, 1955. I could remember that.

Emily pulled out the band that was holding her ponytail, brushed her hair back with her fingers and bound it again, this time up high on the back of her head. It was a small thing, but spoke to a change in her outlook.

23

"THAT'S A pretty big if," Annie said when I told her my plan that afternoon in her office.

The room was strictly functional—a sturdy metal desk, four file cabinets, and some chairs, all dwarfed by the high ceiling and huge arched window. On a bookcase was a stack of take-out menus, some family snapshots, and a framed black-and-white photo of Annie speed skating, her inline skates a blur.

"You might be able to get in there on the pretext of asking Shands to show you your MRI again. But leave you alone long enough so you can sneak around and find the information we need in some file cabinet?" Her look said: *Doomed to failure.*

"And why would he *let* you come back at this point? Wouldn't he want to keep you as far away from the place as he can, especially if he's trying to hide something like a string of accidents or murders?"

I opened my mouth, then closed it. I'd been about to tell Annie why Shands would be eager to see me — that he thought I had Lewy body dementia and wanted to sign me up for his study.

"Peter, what aren't you telling me?" she said, giving me her X-ray look.

"I didn't tell you about this because I thought you had enough on your plate with Uncle Jack so sick. Shands saw something in my MRI. He wants me to participate in his research study. He thinks I've got Lewy body dementia."

Annie gaped at me. "You're only forty years old. How the hell — ?"

"He says the markers are there before the symptoms manifest. Shands says I'm at the lower end of the range for normal, upper end of the range for Lewy body dementia."

"Lower . . . upper," Annie muttered. "Mumbo jumbo. In other words, he can't tell."

"It can be inherited. My father and uncle both had dementia."

Annie stared deep into my eyes, then reached out and touched my face.

"You're taking this seriously, aren't you? Peter, this is a man whose life work is this disease. He's looking for people he can use for his research. He *wants* to see it. If you ask me, he's got his head up his ass."

This was hardly the reaction I'd expected. It blew over me like a gust of air from an open window.

"And don't you dare start living your life as if you're about to unravel. It's not going to happen," Annie said. Then a slow smile came over her face. "But that's not what you're going to tell Dr. Shands. Give him what he wants. You're all worried. You want to do everything you can to prevent the onset of this terrible disease. You can't wait to enroll in his research study. You're interested in the brain, so of course you want to see your MRI again."

Her face clouded. "Promise me you won't let them give you another MRI. Or a shot, or a pill — or anything. Because if you do, I'll kill you."

I put up three fingers. "Scout's honor."

"Shands has the attention span of a gnat," she said. "That'll work in our favor. Just hang in there, ogling that scan. Bet you anything, after five minutes he leaves you alone with it."

"So far so good. Then what? You're the one who knows how to snoop around. All I know how to do is muck about in people's heads."

"First thing, don't get caught."

"I'll try."

Annie put her hand on my arm. "Seriously, Peter. Be careful. Two people have been killed, maybe more than thirty. Every day patients are coming out of there a whole lot sicker than they went in."

• • •

"I'm delighted you decided to participate in the study," Shands told me.

He'd made time for me early the next morning. I'd signed the consent form, and he'd already handed me a packet of pills with instructions for taking them.

"You're our youngest subject with the inherited form of the disease. You'll be helping us to break new ground." I'm sure he thought that would cheer me up.

In my pocket, I had the map Emily had drawn along with the Xeroxed copy of the table Annie had put together listing all the patients. With the information we'd gathered from family interviews and death certificates, it was turning out that more and more patients had succumbed to respiratory illness, flu, or bacterial infection. I'd have needed an actuary or Shands's Cray T3E to tell whether the proportion was typical for this kind of population. I reminded myself that the whole point of coming here was to find out when each of those patients had his or her last appointment at the lab.

"How's Dr. Ryan?" Shands asked, looking as if he'd suddenly developed a headache. "Such a shame. A young woman with so much promise."

"You think she's guilty of two murders?" I asked. "You knew her fairly well."

"Well, I, uh . . ." Shands stammered, "I didn't know her that well."

"I thought she even authored a paper with you."

"Dr. Ryan assisted," he said shifting uncomfortably. "I gave her a credit. I often do that. Help young people who are starting out."

"Mentoring can be very satisfying," I said. "Actually, I'm feeling a bit like a student again myself—there's so much to learn about magnetic resonance imaging." I tried to look sincere. "I hope you don't mind going over my brain scan one more time."

"It's a pleasure to talk to someone who appreciates the science behind this. I remember the first time I saw my own. Practically an out-of-body experience." He chuckled at the lame joke. I managed a weak smile.

I followed him to the control room. We sat at what I thought of as Philbrick's computer. Soon Shands had opened a window on the screen and my brain was floating in it.

"Let's get a better look," he said, enlarging the window.

He ran through the scan, slowing it down to show me what he considered the key indicators. I feigned rapt interest but tried not to pay close attention. The choice was mine whether to see what he saw, and I preferred not to.

"This is so interesting," I said when he'd finished his spiel. "Would you mind if I take some time to go through it some more?"

He gave me an indulgent smile. "By all means. Be my guest."

As Annie had predicted, he hung around for about a minute more and then excused himself.

"Enjoy. Come find me in my office when you've had enough."

At last I was alone. I opened the door to the corridor a crack just to be sure. All quiet. I took a final look at the map Emily had drawn, reminded myself of the combination numbers for the records-room door, and slipped out into the hall.

I peered through the windows in the fire doors up toward the central area. The receptionist was standing there talking to a man in a white coat who was sitting at the counter. I waited until she was gone and the man had returned to his computer.

I'd just pushed through the door and had nearly reached the records room when I heard voices. I ducked into the storage room an instant before Shands and Dr. Pullaski came out of the door across the hall marked PRIVATE. They stood talking quietly for a moment while Dr. Pullaski unlocked the records room next door and let herself in.

I felt my heart pounding in my chest—a minute earlier and I'd have been discovered in the records room, rifling the files. Shands went back inside the private office and I eased myself out from between two six-foot-tall helium canisters. I needed a better place to wait while Dr. Pullaski did whatever she was doing in the records room.

Just then Shands came out into the hall and, without glancing across the hall at me, headed toward his office. I darted across the hall and managed to catch the door just before it clicked shut and slipped inside.

Emily had called it "Bluebeard's Chamber." I don't know what

I expected to find, but nothing prepared me for this. The room was small, no more than fifteen feet wide, and it was at least twenty degrees cooler than the hall. It smelled of formalin, and a chirping sound filled the air, as if baby birds were nesting in here.

One wall was lined with stainless-steel standing freezers. A readout on one of the doors said "−82°F." Not nearly as cold in there as the liquid helium they used to cool the magnets, but plenty cold enough to begin freezing living tissue in a matter of seconds.

I opened the unit and it exhaled a puff of dragon's breath. When that cleared, I could see an interior half-filled with sealed bags. Just visible through the clear plastic were the squiggly reddish veins that crawl all over the surface of a freshly harvested brain. So that's what this was — Shands's own private brain bank. I did a quick count. There were about fifty of them. I closed the freezer.

On the floor were several empty FedEx boxes marked WET ICE, just like the one Shands had found when I'd paid my first visit to the lab. How prosaic, shipping disembodied brains via FedEx.

On the adjacent wall, I found the source of the chirping. There were four shelves of quart-sized glass beakers, each filled with half a brain floating in solution. Each hemisphere was impaled with electrodes like so many meat thermometers. The wires were attached at the opposite ends to small black electronic meters, their needles twitching in time to the sound.

The beakers were each labeled with a date, the most recent one just a few days old. The solution in some of them was bright blue and clear. In others the liquid that had turned cloudy. The oldest brain, nearly a year old, was suspended in a brown, semi-opaque solution. Most of the brain tissue seemed to have disintegrated.

I stood there gaping. Shands's research wasn't confined to a drug trial, periodic MRIs, and postmortems. It looked like he was trying to directly measure cell membrane permeability. Whatever it was that he was doing, it was causing brain tissue to disintegrate rapidly. I remembered Dr. Rofstein's comment: *Brains were being lost at an alarming rate.*

A regulated brain bank would never have allowed it. Brains were their most precious resource. Slivers of brain tissue were rationed to qualified researchers. No wonder Shands had parted company with the Cambridge Brain Bank. And no wonder he kept this brain bank under wraps.

I heard a thump from next door. Just past the freezers was a connecting door to the records room. I put my ear to it. There were footsteps and a file drawer closing. Apparently Dr. Pullaski was still in there. I hoped she'd finish up soon — Shands would eventually return to check on my whereabouts and when he didn't find me, he'd come looking. Plus I was getting damned cold.

On the wall there was a large whiteboard with rows and columns ruled off in green marker. Across the top, columns were labeled, "<50," "50 to 60," "60 to 70," "70 to 80," and finally ">80." Age ranges, I assumed. Down the side, the two rows were labeled MALE, FEMALE.

The table had names written in it. There in the middle of the table, in the seventy-to-eighty male slot, was the name Frank Mosticcio. These were patients, and this was the grand plan Emily had told me about, the one Shands used to target his research. It was just another example of the man's hubris — standard practice at research labs was to use patient ID numbers, not names. But then, this was not your standard brain bank. This locked room was a private sanctuary, and within these walls he could do whatever he damn well pleased.

I thought I heard a door slam. I listened again at the connecting door. Now I heard nothing. Had she left? I needed a peephole.

There was a heavy metal bolt on the door, locking it in place. I pulled on it, but the bar resisted. A little three-in-one oil would have done the trick.

I took my handkerchief from my pocket and wadded it over the end of the bolt, then pressed against it as hard as I could. Slowly, reluctantly, the bolt slid open. I twisted the knob and pulled the door open just a crack. Still no sounds. I nudged the door open wider until I could see into a long narrow room lined with file cabinets. No sign of Dr. Pullaski.

I put a wastebasket in the threshold and slipped into the records room. I found the two file cabinets marked PATIENT RECORDS and pulled one open. Neatly typed labels marched alphabetically on tabs from front to back. Getting the information I wanted would be a piece of cake.

I worked my way through my list, beginning with Anna Abels. Her last appointment had been four days before her death. Could be just a coincidence. Still, I felt my pulse quicken with anticipation.

I looked up the second name. His death had been three days after an MRI. I jotted down the information and quickly moved on. The next patient, a woman, had also died within a few days of a visit to the lab.

As I opened up file after file, outrage coursed through me. How dare Shands pervert medical research in this way? Taking advantage of vulnerable people. Not to mention how, when this became public, it would set back medical research. As it was, not nearly enough people donated their organs.

I was on the next-to-last name when I froze, alert, thinking I heard a noise in the hall. It was hard to tell over the hum of the freezer units and the chirp of the meters coming from the next room. I shut the file drawer and put the list back in my pocket. I had enough data, and there was no point in taking unnecessary risks.

I ducked back into the brain bank. The bolt balked at going back into place. I was struggling with it when I noticed a box just sticking out under the freezer beside me. I edged it out with my foot. It looked like a metal cash box. The lock had been smashed and the top of the box sat unevenly on the base. I nudged the top off with my toe.

It was an odd jumble of stuff. A used tissue with lipstick on it. A pair of women's underpants. I squatted to get a closer look. What looked like a wad of chewed gum. There were also some slips of yellow paper—"Freudian Slips," like the ones Emily used. I picked up one of them. "Thanks for your help!" it said, then a smiley face and the letter E. Another said, "Back at 2:30. Emily." Innocuous notes left for a coworker. It wouldn't have been hard to transform one of these, one that said "See you at 6—Emily," add a few Xs to make it look personal, then tuck it into Kyle's gym bag and leave it for the police to find.

At the bottom of the box was a short stack of magazines—all back issues of *Playboy*. All October issues, in fact. The one on top featured "Girls of the Big Ten." Another boasted "Women of the Ivy League." That one was from three years back. I opened it and flipped through, knowing what I'd find. Sure enough, a page had been torn out. I was sure the missing page was the one featuring Emily Ryan, the one that had ended up in Philbrick's desk drawer. And I knew without smelling it that the chewing gum was Juicy Fruit. I wasn't surprised to find two other fabric hearts in the bottom of the drawer. Whoever had put together this stash had been Emily's stalker. Emily had said only senior staff had access to the room. Philbrick qualified as senior staff. It could have been his.

I started to put the objects back into the box, trying to remember the order in which I'd taken them out. I set the top back on and slid the box under the freezer where I'd found it. Why were the lock broken and the top damaged? There was no time to think about it. I'd already spent more time here than was prudent.

I listened at the hallway door. Footsteps. Getting louder. I held my breath. I could feel my shirt sticking to my back. Then nothing, as if someone was pausing outside the door. Then the footsteps continued on.

I needed to get back to the control room. I'd wait a few more moments, just to be sure whoever it was had really gone. Then I'd leave.

I waited, staring at the whiteboard with its "master plan." What I hadn't noticed before were red checkmarks beside some of the names. Frank Mosticcio's name had a red check. I pulled Philbrick's list from my pocket. It looked as if all the names of dead former patients on our list had checkmarks beside them. But there were other names in the table too, names that were not in my list that also had red checkmarks.

There in the middle of the table was JOHN O'NEILL—Annie's uncle. Beside it, a red check had been erased. Maybe checks meant "deceased, brain harvested." And maybe Philbrick only collected the names of patients who'd been "helped out."

I dragged my gaze over to the "<50" column. There I was, PETER ZAK. Not yet checked.

It felt like ice water was dripping down my spine as I realized what I was looking at. This was more than a grand plan. It was a shopping list. Shands needed brains for every cell of the matrix. Every name that didn't have a red checkmark beside it, including my own, was marked for death. These were innocent people scheduled for appointments at the lab. Maybe it wouldn't be their next visit, or the one after that. I knew I was pushing it, but I had to copy down the names that weren't yet checked. The families had to be warned. I got the paper and a pen from my pocket and began to write.

I didn't hear the door open behind me. All I caught was a glimpse of white lab coat when pain exploded in the back of my head. The last thing I remembered was catching my chin on the edge of the table as I went down.

"DR. ZAK, are you all right?" Through a mist, Estelle Pullaski's face swam toward me.

I had a throbbing headache, and my lip and nose felt bashed in. Something was covering my face. I tried to move it aside, but Dr. Pullaski held my hand.

"You were having trouble breathing," she said. "Just breathe deeply. This will help."

I strained to look around.

"Is he conscious?" It was Shands's voice. He was somewhere behind me.

"He's coming around," Dr. Pullaski said, pressing her fingers to my pulse. "Just try to relax." Her mouth moved as she counted. "Much better," she said, her voice soothing. She gently lifted the oxygen mask off my face.

She and Shands helped me to a seated position. Too fast. My head felt as if it had a fifty-pound weight attached to it. I touched my face. My lip and nose were swollen, but at least my teeth were intact.

Dr. Pullaski had on a white lab coat and so did Shands. The young man I'd seen working at the main desk stuck his head in to ask whether they wanted him to call an ambulance. He had on a white coat, too.

"I don't think that will be necessary," Dr. Pullaski told him.

"What happened?" I asked.

"We found you unconscious in the hall," she said.

In the hall? I remembered being in the brain bank, hearing someone behind me, going down. I didn't remember being out in the hall and I had no idea how I'd gotten up on this stretcher or into the control room.

"We thought you might have had a seizure," Dr. Pullaski said. "You don't have epilepsy or anything like that?"

It was tempting to go along: Yeah, gee, forgot to mention, I do have a mild seizure disorder; must have lost consciousness in the hall. But Dr. Pullaski wasn't waiting for an answer. She was giving me a speculative smile.

The breathing mask was in her hand. I followed the tube from the mask to where it was attached to an oxygen tank. The tank had a piece of yellow paper taped to it, and in black marker it said NON-FERROUS, and beneath that MR-SAFE.

Screwed into the mouth of the tank was a nebulizer, a little gizmo that administers metered doses of medication with every inhale. Suddenly my mouth went dry. I realized this was how they'd done it. Just scrape a little bacteria into the nebulizer, and *voila*. Combine with oxygen in a nice moist body and it was a recipe for death.

I imagined little green bacteria multiplying like crazy in my lungs, forming a conga line as they marched along the bronchial tubes, down to the alveoli where blood gets aerated and, by the way, where the bacteria can hitch a ride into the bloodstream.

I strained to see the clock on the wall. Best guess, I'd been unconscious for about twenty minutes. I wondered how much of that time I'd been breathing poison. Dr. Pullaski was already rolling away the tank.

Even if I got sick, I couldn't prove a thing. I wanted to leap down off the table, grab the nebulizer. I swallowed the red fury that was threatening to boil over in me. Shands was eyeing me anxiously. I needed to get myself out of there and over to the hospital where I could have Kwan start me on antibiotics.

"Sheesh," I said, running my fingers through my hair. "I have no idea what happened. I can't remember. Must have hit my head." Gingerly I felt the goose egg that had grown on the crown of my head. I didn't point out that a goose egg there meant I'd been hit— no way I could have landed headfirst on the floor. "I guess I went looking for you when I finished with my MRI. This is a confusing place, so many corridors."

I slid down off the stretcher. "I'm fine," I said, stumbling as I tried to take a step. Shands moved to prop me up. "Just fine." I took a shallow breath, fighting back nausea as the world threatened to go black again. Deep breathing would only give the bacteria a firmer foothold. I had to get to the Pearce.

It wasn't until I was in my car, driving back, that I thought to check my pockets. I still had Emily's map, but the paper with Philbrick's list with all the information I'd copied from the files and the whiteboard was gone.

• • •

I lay on the bed in the on-call room. I watched Kwan wind the tourniquet around my arm, tap for a vein, and then insert the needle. Slowly he withdrew a syringe full of blood.

"Why am I doing this?" he asked. He was looking at me like I was an unripe melon. Grudgingly, he'd given me a healthy shot of amoxicillin and a prescription for more to take orally over the next week. "You don't look sick. You won't even give me time to get your blasted blood tests back," he complained. "Since when did you get a medical degree?"

"Ouch," I said, as he removed the needle from my arm. "You've got to compare whatever my blood test comes back with to what Mr. O'Neill had—I'll bet anything it's the same nasty bug."

"You don't look sick. Weird, yes. Sick, no."

"I would have been. In about twenty-four hours."

"Are you saying the MRI lab is making patients sick?"

"Sick to death."

"So the mad doctor can get his hands on their brains?" Kwan sounded skeptical but not entirely dismissive. "The only thing I don't get is why anyone would want your brain. Clearly inferior blend."

"I wish I knew who the hell—" I closed my eyes and tried to remember the moment when I was struck. But I couldn't come up with a face to go with the lab coat.

"Maybe they want to add your brain to their Lewy body collection." Kwan said it as a joke, but when he saw my reaction he gaped. "They *do*? Well, that would explain a few things."

I tried to smile but couldn't quite manage it.

He put his hand on my shoulder. "Sorry, old friend, habits die hard. I'll probably be ribbing you on your deathbed . . . which you are *not* on! Peter, if you were losing it, I'd be the first one to let you know. And believe me, I look forward to it."

"Thanks. I appreciate the vote of confidence."

Gloria came in with an ice pack. I didn't know whether to apply it to my face or my head. I chose the latter.

"Dr. Shands called," Gloria said. "Twice. Seems he's very concerned about your health. Went to great lengths to explain to me that you'd fallen accidentally." She handed me a piece of paper. "Asked me to give you this number so you could call him back."

Kwan started to leave.

"Hey, how long do I have to lie here?" I asked.

He wheeled back around. "Damn you. For all I know you don't have to be lying here at all! I won't know until I get your blood tests back. I'll walk your precious bodily fluids over there personally and harass them until it gets done. But I can't pull hats out of rabbits." He marched off, tossing back over his shoulder, "And if you're not good and sick, I'm going to get you certified."

As I lay there waiting, I mentally smacked myself in the forehead for not getting out of the lab with Philbrick's list. I could almost feel a bomb ticking beside me. There were patients whose names would sooner or later bloom red checkmarks on Shands's matrix, and I had no way to warn them.

"I've got to get out of here," I told Kwan when he returned a half-hour later.

"Forget about it. Hemophilus influenza, gram-negative coccobacillus," Kwan said, grim-faced.

"Is that a magic spell or a curse?" I asked.

"The latter. It's the same thing we found in Mr. O'Neill—a particularly virulent type of bacterial infection that can enter the bloodstream and rapidly spread. Could have given you pneumonia. Maybe kidney failure or pericarditis."

"I feel fine," I said. "Except for my head."

"Sure you do. And I intend to keep you that way. You're staying here and resting if I have to tie you down. Seriously, you need to give the medication a good headstart."

I was busy counting ceiling tiles when Annie appeared in the doorway. In my sorry state, to me she looked like an angel in those jeans that showed off her long legs and very nice behind. She must have recognized the look I was giving her because she said, "I thought you were sick."

"How'd you hear?"

"I've got my spies. They say you've got to stay put. I'm here to enforce indolence. I'm here anyway visiting Uncle Jack. What happened?"

When I'd finished telling Annie, she exhaled slowly. "So Emily Ryan really *was* being stalked. And they *are* killing their own patients."

"In the name of research."

"We should call the police. With the evidence you collected—"

I winced.

"You didn't?"

"I did. But when I came to, I didn't have the list."

"Shit," Annie said. "At least we have a copy. But the police are going to want more than that. You think Shands is Dr. Death?"

"Dr. Pullaski was the one who was administering the oxygen."

"Maybe she didn't know what was in the nebulizer."

I remembered Dr. Pullaski's look as I lay there breathing the tainted oxygen. I was pretty sure she knew.

Gloria stuck her head in the room. "It's Dr. Shands again." She offered me a phone.

I took it and put my hand over the mouthpiece. "He's been calling to find out if I'm okay. I think they're afraid I'll sue before I check out."

Annie didn't hesitate. "Get him to meet you somewhere. This

afternoon. A place where there's people around. If we haven't got hard evidence, then you've got to get him to reveal himself."

"What do I say?"

"Come up with some pretext for meeting him. Then, when you see him, be direct. Just lay out the case and see how he reacts."

"Hello?" I said into the phone, trying to make my voice sound weak.

Shands asked me how I was. Just a bad bump on the head, I told him.

"I'm extremely sorry," he said. "I hope you understand. Accidents happen."

"Of course they do. It's unavoidable. Our accident rate here at the Pearce is minuscule." I cleared my throat, making this up as I went along. "I was talking to our safety director just now, told him what happened. He thought maybe you'd like to see a copy of our safety handbook. I don't believe in lawsuits" — I paused on the word, hoping that would make the mild invitation I was about to offer sound a bit more coercive — "but I'd feel better if you'd let me share what we've learned from decades of experience with this."

"I suppose." There was a pause. "Sure you're feeling up to it?"

"I should be fine by later this afternoon," I assured him.

He didn't need more convincing.

25

I WAS sitting at a table at the Stavros Diner, waiting for Shands, munching on one of their excellent olives. The sting of the brine reminded me that I had a cut lip. The place was always pretty empty at that time of day. I couldn't see Annie, but I knew she was listening to me breathe as she sat at the far end of the counter that wrapped from one end of the diner to the other. I was wired.

Jimmy, the owner of the place, was cleaning the grill. When we'd arrived he'd rushed over, making appropriately sympathetic noises. With my swollen face, I looked as if I'd gotten into an argument with a revolving door. He was ignoring Annie only because we'd told him he had to. She'd tied back her hair, pulled a baseball cap low over her forehead, and propped a newspaper in front of her face so if Shands happened to wander into that end of the diner, he wouldn't recognize her.

Shands arrived, still in his lab coat. He looked frazzled, his hair not quite its usual Grecian perfection. When he saw me, his face fell another notch. He came over.

"I feel just terrible about this," he said, his eyes searching my face. He was an amazing actor.

He sat and ordered some coffee. I ordered a Coke. I slid my copy of the Pearce safety manual over to him. He opened it, his eyes flicking over the table of contents.

"We really are very careful, too, you know," he said, "And we have our own safety procedures."

"I know you do. That's what I wanted to talk to you about. Remember when I brought a patient, John O'Neill, over to you for an MRI?"

"Of course I remember him. A shame his family pulled him out of the study."

"I'll bet you were disappointed."

Shands blinked back at me from behind his expensive wire-rimmed glasses. From up close the teeth looked too perfect, as if they were capped. "I was. But I have to say, I don't much like your tone."

"Mr. O'Neill almost died two days after you gave him an MRI. You'd think that would be unusual, but it's not. An awful lot of patients on your treatment protocol die within a few days of coming in to have an MRI."

"We deal with sick, often elderly patients. Death is . . ."

"Inevitable?" I said, supplying the word. "Perhaps. Then why not just wait for them to die?"

"What are you suggesting?" He gave me a self-righteous glare.

"Frank Mosticcio?"

"He . . ."

"Anna Abels?" I reeled off the names of a half-dozen more patients. I laid Annie's copy of the list on the table. "These patients all died of pneumonia, or lung infections, or—"

"That's what old people die of," he said, narrowing his eyes at me.

"Dr. Philbrick collected death notices of all these patients. And he called me the night before we brought Mr. O'Neill in to you for testing. I never talked to him, but I suspect he was trying to warn me. He never got the chance because, as you may recall, he was killed."

"But this is absurd," Shands said.

"And what about Kyle Ronan?"

Now Shands was giving me a blank look, as if the name didn't register.

"The man whom Emily supposedly ran down with her car? I think he was killed because of something he saw—or something that he should have seen and didn't. There he is, following Emily, waiting in the garage for her to return to her car the morning Dr. Philbrick was killed. He sees Emily arrive. He sees the police. He sees me."

Jimmy delivered Shands's coffee and my Coke.

"But he never sees you," I said. "I wonder why not, because when I arrived you were already there." The silence of the diner was broken by the whirring of the milkshake machine. "And isn't that precisely what made him so dangerous?"

I expected to see a flash of anger, the shifting eyes of someone who's cornered. But what I saw in Shands's face was confusion. His jaw had gone slack.

He pushed the coffee away. "Do you have any idea how horrendous this disease is?" he asked. "The data we're collecting is extraordinary." His face became animated. "We're so close to understanding. So close to preventing. Have you any idea how painful it is to watch someone you love become so tortured?" Real emotion, tears even had sprung to his eyes. "How it destroys, crushes the intellect, wipes out personality." He swallowed. "And all you can do is stand by and watch."

That's when it hit me. This passion for his research—Shands had come by it the hard way. He'd lost someone he cared about to Lewy body dementia.

"How old are you?" I asked.

"What?"

"And how old was your father when he started to lose his mind? When he began to show symptoms of dementia? This cure you're looking for. It's personal, isn't it? Your bid to survive. When you look at your own brain scan, what do you see? How long do you figure you have?"

Shands took off his glasses and rubbed the bridge of his nose. "My father was only fifty-nine when he started to become forgetful. His brother was in his early sixties." Shands gave me a hard look. He raised his hand and pointed a finger at me. "I figure I have just a few years less than you do." Was there a slight tremor in his hand, or was I seeing what I expected to see?

"Will I last that long?" I asked. "Or will I get sick, like all those other patients? Suddenly not feeling so well. Will I get to the hospital in time, or will I wait, assuming it's just the flu? Then by the time they put me on antibiotics, the infection is raging and nothing can be done."

I put my palm down on the list of patients, all those people who'd been killed in order to save Shands from the same miserable fate. I pushed the list toward him.

"You're a researcher. Is it even remotely possible that chance alone could account for this number of deaths in this close proximity to a similar event—having an appointment at your lab?"

"What you're suggesting . . ." he began, his voice raspy. I could see the realization taking hold. "I would never, ever deliberately hurt one of our patients."

He picked up the list of names and stared at it. He drew his finger carefully down it, then he gazed off into space.

"No," he whispered. "It's not—" He paused and seemed to gather strength. He stood up suddenly, his chair scraping on the linoleum. "Where's the phone? I have to make a call."

I looked at him, open-mouthed. What was happening?

"You can use my—" I started, taking out my cell phone. But he was already loping toward the pay phone at the back of the diner.

I followed. He barely noticed Annie as he hurried past. When he'd disappeared through the swinging doors marked RESTROOMS and PHONE, Annie gave me a discreet thumbs-up.

I went back to wait. I took a drink of Coke and fished out an ice cube to suck on. I thought about Shands's reactions. First surprise. Then denial. Finally what I thought might be horror. I crunched down on the ice. Was it possible that he didn't realize what was going on? I glanced toward the back of the diner.

I took another sip of Coke. Shands's coffee was growing tepid. Jimmy came over to me.

"Your friend?" he jerked a thumb in the direction of the rest room. "He left the back way."

Annie must have heard because she came bolting from around the corner. She had her cell phone out. "It will take about thirty seconds for them to erase that whiteboard. An hour more to shred the files."

She started out to the parking lot, dialing as she ran. I raced in front of her and opened my car. We both got in.

"He's not in his office?" Annie said into the phone. "Well, page him. It's important."

I accelerated onto the road and almost immediately came to a halt at a red light.

"Mac? It's me, Annie."

The light turned green. I took off again and moved into the left lane.

Annie put her hand on the dashboard to steady herself.

"You know that MRI lab in Cambridge where there was a murder a few weeks ago? Well, it turns out they're killing patients, too. They're making them sick so that they come down with an infection. Peter and I are headed over—" She paused. "Well, I know because I overheard a conversation—" There was another pause.

Now we were heading down a crowded Fresh Pond Parkway toward the river. Rush-hour traffic was starting to build. Cars backed up approaching the rotary—a torture device invented in the 1800s to manage horse-and-buggy traffic. Some drivers dither trying to enter, others just barrel ahead. I'm a barreler, and the guy in front of me was a ditherer. I leaned on the horn.

"Well, we *had* some evidence, a list with names and dates that makes it pretty obvious what's going on. But it got stolen."

There was another pause. Annie listened, shaking her head as she stared the window. "What do I want you to do?" Annie said. "Meet us over there. If we don't move fast they'll destroy the records."

Now we were merging onto Memorial Drive.

"Search warrant? Are you kidding? You know how long that's going to take. There was already a murder there. Can't you get a follow-up search, an extension of whatever search warrant you've already got?"

I accelerated as the light turned yellow at JFK Street, swerving around the crowd of pedestrians nudging their way into the crosswalk. A short distance later, we passed the big Shell sign, which that day was reading HELL.

"Yes, I know you can't turn on a dime. Uh-huh, probable cause." Annie leaned her head against the window. "Right. I know you need evidence. But if we don't get over there now there won't be any."

I wove my way through pothole-ridden streets lined with warehouses and pulled into the driveway of the Sidney Street garage.

"Damn," Annie said, turning off her phone. "Bureaucratic bullshit."

I pulled into a spot on the first level and we got out of the car. The elevator was open, waiting for us.

As we rode up Annie said, "Let's make sure that one of us comes away with enough information to jumpstart an investigation. Why don't I do patient records while you keep Shands and Pullaski occupied?"

"You've got the list?"

Annie nodded. She followed me across the lobby to the MRI lab entrance.

"Just look like you know where you're going," I said.

We walked into the waiting room. Apparently business had bounced back because there were about a half-dozen people there. The receptionist was on the phone. Without hesitating, I strode through, reached for the door to the inner area, and pulled it open.

"Can I help you?" the receptionist said as we blew by. "Hey!"

"It's okay. Dr. Shands is expecting us," I said. We were inside.

We walked through the central area. One of the young men working at the counter looked up. His face registered confusion as he looked back and forth from Annie to me, not recognizing either of us.

I nodded to him. "We were here visiting with Dr. Shands. I know the way."

In a moment we'd pushed through the double doors and were out of sight. We passed the room with the helium tanks and the brain bank. Now we were outside the records room. I had my hand poised over the keypad. Emily said the combination was Shands's birthday. *Please tell me they haven't changed it.* I punched in the numbers. The keypad beeped, and Annie opened the door.

"Meet you at the car later, and remember to keep your head down," Annie said, and slipped inside.

I BACKTRACKED to Shands's office. The door was standing open. He wasn't there, but his lab coat was thrown over the chair.

I doubled back, past the records room again where I hoped Annie was already gathering the evidence we needed, then past the yellow sawhorse barriers. I paused outside the scan room. The door was closed and at first I couldn't hear anything. I held my breath and listened. A woman's voice was audible. Then the low rumble of a man.

I went down the hall and let myself into the control room. Through the window I could see Dr. Pullaski and Shands in the scan room. They were locked in a struggle. Crouching, I approached the control console and switched on the speaker. "You have to . . . stop . . . can't keep . . ." said Shands, his voice coming in tinny bursts.

I hung back in the shadows of the darkened room and watched. Shands was trying to pull something away from Dr. Pullaski. Beside them was a patient in a wheelchair. The gray-haired woman in a hospital gown was whimpering and cringing.

"I never . . . meant for you — " Shands wrenched an oxygen mask free of Dr. Pullaski's grasp and was backing away.

"What on earth has come over you?" Dr. Pullaski said.

Shands bent over the woman in the wheelchair. Hesitantly, he put his hand on her shoulder. It was an awkward gesture, as if he were trying out a dance step he'd never done before. He got down on one knee, steadied himself against the wheelchair, and lowered the other knee. The effect was clearly calming as the woman became less rigid and the mewling subsided.

"Is she going to be all right?" Shands asked, looking up at Dr. Pullaski.

"She'll be fine, once you stop leaning on her."

"How many have there been?"

Dr. Pullaski gazed at him steadily without answering.

"How many?" he demanded.

"You're telling me you don't know?"

Shands staggered to his feet. "God help me. It's true, isn't it? What could you have been thinking? I'm a doctor. I don't kill people."

"Of course you don't." Dr. Pullaski went up to him and put her hands on either side of his face. "Which is why you need me." He pulled away. "Why you've always needed me. We're the perfect partnership. That's how we got all this. The most powerful magnet in any lab in the country. Patients clamoring to be included in your research." Her voice turned hard. "Beautiful young research assistants. You can't suddenly get cold feet. We have a bargain."

"Bargain? What the hell are you talking about?" Shands said.

The patient gave a yelp of distress.

Dr. Pullaski put her finger up to her lips. "Keep your voice down," she told Shands, as if she were talking to a child. "Maybe you've forgotten that the girls come and go. I'm the constant, the one who keeps it all happening. Surely you know that after all these years. I do it for you. Because of the special relationship we have, that we've always—"

"You're out of your mind," he said, cutting her off. The woman in the wheelchair started to mutter heatedly to herself. Shands dropped his voice. "I've tolerated you because you do your job better—"

"Tolerated?"

"You're not an easy woman. With your petty jealousies."

"My *what?*"

"Your fantasies about us."

Dr. Pullaski's mouth dropped open. "Fantasies? You . . . need . . . me," she said, biting off each word.

"Like hell I do. You've endangered everything that means anything to me. I might have loved you once. But that was a long time ago. Now? How could I? You're cold. You're all dried up."

"You bastard."

"Bitch!"

The woman in the wheelchair let loose with a long, protracted scream that sliced through the air.

"Would you shut her the fuck up!" Shands yelled.

The woman in the wheelchair flinched, shrinking down, bringing her chest to her knees. She began to screech, and the screech turned into a prolonged moaning that seemed to set the air vibrating. Dr. Pullaski tried shushing her, but to no avail. Now the woman was thrashing around. Any minute she'd have thrown herself out of the wheelchair.

As Dr. Pullaski reached for the woman's neck, I bolted for the door to the scan room and pulled it open. When she saw me Dr. Pullaski took a step back.

The room fell silent, the only sound the patient in the wheelchair keening, her gray hair hanging over her face.

Shands and Dr. Pullaski exchanged a look.

"He knows," Shands said.

Dr. Pullaski absorbed the news without changing her expression. She smoothed her lab coat. Shands picked up the phone in the room, punched in a few numbers, and asked whoever answered to send someone down to get the patient. A few moments later one of the men I'd seen working in the lab came and took her away.

Dr. Pullaski began wheeling the oxygen tank to the door.

"You aren't very fond of Dr. Ryan, are you, Dr. Pullaski?" I said.

She paused, an amused expression passing over her face. "Should've thrown that one back."

"And why was that?"

Dr. Pullaski set the pushcart upright and gave me a direct look. "She—"

"Estelle," Shands said, a warning in his voice.

"You're not only an able administrator who keeps this place humming and the money flowing in, are you?" I said. "You keep the young women flowing in as well. You hire them knowing full well what's going to happen. One after another, they get seduced by the good doctor. They get chewed up and spit out. They come and they go, but you're still here, the irreplaceable helpmate. Only you made a little mistake with Dr. Ryan."

"Me? Oh no, I never would have hired that one. She applied"— she paused—"directly to you, James, didn't she?" Dr. Pullaski's thin smile turned into a sneer. "Oh, she knew how to appeal. How to make you stand up and take notice. Little Miss Innocent. Then she wouldn't have you, would she?"

"She would have, if it weren't for your . . . your interfering," Shands sputtered. "Besides, she's different."

"You think so?" She shot Shands a pitying look. "Ambition. That's what that girl's about. That's what they're all about, really. She'd have made love to *me* if it had gotten her what she wanted. All she's done is distract you from the important work. It was pathetic, really. The way you followed her—"

"I think you've said quite enough," Shands said.

"You just couldn't take no for an answer, could you?"

So I'd been right in my first impression of Philbrick—odd, intense, socially awkward, but not a stalker. Now I recalled the undercurrent of anxiety I'd felt from Shands when he'd asked if I'd seen anything the night I'd found Emily terrified in the parking lot at the Pearce. His obvious relief had been because I hadn't seen *him*. Shands was obsessed with Emily, all right, the woman who'd pose for *Playboy* but wouldn't fall into bed with him.

Had something changed? When had Shands turned from pursuer to executioner? The fabric heart and the pages from *Playboy* had been planted in the desk to make Philbrick look like the stalker—and to give Emily a motive for murder. Emily's earring and her "Freudian Slips" had been planted by the same person who ran Kyle down with her car. It would have been easy to take Emily's car keys, her apartment keys from her bag while she was working at the lab, have copies made, and then return them before she knew they were missing.

But Philbrick's and Kyle's deaths weren't about stalking. That was just a convenient ruse to divert attention from the real reason they were killed.

"I ran into one of the doctors who served on the board with you at the Cambridge Brain Bank," I said. Now I had both of their attention. "You both left at the same time, didn't you? Why was that? One too many complaints from young women? Too much research funding vanishing from other budget lines and showing up on yours?"

Dr. Pullaski and Shands exchanged a look. In that instant they'd morphed from adversaries to allies.

"We didn't belong there," Shands said. "It was too conservative, stodgy. Our research was . . . is . . . light-years ahead of theirs."

"So why haven't you published it? Why not let the world know about the radical, groundbreaking work that's going on here?"

Together they presented me with an impassive wall.

Now I spoke directly to Shands. "It's not just women that you collect, is it? You need brains to feed your research, and you need a lot of them because whatever you're doing, it causes the tissue structure to break down. And time is of the essence, isn't it? Who knows how long before you start to feel the effects of the disease yourself?"

"Shut up!" Shands roared. "You know nothing."

The room fell into silence, the only sound the humming of the overhead fluorescent lighting and an occasional clicking from the scanner. It had been twenty minutes since I left Annie.

"This has been an interesting discussion, but I'm afraid we have work to do," Dr. Pullaski said, busying herself straightening the room. "We have a full schedule today, and there are patients waiting to be tested."

She removed the paper covering the scanner table, threw it away, and tore off a fresh sheet from a roll under the counter. She placed it on the table and smoothed it in place. She began to wheel the pushcart holding the oxygen canister from the room. I started to follow, but Shands put his hand on my arm, holding me back. The door swung shut behind her.

"You have to believe me, I had no idea," Shands said. "She must be insane. She set Emily up."

"The police will have to be told," I said.

"Isn't there some other way?" Shands said, sinking down onto a stool. "Think of all my work. The benefits to mankind. There are four million people in this country alone with dementia. Think of the quality of life lost." His tunnel vision took my breath away. Not a moment spent pondering the patients who'd been killed, never mind Leonard Philbrick and Kyle Ronan. "You understand how important it is, don't you? There has to be a way to save it."

I thought about the brains, stuck with electrodes like cloves in so many Christmas hams, dissolving in whatever he had them suspended in. Was that research worth saving, or the quest of a madman intent on only one thing—saving himself?

"She can be very jealous, you know," Shands continued. "A brilliant administrator. Seemed like early on, when we were just getting started, she could just about pull money out of the air." He seemed to settle into a kind of reverie. "I remember the first time I saw her. That dark hair, flashing eyes. She wasn't pretty, but she had a kind of electricity about her. Raw power.

"Now she's turned into something else. Something ugly. I've kept her on because she's made herself"—he paused, looking for the word—"indispensable."

Over Shands's shoulder I could see Dr. Pullaski had entered the control room. She was staring at Shands's back, listening.

"I don't think you should—" I began, putting up my hand to silence him.

"I've already laid the groundwork. A deal that will make the lab financially independent and free me of her—"

Shands looked up sharply as a thud sounded overhead. The sound had come from the ceiling over the scanner. Shands spun around and looked through the window into the control room. Dr. Pullaski had disappeared.

There was another thud. Shands froze, like an animal listening for a predator.

"What was that?" I asked.

"The vents." He cleared his throat and looked up at the ceiling. "Closing, I think."

Now Dr. Pullaski was standing there, her eyes fixed on Shands. She raised her index finger, then reached for the desk. I remembered what was there — the control panel with emergency buttons. Philbrick had nearly jumped out of his skin when Annie had gone for them.

"No!" Shands screamed, spreading his arms protectively over the MRI system.

Dr. Pullaski ignored him. She pressed her hand down.

There was a pause and, for a moment, I thought nothing was going to happen. Then there was an explosion, like a jet engine coming to life. It seemed to come from the MRI system itself. Clouds of vapor began belching from the smokestack vent atop the scanner, cascading over Shands. He gave an agonized scream and he fell back, his hands outstretched. His splayed fingers had turned pale yellow and waxy. A two-tone blaring sound began, like a foghorn.

"Quench!" Shands screamed. Dr. Pullaski stood there, staring at him impassively. "For God's sake, Estelle, open the vents!"

Philbrick's words came back to me: *The system holds over a thousand liters of liquid helium.* And all thousand of them were now boiling over and vaporizing. I could see my college chemistry professor, Hiram Bucholtz, lecturing to us on the dangers of working with cryogenic gases. "It cannot be overstated," he'd intone for the umpteenth time, "compressed gases are hazardous by virtue of their temperature and their compression." Somewhere from the recesses of my brain I recalled that helium expanded at a ratio of about nine hundred to one when it vaporized. We had to get out of there, and fast.

My head felt as if it were about to explode. I lunged for the door, took hold of the handle, and pulled. It wouldn't budge. I wondered if Dr. Pullaski had locked it from the outside, or if the pressure buildup in the room was already holding it shut. I tried to yell to Shands to help me, but ended up bending double with my hands over my ears. It felt like nails were being driven in.

Then, it was as if someone suddenly turned off the sound. The foghorn turned muffled and my ears were ringing. The room seemed to be revolving around me, and I found myself sitting on the floor, breathing rapidly. A red sensor on the wall started blinking, telling me what I already knew. Oxygen levels in the room had dropped.

It was getting colder by the second. Eyeballs freeze, I thought distractedly. I should have closed my eyes to protect myself, but I couldn't. Now the ceiling was completely obliterated by a white cloud that was descending as vapor filled the room. Soon, all we'd need was a gondolier's boat and candelabra and we could do *Phantom of the Opera*, I thought in a wave of dizziness. Only the candles wouldn't stay lit, would they?

Shands staggered toward me. He had his arms crossed and his hands tucked into his armpits. Blood trickled from his ear. I felt the side of my face. My right ear was bleeding, too. Ruptured eardrum.

In elementary school we'd learned about crawling out of a smoke-filled room. Hot air rises. What does cold air do, I wondered as I lay down on the floor and stared up as the cloud of white descended to meet me. Now my eyes were burning in the cold. I could barely see into the control room.

I felt heavy, tired. So it wasn't going to be Lewy body dementia after all. Asphyxiation was ever so much more tidy and quick. Though not all that different, really. Diminished mental alertness. Impaired muscle coordination. Faulty judgment. And a very cold nose.

I could barely see Dr. Pullaski, still staring through the window, her head tilted to one side as if she were watching something growing in a petri dish.

Suddenly, it seemed like the flashing red lights were forming words. BREAK THE GLASS, BREAK THE GLASS. I hoped it wasn't too late.

I managed to roll over onto my knees. Painfully I made my way, crawling under the descending cloud of vapor to the legs of the nearest chair.

Finally I got to it, reached for the plastic seat, and pulled myself up to my knees. Shands was a few feet away, already passed out. *Move*, I told myself, imagining that I was on the river, trying to conjure the feel of the sun on my back, the feeling of elation as I pushed past the pain that always threatens to engulf me early in a row.

But it was no good. I just hung there, my head in the chair seat struggling for air, staring at the outline of the window. *Come on*, the voice in my head hectored. I pictured myself standing, lifting the chair, and aiming at the window that I could barely see.

In slow motion, as in a dream, cracks appeared in the glass and a chair came hurtling through the window. Confused, I saw it soundlessly hit the floor beside me and slide to a stop alongside

Shands. The white cloud rushed out through the opening and into the control room.

In a moment of clarity, I screamed, "Open the control room door!" Then everything descended into darkness.

. . .

Someone was holding my hand. The warmth was almost painful. I opened my eyes. Annie was kneeling over me. I was on the floor of the MRI lab, covered in a blanket. I wanted to smile but I couldn't make one happen—my face felt numb. Annie's lips moved, but if there was sound I couldn't hear it over the persistent ringing in my ears. Her lips formed a kiss. That message I got.

The chair beside me was lying on its back. I remembered. Someone had sent the chair through the window. Had to have been Annie. Jagged bits of glass were all that remained in the window frame. Why wasn't there any glass on the floor? Glass must have imploded into the control room. With the increased air pressure in here, it would have done so with considerable force.

Annie had a towel wrapped around her forearm and blood was seeping through. As numb as my face was, it must have contorted with concern because Annie mouthed, "I'm fine. Really."

"Dr. Pullaski?" I asked, feeling the sound in my throat but barely hearing it.

Annie's eyes flicked to the control room. She shook her head.

I felt the floor vibrate as a pair of medics rolled a gurney past me. "Shands?"

Annie put out a flat hand, fingers splayed, and tilted it side to side, as if to say, "Touch and go."

Annie moved aside and a pair of medics took over. One of them had a clipboard and talked to Annie. The other felt my pulse. Then he rotated my head to one side and peered into my ear.

The scanner, the wondrous 4.5-tesla system, stood in its corner looking benign. Like a huge elephant that had just gone on a rampage and was now anesthetized. I wondered how badly its innards had been damaged by the quench and explosion.

The medic turned my head the other way. The only hint of what had happened was the broken window and the overturned chair.

No, there was more. A three-inch fissure had opened between the ceiling and one of the walls. Air pressure had literally blown the lid off the lab. No wonder I felt like shit.

27

"YOU SURE you want to do this?" I asked Emily. We were standing in the parking lot. It was a hot muggy afternoon in the middle of summer's first heat wave, the sun glowing low and sullen in the sky.

"Absolutely," she said.

Emily had been released and the charges dropped. Shands had survived, though his hands were badly damaged from direct contact with the evaporating helium. In the three weeks since her death, there had been no funeral service for Dr. Estelle Pullaski, who'd nearly been decapitated by a shard of flying glass.

The collection of brains had been transferred to the medical examiner, evidence in a multiple homicide investigation. Every day there were new revelations in the paper, another family coming forward to question a relative's death. The official count was up over twenty. Shands was cooperating with the investigation, and word was that his attorney had worked out a plea bargain.

Among other things, Shands admitted that both he and Dr. Pullaski had been at the lab early on the morning Philbrick was killed. He claimed he'd been working in his private laboratory and heard nothing until later, when he found Emily trying to remove the oxygen tank from the scanner.

Beyond that, what happened was pure speculation since Dr. Pullaski was dead. The most likely scenario was that the evening before, Dr. Pullaski had indeed asked Philbrick to call Emily and tell her she'd left her beeper at the lab. Only Emily hadn't left it there. Dr. Pullaski had taken it from her bag. Philbrick arranged for Emily to come in at seven to pick up her beeper the next morning. Maybe he went to Dr. Pullaski's office to tell her, and that's when she offered him a drink. I wondered if he'd been surprised by the sudden burst of friendliness. The drink had been laced with Valium. In a semiconscious state, she'd probably gotten him to climb up on the platform where he'd passed out. That must have been around the time I was trying to call Dr. Philbrick at his home.

We knew how she'd kept him unconscious—the coroner had overlooked a tiny puncture wound in Philbrick's foot where an IV had been used to administer more of the alcohol-and-Valium cocktail during the night while Dr. Pullaski went home.

She and Dr. Shands returned early the next morning. Just before seven, when Emily was supposed to arrive, Dr. Pullaski got rid of the IV setup, started the scanner, and finally brought in the oxygen tank. The only thing she hadn't counted on was Kyle Ronan waiting in the garage, watching Emily's back. He never saw Shands and Pullaski arrive because they were already at the lab when Emily got there. Later, it must have been Pullaski who called Emily, pretending to be an administrator from outpatient services. The nonexistent new patient had been a ruse to keep Emily out of the way so Pullaski could deal with Kyle.

Maybe Shands would be able to convince the prosecutors that he knew nothing about what was going on. People did things for him, he'd say, things he never even asked them to do. He'd certainly never asked Dr. Pullaski to kill patients.

After he'd dug himself out from under criminal charges, there would be an inevitable avalanche of civil suits. University Medical Imaging was shuttered, and I wondered if it would be indefinitely.

Emily had taken two weeks off. When she'd returned her mood had been subdued and somber. Her car was still in police custody and she'd had to rent one to get around. "It doesn't matter," she'd said. "They can keep it forever as far as I'm concerned. I'll never be able drive it again, much less look at it."

Made sense. After all, it had been used to kill a man she'd cared for and who'd cared deeply for her. Too bad, I couldn't help thinking, it was a very nifty car—something that my Subaru was so not.

In a fit of self-serving selflessness, I found myself offering to swap cars. I didn't mind waiting until the Miata was un-impounded. I'd get the fender fixed and the body painted silver. Emily had jumped at the offer.

"Thank God," Gloria had said to me when she heard the plan. "I can't stand another minute of you whining about that stupid car of yours."

In the summer heat, I gazed about at the underbrush surrounding the asphalt. No menace lurked there today.

"Peter?" Emily said.

"Sorry, did you say something?" I asked. My hearing was coming back, but it wasn't a hundred percent yet.

"Ready?"

I put the title certificate on the hood and with a flourish, signed it over to Emily. Then I gouged the keys out of my pocket.

"The sunroof leaks," I said.

"I know. You told me that already." She took the keys and title from me. "Believe me, this will be much better. Discreet, service-able. Just what the doctor ordered." She opened the driver-side door. Then she set her briefcase on the seat and opened it. "I brought you something." She pulled out a small plastic CD case and handed it to me.

"What's this?" I asked, turning it over.

"Your brain scan."

I had to squeeze my fingers around the case to keep from drop-ping it.

"It's just a video file. It'll run on any PC."

How reassuring. It was the kind of gift I'd have expected from Shands, not Emily. I looked up at her slowly as a realization took hold.

"How did you get this? I thought the lab was closed."

She looked away. "I've been in, helping with the cleanup. I need to give you this, too." She reached into her briefcase, drew out an envelope, and handed it to me. "I'm quitting the clinical fellowship here. I've decided to devote my life to research."

"You know, there's a lot of research going on at the Pearce."

She nodded, looking at the ground. "I've lined someone up to take over my patients. At least I helped get Mr. Black back on the path."

"You have another position, don't you?" She didn't answer. "Uni-versity Medical Imaging?"

"He's selling that lab. Already sold it in fact. It's going to be renovated, renamed."

"Who's the buyer?"

Emily colored slightly. "It hasn't been formally announced."

It didn't take much to figure out the likely buyer. My guess was Cimgen Pharmaceuticals, the company behind Cimvicor.

"They've offered me the position of clinical director, and I've accepted. We're going to refocus on our core mission. In the meanwhile—"

We? "You can't be serious. Emily, this is the man who stalked you. Even if he doesn't go to jail, he's probably going to lose his license to practice medicine. The lab will lose its accreditation."

She swallowed. "He needs me. It's what I wanted from the beginning. To be a part of something really important. The work has to go on, even if we have to start over to do it."

She seemed to search my face for some indication that I understood. She didn't find any.

• • •

"I once had a friend who kept getting into relationships with the same kind of guy," Annie said. We were standing on the Weeks footbridge looking over the Charles. It was late in the afternoon and the sun was at our backs. The week before, I'd helped her get Uncle Jack settled in a long-term care facility. An eight shot out from under the bridge and skimmed up the river, the rowers pulling hard. "Over and over, she'd start going out with these attractive, egotistical, self-centered jerks. And over and over again, she kept getting dumped."

"You think that's what Emily's doing?" Shands seemed to me nothing like Kyle.

"I don't mean Emily. I'm talking about Shands."

As different as Emily Ryan and Estelle Pullaski were, there was an essential similarity. Both were looking for that other half to make her feel complete, someone in whose reflected glory she could bask.

"He needs an Emily," I said. "But she needs him, too."

"You're right. It's hard to tell who was seducing whom," Annie observed. "I know it's not politically correct of me to suggest this, but isn't it just possible that Emily's the one who made sure Dr. Shands saw that *Playboy* spread at around the same time that he saw her resume? His reputation wasn't exactly a closely guarded secret. It wouldn't have taken a rocket scientist to recognize his vulnerability. Who knows, maybe her goal all along was to replace Dr. Pullaski. Become the great man's partner."

As Annie said, it wasn't PC, but it was plausible. Emily had as much as admitted to me that becoming his partner had been her fantasy.

"Gal sure knows how to go after what she wants," Annie said. "I'm glad she wasn't able to sink her little teeth into you. Though God knows she tried."

I felt my face grow warm as I remembered the kiss that I shouldn't have enjoyed nearly as much as I did. Annie just looked at me and laughed.

"I wonder who he had before Dr. Pullaski. Lucrezia Borgia?" Annie said.

"You know the charges against her are trumped up."

"Dr. Pullaski?"

"Lucrezia Borgia." I put my arm around Annie and she leaned back against me. I nuzzled her neck. "I wonder. Is that what scares you about me? Making a mistake you've made before?"

Annie twisted around to face me. "Actually, I don't think I've ever made this particular mistake before."

She kissed her fingertips and placed them first on my right eye, then the left, then on my mouth.

"You're not like anyone else," she said. "You're solid, dependable." I groaned. Was I also boring and predictable? "Men I've been with in the past have been fine as long as things are uncompli-cated."

"Life seldom is."

"Not for long, anyway. Having to depend on another person? Makes my teeth itch." Annie squinted into the sun. "So what are you afraid of?"

I took a breath. Mortality? Illness? Losing my mind?

"Who knows. But I do know that you don't scare me one bit."

"No? I didn't think so. But it sounds like you're still chewing on whatever it is that Dr. Shands saw in your brain scan. Or should I say it's chewing on you?"

I had the CD that Emily had given me in my pocket. I took it out.

"It's on here. Emily gave me a copy."

"It would make a good coaster."

"Not really. It's got a hole in the middle."

"You know what I think?" Annie said.

"That Shands is full of shit?"

"That. And that even if you have the inherited form of this blasted disease, so what?"

If I'd been my own therapist, this is exactly what I'd have been thinking. What was the point of knowing, if it was going to make you live each day dreading something which may or may not happen, and over which you had no control?

"I wish I'd never had that scan," I admitted.

"Ah. But how to close Pandora's box?" Annie said, leaning on the bridge railing.

I leaned over, too, and held the CD case over the water. Our elongated shadows stretched out in front of us. Knowledge or ignorance? Acceptance or denial? In both cases, I'd normally opt for the former. But this was different.

I took the CD out of the case and sent it spinning off the bridge. It sparkled in the sunlight before it settled on the surface of the water, floated a ways, and then sank.

Dear Patron: You are invited
or two, signed or
Your com